a MATTER of SEMANTICS

A YOUNG OFFICER'S DECISION:
DUTY OR LOYALTY IN THE VIETNAM WAR

a novel

FRANK LINIK

A Matter of Semantics
Copyright © 2018 by Frank J. Linik

All rights reserved. This book or any portion thereof may not be reproduced or used in any manner whatsoever without the express written permission of the publisher except for the use of brief quotations in a book review.

Printed in the United States of America

First Printing, 2018

ISBN (Print Edition): 978-1-54393-353-6
ISBN: (eBook Edition): 978-1-54393-354-3

To Janet, my wife, without whose love, support, and encouragement this book would not have come to completion.

ACKNOWLEDGEMENTS

First of all, I need to thank my Writer's Group: John Davis, Ron Humason, Gary Biggs, Joe Barba, and Joe Engelbrecht. Their constructive criticism made me a better writer and this book a better story.

And to all my friends, too numerous to list, for their encouragement, reading and feedback. They have accompanied me on this journey from the beginning. You know who you are and I thank you.

And to Joyce Rhia Linik, my sister-in-law, Irene Dickson, my cousin, and Kasia Wilson. In the final preparation of this book, they provided invaluable reading, editing and ideas.

And one special acknowledgement: Steve Winston, a journalist whose questions about my Vietnam experience proved to be the catalyst for this book.

And finally to Bill Brandt, my main character, who led me down paths I never expected to write about and created a novel.

This is a work of fiction. The characters, incidents and dialogue are drawn from the author's imagination and are not to be construed as real. The incidents and characters portrayed are based on my experiences and those of other infantry lieutenants I knew but have been transformed by the demands of storytelling and crafted into an exploration of how war impacts individuals. I wanted to say more than just my personal experience and not be constrained by historical accuracy.

Place names are real except for a few small villages. In some instances, radiotelephone protocol has been abridged to facilitate the flow of the story. Military unit designations are real, but the characters who populate them are fictional. Any resemblance to actual events or persons, living or dead, is entirely coincidental.

I had the privilege of serving under three fine battalion commanders and two captains. They set a model and standard for leadership that has continued to serve me well in civilian life. I am also honored to have served with some of the finest enlisted men a platoon leader could wish for, paratroopers all.

a MATTER of SEMANTICS

A YOUNG OFFICER'S DECISION: DUTY OR LOYALTY IN THE VIETNAM WAR

CHAPTER 1

Here I am. My first night in Vietnam. I'm naked, sitting in a muddy hole in the ground, listening to a macabre symphony. Welcome to Nam.

Brandt leaned back against the wall of the bunker, breathing hard, his heart racing. All he could see were dancing balls of color in deep darkness.

I'm safe.

The ground shook. The wall of the bunker shoved Brandt away. Sand sprinkled onto his head from above.

Damn. That was close.

He brushed sand from his head.

Well, not completely safe. Got no rifle. I'm helpless.

Danger wrapped in a veneer of safety.

Brandt's attention shifted. Some guys had been counting the incoming rounds but stopped because too many rounds hit at once, beating a strange rhythm of varying frequency and intensity. Explosions ranged from cracks to thuds to thumps, depending on how far away the rounds landed. He listened. He waited and listened. The bunker filled up fast. Grunts and splashes died down, replaced by names called in low tones as friends checked on each other. Brandt ached to hear his own name, to call someone else's name, but he knew no one.

He flexed the fingers in his clenched fists, inhaled deeply, and exhaled slowly. His breathing and pulse gradually returned to normal, followed by an unusual sensation. Brandt's brow furrowed; his head tilted to the side. He remembered lying awake in the oppressive heat, stripping off every stitch of clothing and tossing the sweat-soaked sheet against the wall. Only then had he been able to drift into sleep. Brandt laughed to himself, and calm replaced initial terror. His balls were resting on the muddy floor of the bunker.

He leaned back against the cool dampness of the sandbags and closed his eyes.

How the hell did I get here?

Confusion subsided and he replayed the scenes from his memory.

The deafening blasts jolted him awake. He scrambled out of a top bunk, one foot on the floor and the other in mid-air, eyes blinking, and heart pounding. Bursts of light illuminated unfamiliar surroundings. Rows of beds flanked him. Other men struggled to the floor. Orange-and-white glare alternated with solid darkness. Men seemed to move in stiff, jerky motions, like in an old movie. A siren pierced the thundering of the shells. Sounds and flashes registered as explosions. Someone shouted, "Mortars. Mortars!"

Fully awake, Lieutenant Bill Brandt remembered that he was in Long Binh, Vietnam. His first night in-country. He completed his second stride and sprinted toward the door. Brandt threw his forearm up as he collided with the screen door, flung it open, and leaped into the muddy street. He made a sharp turn to the right but slid in a wide arc through slick mud. Out of the corner of his eye, Brandt saw a human flash flood choked into a doorway funnel.

Brandt lowered his head and charged to a bunker alongside the barracks. The ground beneath him shook, and a wall of solid air hit his right side and slammed him to the ground. He landed on his left shoulder and plowed a wide muddy furrow. Brandt clawed at the edge of consciousness and struggled to think, to see, in the stroboscopic storm around him. He began to drift into the personal silence of semiconsciousness. He heard a voice inside himself, one he'd always heard people describe as "soft, little, or small." It screamed, "Move! Move!"

Brandt blinked, looked around, and spotted the dark bunker opening ten meters to his left. He gathered his feet under him to make another dash when he heard someone yell, "Crawl, you dumb shit. Don't run." Brandt started a crawl, more like a swim, through the muck of the street. An agonized cry pierced the explosions just to his right. He froze, poised between safety and danger. Every fiber of his being drove him toward shelter. His training demanded that he turn away.

A few muddy strokes brought him to the source of the cries. Brandt reached out and felt a warm, soft slickness. His hand recoiled like a rattlesnake after striking. He searched the darkness again, found an arm, and pulled. No movement. Brandt placed the arm back, reached across the body, grabbed under the opposite armpit. His forearm and biceps felt warm slickness. He pulled again, but the body only moved a few inches.

"Whaddya got?" The same voice that had told him to crawl came from the other side of the body.

"He's wounded," Brandt gasped.

"No shit. Well, you pull from the shoulders. I'll push from the waist," he ordered. "Go, Cherry."

Brandt pulled. This time, the body slid over the muddy ground. At the entrance to the bunker, he looked over his shoulder.

"We're here."

A flash of light revealed the face of his helper. Not a hulking, grizzled sergeant. The man staring back at him looked smaller and younger than himself.

"Go in first; then pull him through. I'll push."

Brandt started to look down at the wounded man.

"Get in there," the younger man said.

Brandt dove through the entrance, slithered on his belly, spun around, and felt for shoulders.

3

"O.K., I have him."

Brandt tugged. The body slid through the low, narrow tunnel.

"Let's move him to the back. Got to make room behind us."

Inside, the man-made cave widened. Brandt bumped his head on the low ceiling and had to duckwalk, the floor muddy as the street, the darkness deeper than the night, the air muggy and rank. Mud oozed up between his toes with each step.

A raspy voice drifted through the darkness. "You're at the back. Who's there?"

"Bill Brandt. How'd you get in here so fast?"

"I was already in here. I'm going home tomorrow," he said. "No way in hell are they going to get me tonight."

A gurgling scream wrenched Brandt's thoughts back to the present.

Now what do I do? I can't even see the man. I don't even know what he looks like.

The now-familiar voice called, "Anybody in here a medic or a doctor? We got a man hurt bad. Shoulder and chest. It's sucking."

Squishing approached from the opposite wall. "I'm a doctor. Anybody got a lighter or matches? I hate this fucking medicine by Braille."

Squishing sounds converged on the doctor, and several lighters clicked on and cast a weak glow. Brandt gasped. The crimson chest glistened. Ragged pieces of flesh stuck up through the pooling blood. A thick smear of mud obscured the face, the man's mouth and lips, the only features Brandt could see.

Doc cleared the airway.

"Anybody got a shirt on? Drape it over the entrance," somebody yelled. "Don't let any light out."

"I got a T-shirt," a voice called. "You wanna use it for bandages?"

"Hell, yes. Get it over here," the doctor ordered. "Anybody got a piece of plastic, get it over here quick." One of the men with a lighter pulled the plastic wrapping off a pack of cigarettes and handed it to the doctor.

The wheezing sound turned into a gurgle.

Plastic? Oh, yeah. It's a sucking chest wound. Air is going directly into the lung through the hole in the chest. The plastic will plug the hole.

Brandt leaned closer, transfixed.

This isn't a demonstration class.

The doctor's hands flew in a blur over his patient. His voice became soft but strong.

"What's your name, son? Can you hear me?"

Silence.

"Hell, I know you can hear me. Hang in there with me, kid," the doctor ordered. He listened again. This time he pleaded, "Help me, kid."

A long, slow breath blew through the doctor's lips. His shoulders slumped. He looked up. "Anybody else hurt?"

After a silent moment, he withdrew.

The man spending the night in the bunker moved past Brandt, knelt next to the body, cleaned the face with his shirt and placed a hand on the forehead.

The lighters clicked shut. Darkness reclaimed the bunker.

"He drowned in his own blood," Brandt blurted.

A hand grasped Brandt's arm. "It don't mean nothin'," said the familiar voice, shaky and punctuated with sniffling sounds. He's out of this fucking place." A deep breath.

"Ya done good, Cherry." Strong voice again. "You just might make it to your DEROS if you go down to the aid station and get the doc to give you some cure for that natural stupidity."

"Thanks," Brandt answered.

Did a man just die? Right next to me. Someone I held a few minutes ago? I don't even know his name. No one does. Death is an acceptable way out?

Brandt leaned back and took a deep breath.

That abrupt change in the familiar voice. How could he put away his feelings so quickly?

Brandt rubbed his forehead. "Uh, what's DEROS?"

"A lifetime, man. Date Eligible to Return from Overseas. If somebody asks you how short you are, you count back from that date. Now, in your sorry case, you got 365-and-a-wake-up."

"How long you been here?" Brandt asked.

"Six months. I just got back from R&R today. I'm looking at 175-and-a-wake-up."

"What unit you in?"

"173rd Airborne. Way up north. Central Highlands. Know where you're headed yet, Cherry?"

"101st Airborne."

"Hot damn, Cherry. I knew you couldn't be a straight leg."

"What's your name?" Brandt asked.

"Wally Jenkins."

Another unfamiliar sensation grabbed Brandt's attention. He sniffed the air and then held his arm up to his nose and sniffed again.

The man who was spending the night in the bunker said, "That's blood you smell, son. Human blood." After a pause, he continued. "I'm a chaplain, and it sure doesn't smell like the wine I drink every Sunday." Another pause. "Brandt, you said you were a paratrooper? An infantryman? Better get used to it."

Brandt's left hand moved to his right forearm. The blood was now sticky. He wasn't sure how to respond. He kept his mouth shut and rested his head on the sandbags. His thoughts drifted back to the plane flight.

Today?

He glanced at the green fluorescent dial on his watch.

Yesterday.

It seemed like a long time ago. He remembered how he walked down the aisle of the plane and past the stares of the young draftees. Their eyes scanned the mirror-like jump boots with pants bloused at the tops, the paratrooper's wings on his chest, 101st Airborne patch on his shoulder, and finally the Ranger tab. Then they searched his face. He knew the swagger in his walk projected the confidence he'd gained from specialized training and service in elite units. They wanted to draw some of that confidence from him.

Training was never like this.

Brandt leaned forward and held his face in his hands.

In a few days, I'll lead men like that. Through nights like this?

A siren blared. Someone said, "All clear." Hushed voices repeated the phrase several times. Brandt noticed a time lag before anyone moved toward the entrance.

"Brandt," Jenkins said, "you might still be an FNG, but at least you ain't a Cherry no more." He started moving toward the entrance.

"FNG?"

Jenkins chuckled. "Fuckin' New Guy. Let's go."

Brandt listened for the sounds of movement around him, began a slow duckwalk, and made his way patiently to the entrance, the last to get out. Just before he slid through the entrance, he paused. "Padre, you still there?"

"Yeah," the voice drifted from the back.

"You got a special blessing for infantry lieutenants?"

"Sure. What religion are you?"

"Catholic."

"May God the Father be your jump master, God the Son, your RTO, God the Holy Spirit, your point man, and may St. Ignatius of Loyola help you kick butt."

Brandt's head snapped back as if punched. He gasped.

"Son, when was the last time you went to church?"

"Uh, eight months."

"It's Bill, isn't it? Listen, Bill. You asked for a blessing because you're scared. You'll start going to services whenever you can. During your first firefight, you'll promise God you'll never miss a Sunday mass for the rest of your life, if He'll just let you live. After a few firefights, you won't believe in God anymore because no god would allow war to exist. But you'll still go to services just for insurance. Then you'll spend the rest of your life trying to reconcile what you learned here with what you're taught back home. That's as far as most men go. If you're lucky, you'll take one more step here. You'll find God. You'll talk to God and experience an intense personal relationship. At that point, you won't need me. I'm just a middleman."

"Thanks, padre." Brandt ducked into the entrance.

"Bill," the gentleness in the voice held him a moment longer. "I wish you luck. I'll mention your name today."

Brandt crawled through the tunnel and emerged into the half-light of dawn. Smoke drifted and cast an eerie spell. Acrid odors scoured his nostrils as he breathed. He stood, legs stiff, and took a few awkward steps. He searched for Jenkins, but men scurried in all directions, and he recognized no one. Pairs of men carrying stretchers hurried to the aid station, winding their way around the holes in the street. Shredded canvas draped building frames like Spanish moss. Remarkably, most of the wooden frames remained standing. The few permanent structures bore splintered wooden walls and twisted metal roofs. Mangled vehicles burned. Maroon stains on the ground tattooed a path to the aid station.

Brandt stood in the midst of bustle and destruction, but his heart beat faster, his chest expanded, and a smile spread across his face.

Why am I feeling this way?

The answer pulsed almost immediately through the confusion.

I survived. I'm alive.

He savored the feeling, sharp and exquisite, more intensely than ever before but only briefly. Then his shoulders sagged and fatigue tugged at every muscle of his body.

My God. A whole year?

CHAPTER 2

Brandt pushed open the mess hall door. A sergeant seated behind an OD-green field table snapped to attention. "Ten'hut!"

Everyone in the front section of the mess hall placed their forks down and stopped eating.

"At ease," Brandt said without hesitation.

The sergeant nodded, then sat down and made a mark in the register before him. Enlisted men resumed eating. Brandt picked up a tray and strode to the front of the line. Slaps, plunks, and splashes were the only sounds as he moved down the chow line.

Typical army breakfast. Everyone still half asleep, silently accepting what is offered as food. At least I can recognize it today.

Brandt walked with a deliberateness characteristic of second lieutenants past the enlisted men toward the area reserved for officers in the back of the mess hall. He saw an empty chair available at the nearest table, but a captain asked a lieutenant colonel if he wanted more coffee. Brandt veered away. He spotted two lieutenants at a table in the far corner, thought he recognized them from the barracks, and headed in that direction.

"Mind if I sit down?"

A smile burst through a galaxy of freckles. The redhead rose to six feet three inches with broad, husky shoulders and extended his hand. "Bob McKnight. Call me Mac."

Brandt shook his hand. Not a bone-crushing grip, but firm and businesslike.

"Bill Brandt."

Brandt faced the other lieutenant.

"Hi, Bill. I'm Doug Lowery."

"Glad to meet you," Brandt said and clenched his teeth. A vise attached to a small, wiry body clamped on his hand.

Mac gestured to the empty chair. "Have a seat."

"How's the food?" Brandt asked.

"Not a bad breakfast," Lowery said, "by Army standards."

"Anytime," Mac raised a finger in emphasis, "you don't have to drink the scrambled eggs."

Lowery chewed limp toast and sipped coffee.

"Which unit you going to, Bill?"

Brandt sat back, relaxed his shoulders, and sighed. Friendly faces. Food. And hearing his first name. It seemed so long since he'd heard it, though it was only a few days ago when he left home. He'd found new friends in a sea of scowls among high-ranking officers.

Brandt straightened. "101st Airborne."

"No shit? That's where we're going, too."

"All right." Brandt paused, then added, "I don't know why it takes so long to process through here. How could it take three or four days? They already know where we're supposed to go."

"Yeah," Lowery agreed. "I don't want to spend any more nights here than I have to."

Mac shook his head. "I'll second that. I was scared shitless."

Brandt looked up, eyes wide. Mac had verbalized the feeling that Brandt saw in everyone's eyes and which yet remained unspoken.

"Yeah," Brandt said and nodded in emphasis, "first time for real. For everyone here, I guess."

"The worst part," Lowery added, "was not having a rifle. Not being able to fight back."

"Right. I felt helpless," Brandt said. "What were we supposed to do if the VC got through the wire?"

"You know," Mac said, "there was a guy in our bunker that died last night. I didn't even see him."

"Neither did I," Lowery said. "Doesn't seem real, but I know it happened."

Brandt put his fork on the table and his eyes followed it down. "I was next to him. I watched him die."

After a moment, Brandt felt a punch on his shoulder. Mac said, "Hey, you guys done? Let's save the rest of this slop for the hogs."

Brandt looked up into a smile that drew him into its cheerfulness.

"Where are you from?" Brandt asked.

"Iowa."

"Where in hell is Iowa?" Lowery sneered as he stood.

"God's country, son. God's country. And don't you try to move there either. The corn grows as high as an elephant's eye. You'd get lost."

They deposited their trays in the kitchen wall pass-through. Brandt recognized a private straining to carry a large tray of dishes, groaning in relief as he rested the heavy tray on the edge of a stainless steel sink. His mouth hung open in the center of his flushed face, gasping for air. Rivulets of sweat ran down his temples as he leaned over the steaming rinse water. He was on the same plane, then the same bus coming into Long Binh. Brandt hurried to the door.

"Let's go check the bulletin board," Brandt said as he stepped down into the muddy street. "See if orders are posted."

"Good idea," Lowery said.

Long Binh bustled with activity. Trucks and jeeps everywhere, some parked, some rumbling along, enlisted men, sergeants, and officers all in constant motion, some purposeful, some seemingly aimless.

"Damn, this is weird," Brandt said. "This looks like any small town beginning the activity of day-to-day life after a calm and restful night."

"Yeah," Mac said as he gazed around. "Like nothing happened last night. I keep looking around expecting to see another explosion."

"You're not alone, there," Lowery said.

The trio weaved their way down the street in their stateside uniforms and spit-shined jump boots. Everyone looked at them as they passed. No one stared—they just looked and moved on—but it was the way they looked.

"Anyone feel out of place?" Mac asked.

"Yeah," Brandt said. "A guy in the bunker last night called me an FNG. Fucking New Guy. This is what it must be like in a zoo. For the animals."

One man in particular drew Brandt's attention, a sergeant wearing a steel helmet, carrying an M-16 rifle, clad in jungle fatigues no longer OD green but faded and pale and jungle boots no longer black but scuffed to a coarse buff color; above his left breast pocket he wore a CIB. Combat Infantryman's Badge. This man had been in combat. His steel-like eyes were cold and hard. On his shoulder, a patch bore the head of a bald eagle on a black shield, the insignia of the 101st Airborne.

The sergeant examined the jump wings on Brandt's chest, the gold bar on his collar, his 101st patch, and finally the orange-and-black Ranger Tab—a virtual tape measure. Brandt pulled his shoulders back and raised his chin.

The sergeant passed by without comment, just a snappy salute as they passed by.

"Hey, Bill." Lowery tugged on his sleeve and led him to a blank bulletin board. "Nothing. Can you believe it?"

Lowery stepped over to a portable table blocking the doorway to the personnel office. An enlisted man, a specialist fourth class named Terell, sat behind it, scanning papers on a clipboard. Lowery cleared his throat. Terell looked up.

"Do you have any idea what's taking so long? We already have our orders for the 101st."

"Orders?" Terell snorted. "Orders from the Pentagon don't mean diddly. We decide where you go. Just keep checking the lists on the board like I told you to."

Brandt strode to the table, leaned forward and placed his hands on the tabletop. "Like I told you to, what, specialist?" He glared into the young man's eyes.

"Like I—like I—asked you to, sir."

Brandt nodded and ignored the tone of the last word.

"Now, would you explain that to me again?"

"Uh," Terell glanced down, breaking the tension.

Brandt waited, still only inches from the man's face.

"Sir," he said, looking up. "Part of the job of the replacement depot is to balance incoming personnel with the immediate needs of units in the field. Orders from Washington are often changed. Like, if a unit gets hit bad and needs replacements fast."

Brandt stood erect as he said, "Thank you, specialist. I'll continue to check the bulletin board as you suggested."

A green bulk filled the doorway, arms akimbo, bearing master sergeant's stripes. The deeply lined poker face revealed nothing. Brandt held his breath. Terell glanced up over his shoulder, aware of the ponderous presence above him. Sweat beaded on his forehead. The sergeant winked and walked back into the office.

Brandt spun around and marched down the street. Lowery and Mac caught up with him.

"Damn, what did you do that for?" Lowery exclaimed. "Now he'll probably send us to some unit that guards latrines somewhere."

"Spec 4s don't make those decisions. Besides, even if you weren't an officer, he didn't have to talk to you like that. If I were out of line, that sergeant would've jumped in."

"Yeah, I guess you're right."

"Damn right," Brandt said. "Give some people a clipboard and they think they're a first sergeant."

They turned a corner and continued down a new street, silent for a while. Brandt lifted his hat and drew his forearm across his forehead in a vain attempt to wipe sweat, but his forearm was just as wet. Rivulets of sweat trickled down his temples, the middle of his back, and the inside of his thighs. He glanced at Lowery and Mac. Large, dark blotches stained areas of their uniforms. The same spots plastered Brandt's uniform to his skin, and the starch in their stateside fatigues added stickiness to discomfort.

"I can't imagine carrying a pack and a rifle in this weather," Lowery said, breaking the silence.

"Yeah." Mac tugged at his fatigue shirt. "I thought I was in good shape. This heat is kicking my butt."

They looked at Brandt expectantly, but he looked away without comment.

"Hey, what's that?" Brandt said, changing the subject.

Mac and Lowery followed Brandt's gesturing finger to the right side of the street. A high barbed-wire fence surrounded a tent. The fence extended back a long way, but the tent hid the interior. Two armed guards stood at the entrance.

"There it is," Lowery said, pointing high above the gate. "L B J," he read from the sign. "Must be Long Binh Jail. Why the hell do they need a prison in a war zone?"

Mac chuckled. "Funny it has the same initials as the president."

"Yeah. Let's get moving," Brandt said.

They rounded another corner, walked down the block, and found themselves back at their barracks. A new tent sat atop the frame.

"I'm going to sack out for a while," Mac said through a yawn. "See you guys later." He climbed the wooden steps and opened the door.

"Doesn't take long to rebuild, does it?" Brandt said. "I guess that's why they build them that way."

"Bill, you want to play some catch?"

"What?" He looked at Lowery in disbelief.

"I brought my glove and a baseball. Follow me. They're in my duffel bag."

Lowery led Brandt into the barracks, where they shed their shirts. Lowery dug into his duffel and they headed out the back door.

"You pitch." Lowery flipped Brandt the ball. "This is home plate," he said, and squatted behind a small crater in the ground.

Brandt shook his head, stepped off thirty paces, assumed a pitcher's stance and threw the ball. A sharp slap sounded as it hit the glove followed by silence as Lowery tossed it back and Brandt gingerly plucked it out of the air. The ball sailed back and forth between them, motions became automatic, and Brandt's mind drifted with the rising heat waves.

Rows of tents on my left, concertina wire and mines on my right. In the narrow corridor, my friend and I are bare from the waist up, wearing fatigue pants and combat boots. We're playing catch using a crater from a mortar round as home plate. Lowery looks like Steve McQueen in the movie, The Great Escape. *Baseball after a rocket attack last night. Something's wrong with this picture.*

Brandt held on to the ball and shook his head. Sweat flew from him like a sprinkler. "It's too hot. Let's go in."

"You're right."

They plodded across the pockmarked ground and entered the barracks.

"The shade does feel good," Lowery said.

Mac rolled to his side and propped his head up with a hand. "It's so hot, I can't even sleep."

Brandt and Lowery each saturated a towel wiping off sweat. Lowery tossed his on the floor against the wall.

"The temperature is the same inside," Brandt said, "but you get relief from the sun's rays that beat down on you."

Like the feeling a quarterback has after the pile of defensive linemen get off him.

Lowery said, as if reading his thoughts, "Damn, Bill, you're built like a brick shithouse. You play football in college?"

"A little." Brandt draped his towel over the bed frame.

"No, really Bill," Lowery persisted. "What position did you play? What college?"

Brandt sighed. "Quarterback and safety. Virginia Military Institute."

Mac jumped in. "So, a military school. No wonder you're a Ranger. What was your major?"

"English. With a minor in ancient Greek and Latin."

Lowery snorted. "English? Not engineering, math or science? How are you going to use that? Write a poem to the enemy?"

Brandt shook his head. "Actually gentlemen, the ability to write clearly and effectively is an essential skill for an officer. History is full of examples."

"Like what?" Lowery sneered.

"The Charge of the Light Brigade."

"A poem. I was right."

Mac sat up. "I can't wait to hear this."

Brandt cleared his throat and raised his chin. "A poem about a military disaster. But why?" He glanced questioningly at each man. "Ever study the Battle of Balaclava?"

No response.

"At VMI, we studied military history." He paused. "In addition to English. An integrated curriculum."

Lowery leaned against his bunk. "So get on with it."

"The famous cavalry charge was part of that battle. In the second stanza, Tennyson says it was a blunder. But of what kind? Tactical? Strategic? Intelligence?"

Brandt shook his head.

"British, French and Turkish forces attacked Russian fortifications in Crimea. During the battle, the Turks abandoned their artillery positions on the hills surrounding the infamous valley of death. The British commander saw this from his position and sent an order to his light cavalry commander to prevent the Russians from getting the guns."

Brandt paused.

"But from his position at the mouth of the valley, the light cavalry commander couldn't see the artillery guns on the hills, just the Russian guns at the head of the valley about a mile away. So he attacked the guns he could see. They charged straight down the valley and were slaughtered by fire from guns on three sides."

Brandt paused and glanced at each of them again.

"A military disaster caused by a poorly written, unclear order."

"Damn," Mac said, "I never knew that."

A sheepish look on Lowery's face. "I stand corrected, professor."

"So gentlemen, the next time you write an operations order, give me a call."

Brandt climbed on the bunk and sat opposite Mac. "In the meantime, let's get back to the present. What unit do you think we'll end up in?"

"Could be anywhere, I guess," Mac said. "I just hope we can go to the same unit." He let out a deep breath. "Kind of bothers me, what that specialist said. I mean, he implied that Washington doesn't have any idea what's happening over here. Know what I mean?"

"I know," Lowery said. "Then why do they assign us to units from over there? Makes you wonder, doesn't it?"

A MATTER OF SEMANTICS

"Washington's perception," Mac said each word slowly and deliberately, "does not necessarily coincide with reality on the ground in Vietnam." He shook his head slowly. "Damn."

Their eyes met as they considered that statement.

Mac broke the silence. "And we all volunteered for Vietnam, right?"

"Yeah," Lowery said.

Brandt nodded and said, "It's expected of a career officer. Combat experience is essential."

"So you guys are lifers," Mac said. "Not me. I'm going to law school and then maybe public service. The military isn't the only profession in which combat experience helps. It's also worth a lot of votes."

"Well, I just hope it's Airborne," Brandt said, bringing the discussion back to the issue at hand. "Damn if I want to go to a leg unit."

Lowery jabbed him in the ribs. " You're supposed to spit when you refer to a non-Airborne unit."

"Hey," Mac said, "where did that term 'leg' come from anyway?"

Brandt raised a finger. "I asked a sergeant at Fort Bragg about that. He said it goes back to World War II. Airborne soldiers wore special pants with extra pockets for all the stuff they had to carry and they bloused the pants into the tops of their jump boots to keep them from getting caught in the wind coming down. Regular infantry soldiers wore leggings, so their pant legs were straight. Hence, "straightleg" or just "leg" when referring to non-Airborne units."

"Interesting," Mac said. "I guess it's like team pride, school pride in high school and college. Everyone wants to think they're better than the other guys."

Lowery continued the banter. "You just don't want to miss out on that jump pay."

"Hey, that hundred dollars a month will add up, man," Mac shot back. "Hell, once we get to a line unit, there won't be any place to spend it. We'll be slightly rich when we get home. We'll be able to invest it."

Brandt leaned forward. "I don't know any paratrooper that would want to go to a non-Airborne unit, and jump pay doesn't have anything to do with it. That's why I volunteered for Jump School and Ranger School. If I'm going into combat, I want to be with the best."

"I know. Just kidding," Lowery admitted. "I feel the same way. But there's not much choice. Besides the 101st, there's the 82nd, with only a brigade here, and the 173rd, a separate brigade. Not a lot of jump slots available." He paused and poked Brandt. "And there aren't any Ranger units anymore."

"The Army's thinking," Brandt said, "is to put Ranger-qualified men into regular infantry units, thereby raising the performance of the Army as a whole."

"Well, the 101st is my first choice," Lowery said.

"Me too, but I wouldn't mind going to the 82nd either," Brandt said. "I've been in both units back in the States. The one unit I wouldn't want is the 173rd."

"Why's that?" asked Mac.

"All of the units are taking more and more casualties," Brandt continued, "But when the 173rd makes the evening news, it seems like they lose whole units, whole platoons, even whole companies. Something must be wrong."

"I'll tell you what's wrong," Lowery said. "I know a guy, a Jump School classmate, that was in the 173rd. He said that they never had an Area of Operations. Headquarters used them as a quick reaction force. They sent them to places like the Iron Triangle. When the action calmed down, they sent them to another hotspot like War Zone D. After that, they sent them up north into the Central Highlands." Lowery paused for emphasis. "He told me that at Hill 875, one battalion, about 500 men, was sent to find an NVA division, about 3,000 men. They found it, and kicked ass, but by the time reinforcements arrived, they lost nearly the whole battalion."

"When was that?" Mac asked.

"A few months ago."

Brandt shook his head. "Who's making those decisions? Doesn't sound like a good strategy to me."

"Beats me," Mac said. "All I know is I'm getting hungry. Let's get ready for lunch."

"All right," Brandt said, as he hopped off the bunk. "I'll go check the bulletin board again while you get ready."

A few minutes later, Brandt ran his finger down an assignment roster. His heart stopped along with his finger at "Brandt, W. F.," and below his name, Lowery's and McKnight's. His finger followed the dotted line across to the next column.

"Holy shit."

Brandt ran back to the barracks and threw open the door. "Doug. Mac. We got our assignments. We're going to the 173rd. All three of us."

"Go-o-o-ddamn!" they blurted in unison.

The trio ran back to the bulletin board. Brandt pointed and they gaped.

A voice behind them broke the silence. "You better get your gear and bring it down here," Specialist Terell said. "The plane for An Khe will be leaving soon." A smirk creased his face. "Sir."

CHAPTER 3

Brandt arched his back and straightened his legs, a futile effort. All military aircraft seemed to be designed for the same level of discomfort. No matter how big the plane, seats like large-gauge nets crammed passengers together. Shifting position no longer relieved the discomfort but only moved the ache to another part of his body. For a while. The cotton-strap webbed seats cut into his thighs and back, his shoulders jammed between Mac's shoulders on his right and Lowery's on his left. When he stretched his legs, he had to place his feet between those of the men across from him. Rumbling engines shook the fuselage, Brandt's feet absorbed the vibrations, and his whole body tingled. Turbulence jostled and bounced everything in the plane, and three men had vomited, adding stench to stale air.

Just like flights to practice jumps at Fort Bragg. Rumbling engines churn your gut into a milk shake. One person throws up, and that starts a chain reaction.

Brandt nudged Lowery. "Can you believe we're used to this?"

Lowery glanced at Brandt but didn't respond. He looked bored and uncomfortable. Brandt scanned other faces in his field of vision. All but one wore the same look. It belonged to a lieutenant colonel sitting across from him. The man, tall and rangy, wore a field pack, a pistol belt and suspenders with a .45 caliber pistol, three knives, and a canteen attached. The 173rd shoulder patch rested beneath a Ranger Tab. He held a camouflage-covered steel helmet in his lap.

First high-ranking officer I've seen dressed like a real soldier. Tough looking son of a bitch, too.

The name tag read "Everett." Above that sat a CIB with a star.

Damn. Twice in combat. Must have been in Korea. He's no FNG.

Everett exuded a surly disdain and seemed very self-contained.

Brandt felt a jab in his right side. Mac leaned toward him and whispered, "Bored?"

Mac winked. He leaned forward to address the lieutenant colonel.

"Quite a collection of knives you have there, sir."

Everett barely acknowledged the remark with a grunt.

"Are you a cutlery salesman?"

Shit. Lieutenants just don't talk to a lieutenant colonel that way. Let alone one who looks like he knows how to use those knives.

Brandt tried to move away from Mac. About three inches was all he could manage in the tight quarters.

Mac was now the center of attention, and the smile on his face bore witness to the fact that he loved it. Brandt stared at him, barely breathing. He caught another wink from the corner of Mac's eye.

Everett stirred like an awakened giant, slowly sat erect, leaned forward, and directed the full energy of his attention toward the upstart lieutenant. The aggressiveness that emanated from him was palpable to Brandt but seemed to wash around and away from Mac.

"No, lieutenant," he said, breaking the hush that had seized the plane. "I don't sell knives. I use them." He paused, holding Mac in his gaze.

Mac held his forward lean, his shining face expectant.

"Which one interests you the most, lieutenant?" Everett continued.

Mac pointed to the largest one. It hung upside down on the left suspender.

Everett unsnapped the safety strap, drew the knife from its scabbard, and offered it handle first. Mac took the knife by the leather handle and inspected the hexagonal metal butt, curved hand guard, fine edge and partially serrated top. Mac examined it, almost reverently, and kept his fingertips off the gleaming blade.

Mac whistled. "A fine piece of workmanship, sir. A custom Randall?"

"Not a bad eye for a farm boy. Ever use a knife like that, son?"

Mac shook his head. "No, sir."

"Well, I have. You better stick to whittling willow branches with a jackknife."

Brandt was breathing normally again, and he noticed that everyone else was, too. He marveled at the exchange. Mac moved from challenging, to disarming, to respectful without retreating. Everett deterred insolence and established credibility.

The conversation grew into an animated discussion of knives. Everett passed the knife to Brandt and Lowery and brought them into the discussion.

"I've got a Gerber," Brandt said.

"The double-edged dagger they make?" Everett asked. "Where is it?"

"In my duffel bag." Brandt pointed toward a pile of baggage at the rear of the plane.

"Not doing you any good in there, is it, lieutenant?"

"Guess not, sir." Then Brandt added, "You know, sir, you're the only field-grade officer I've seen wearing combat equipment."

"I know I seem out of place, but I don't care what anybody thinks. That rear-echelon atmosphere can lull you into a false sense of security. It can get hot anytime, anywhere."

Brandt took a deep breath. "Speaking of anywhere, sir, do you have an idea how much longer this flight is? We don't even know where An Khe is."

Everett feigned a serious look. "You mean to tell me, Ranger, that you don't know where you are now? Didn't you study a map this morning?"

"Map, sir? I don't even have web-gear to hang my knife on, let alone a map and rifle. I feel helpless. Like a sheep being poked by the shepherd's staff and just following the herd."

Everett laughed. "Relax, lieutenant. I'm just having a little fun. I understand your feelings. But enough of that. Actually, it's 'flock' when you're referring to sheep. Interesting that you said 'herd' because the nickname of the 173rd is 'The Herd.'"

Everett paused, checked his watch, and glanced at the crew chief strapping himself into a seat at the back of the plane. He cleared his throat. "An Khe is located," he began in a professorial tone, "in the Central Highlands, about 400 miles north of Saigon, more than half way to the DMZ. It's in the middle of the country between the coast and the Cambodian border."

Everett shrugged his shoulders. "Basically, in the middle of nowhere."

Brandt asked, "Why are we going to the middle of nowhere?"

Everett chuckled. "Actually, An Khe is a district capital in Gia Lai Province. The 1st Cavalry Division built the base and named it Camp Radcliff to honor their first combat death. When they moved farther north, the 173rd took it over because the brass in Saigon finally decided to give the brigade its own Area of Operations. Most people now refer to it as An Khe Base."

Brandt leaned forward. "So the 173rd has its own AO now?"

Everett nodded. "Yes. Essentially, it encompasses all of the Central Highlands from the coast to the Cambodian border. The mission is to interdict the main supply spurs off the Ho Chi Minh Trail. Highway 1, the main north–south road runs along the coast, and Highway 19, the main east–west road, runs from Qui Nhon on the coast through An Khe to Pleiku, the province capital."

Everett glanced at the crew chief again and saw him talking into his headset. Again he feigned the serious look and tone. "So, if this plane goes down, I at least stand a chance of making it back."

Brandt's stomach lurched up. He found himself leaning on Lowery. Mac pressed against his shoulder. Men on the other side of the plane canted at the same steep angle. The plane leveled out of the sharp turn, nosed down, and plummeted. Brandt's eyes widened. He struggled to suck in the breath that had been squeezed out of him.

Everett laughed. "Relax, gentlemen, we're just landing."

Brandt stared at him, mouth open.

"It's O.K. Pilots in Nam don't make long, slow approaches to a runway. They drop in fast. Gives snipers less time to line up a shot."

The plane slowed rapidly. Everett smiled. "You boys seem like you've jumped from more planes than you've landed in."

Brandt was about to answer when the plane shuddered. He bounced in his seat. The engines roared. Brandt felt the floor slam into his feet. Gravity threw him on top of Mac this time. Then his back bounced against the fuselage as the plane banked sharply to the left. Men opposite, actually above him now, were straining forward against their seat belts.

Level flight.

"Damn," Brandt gasped. "What the hell is going on?"

"A sniper probably took a shot at us. Pilots don't like to land when that happens."

"A sniper? What'll we do?"

"No big deal. Happens all the time coming into An Khe. The pilot will circle while a squad of infantry goes after them, but they're gone already."

"What?"

"It's just harassment. A team with a .50 caliber machine gun sets up on a ridge at the head of the runway. They take a few shots at an incoming plane, disassemble the .50, and run away. We'll be landing in a few minutes."

Brandt shook his head. "But this plane just about had its wheels on the ground. How did it do that?"

Everett smiled. "I know. It's hard to believe what some of these planes, choppers, and the pilots can do. This is a C-7, a Caribou. It's a workhorse over here. Lands and takes off from incredibly short airstrips."

Brandt eased his grip on the seat. He nodded but knitted his brow. A sniper had just shot at them. Everett only seemed inconvenienced. No more than trying to cross a busy street during rush hour. Brandt gazed around. Most passengers looked like he felt. A few projected the same air of annoyance as Everett. The crew chief scowled. Brandt caught part of his comment into the radio headset, "If only those fucking ground-pounders would do their job."

The plane dropped and leveled again. Brandt tightened his grip again. The wheels touched. He heard a low-pitched rumble that translated into a steady vibration through his body, like landing on a washboard. The vibration tapered to a tingle and then stopped. The rear cargo door of the plane lowered, revealing blue sky and a distant hazy horizon. Brandt struggled out of his seat and stretched kinks in muscles. Everyone groaned. Then they waited while the crew unloaded cargo.

The crew chief raised his hand high, circling it above his head. "Move it out."

The throng moved forward and Brandt followed, welcoming the fresh air. Then he collided with heat. Sweat beaded on his forehead and neck as he stepped onto a corrugated steel runway. He looked around and a curt laugh escaped.

Just like a giant washboard.

Brandt joined the others and picked through the pile of duffel bags, rucksacks, and boxes. He found Lowery's first, rolled it to him, and then spotted his own. Mac was waiting for them at the edge of the runway.

Brandt scanned the area. "Where the hell are we?" A few buildings and steel shipping containers clustered near the runway, but beyond that, all he could see were open fields, hills, and mountains. Everything seemed normal. Too normal. No barbed-wire perimeter, no guard towers. At least none in sight. Everyone hustled away. Apparently they knew where they were going.

"Where's the base camp? Is this place that big?"

Mac shrugged and stepped over to an air force sergeant holding a clipboard, checking off the remaining cargo. "Sergeant, where's the headquarters of the 173rd?"

"About a mile from here." He pointed with the clipboard. "Down that road."

"Thanks." Mac looked at Brandt and Lowery and shrugged. "I guess we follow that road."

Brandt picked up his duffel, balanced it on his shoulder, and followed. The bag got heavy fast, and the pace slowed as they plodded down the bumpy, rutted dirt road wide enough for two vehicles to pass. Fields of tall grass flanked both sides of the road.

Thirty yards ahead a snake slithered onto the road from the right. Thick-bodied, brown, and no pattern markings. As its head neared the left edge of the road, it stopped, and they still could not see its tail.

The trio froze. Brandt gasped and dropped his duffel. In the blink of an eye, the snake coiled in the center of the road. Beneath its raised head, the neck flattened into a wide hood with a distinctive mark. A cobra.

The snake stared at them for what seemed to Brandt an eternity. Sensing no threat, the snake slithered into the grass to the left of the road.

Brandt heard a truck on the road behind him, picked up his duffel, and hesitantly stepped to the side of the road, peering into the grass. No snakes. Mac and Lowery followed. The truck stopped. Everett leaned out the passenger side window. "You boys are officers, now. Better start acting like some." He motioned with his thumb. "Hop in the back."

★ ★ ★

A MATTER OF SEMANTICS

Bleachers. The Army's all-purpose, portable, open-air classroom. Blazing sun overhead. Bodies crammed shoulder to shoulder, knees of one row jammed into the backs of the row in front. Row upon row. The instructor stopped his description of the Central Highlands terrain and glared. Brandt nudged the private sitting next to him. The man started.

"Sorry, sir."

"Don't apologize to me," Brandt said. He gestured toward the instructor.

The instructor said, "O.K., gentlemen. I can see you need a wake-up."

He started telling a funny story about the Fuck-You Lizards of Vietnam. Young enlisted men and newly made NCOs listened with rapt attention. Brandt smiled. This instructor had style.

Right. Been through enough initiation rites to spot this one coming from a mile away.

In fact, his company commander at Fort Bragg warned him about the "new guy" practical jokes they pulled in Nam. "Bill, when you get there, somebody will tell you that you need to get measured for a body bag."

"What?"

"Yeah, they go through this big explanation of how body bags come in different sizes and they'll have to requisition one for you. If you get killed, they'll have the right size to send you home."

"First time I've heard that one, sir."

"Don't let them scare you with that shit, Bill. You'll be scared enough already. And don't let that bother you either. We all were scared."

Brandt nodded, as if agreeing with the instructor.

Yeah, a lizard that's going to tell me to get fucked. Probably part of the VC psychological warfare program. They can't afford a Tokyo Rose and a radio station so they train lizards.

★ ★ ★

Brandt wandered the streets of An Khe Base. After sitting in bleachers most of the day, he decided to walk and explore. Mac and Lowery caught some shuteye before going to dinner.

Dinner at the NCO Steakhouse. A restaurant in a war zone?

He shook his head. That was not his image of war—based on history and what he'd seen on television. And he'd already been to the Post Exchange, as large as most department stores back home.

Why did you need a PX in a war?

He passed one of the now familiar structures, a wood-framed building with screens for walls, green plastic sandbags stacked a third of the way up the sides, called a hooch in Vietnam. The sign in front caught his eye—the winged bayonet of the 173rd Airborne and the words, "Inspector General." He stopped and peered through the screen door.

"Come in," boomed a strong voice. Brandt hesitated, then pulled on the screen door and stepped in.

Why did I do that?

Lieutenant Colonel Everett sat ramrod straight behind a plywood desk. He gestured toward a folding chair. "Have a seat, lieutenant."

Brandt stepped smartly forward and sat at attention.

"Relax." Everett glanced down and read the name tag. "Brandt. I remember you from the flight into An Khe." He smiled. "And the ride into headquarters. Just thought I'd see how you were doing. After all, that is my job."

Brandt relaxed his shoulders. "Pretty well, sir. Getting used to the heat."

Everett glanced down. "And I see you're wearing your Gerber now."

Brandt grasped the knife in its leather sheath. "Yes, sir. And I feel a little more comfortable, thanks to you. But I sure get a lot of funny looks around here."

"Don't let that bother you. We're surrounded by REMFs." He pronounced the acronym as a word.

"Sir?"

"Rear-Echelon Mother Fuckers. It's what grunts in the field call people who work in rear areas. REMFs get lulled into a false sense of security. In reality, they're surrounded by the enemy. There are no rear areas in Vietnam, only varying sizes of base camps."

Brandt nodded.

"May I see it?" Everett extended his hand, palm up.

Brandt slipped the double-edged dagger out of the sheath and presented the handle to him. Everett examined the knife like a jeweler appraising a gemstone. "The blade is at a five-degree cant from vertical. Do you know why?"

"It's so the blade will glance off a bone instead of getting stuck in it."

"Right. Do you know how to use this?"

Brandt sat back and took a deep breath. Everett offered the knife to him, stone faced, eyes riveted on him. Brandt took the knife and replaced it in its sheath. Everett remained silent.

"Sir, that's the first time anyone's asked me that question. My father told me I should say that there's only one way to find out the answer to that question. But a little voice in my head is telling me that I shouldn't say that to you."

Everett smiled. "Your father gave you good advice. That is the correct answer." He sat back. "But you were right to listen to that little voice."

Everett waved a dismissive hand. "But enough of that. What's your first name?"

"William, sir. Bill."

"Well, Bill, tell me about Jungle School. Are you learning anything?"

Brandt hesitated, still unsure about this situation. "To be honest, sir, not much that's new. But only because I learned most of it in Ranger

School. It's all good stuff, and others in the class say they're learning a lot."

"Good to hear you say that, Bill. You'll find your Ranger training invaluable, but it will also place more responsibility on you. You know the motto: 'Rangers, lead the way.' And people will expect more of you." Everett patted the Ranger Tab on his shoulder. "I know."

Again, Everett waved a dismissive hand. "But enough of that. I'm interested in what you think of Jungle School because it's unique in Nam. The 173rd is the first unit that I know of to do something like it. And it is my job to know if it's helping my soldiers."

"Uh," Brandt hesitated again.

"Go ahead, Bill."

"Well, just what is your job, sir?"

"Actually, George Washington created the position of Inspector General during the Revolutionary War. He based it on models in European armies. It has evolved over time. Essentially, the Inspector General is the eyes, ears, and conscience of the commander. It's my job to be aware of any problems in the command. Any soldier can come to me with a complaint and I can investigate any officer from a full colonel on down. So the IG wields a great deal of power and needs to use it wisely."

He raised an eyebrow.

"But enough of that. Besides getting used to the heat, what's the value of Jungle School?"

"Well, sir." Brandt thought for a moment. "For me, it's bringing my knowledge down from a general level to a specific, local level. The instructors have come in from the field after about six months out there. It's usually their second tour in Nam. I'm hearing about types of booby traps the enemy is using here, their tactics, what the terrain is like, and so forth. They share modifications in our basic infantry tactics they developed here. What seems to work and what doesn't."

Brandt stopped talking. Everett nodded but remained silent, waiting expectantly. Brandt squirmed in his chair and looked up and to his right.

"And from what I've heard," he continued, "veterans don't want to befriend the new guys because they're likely to do something stupid and get themselves and others around them killed. Nobody likes to see a friend die. That means the new guys are the most likely to get killed. What they're learning here means they won't go into the field completely clueless. It should break down that vicious cycle. Seems like a great idea to me."

"Thanks, Bill. That kind of information helps me a lot. Anything else?"

"Last night we pulled guard duty on the Green Line. Small groups were assigned to the guard towers on the base perimeter along with the regular guards. Nothing happened at our post, but the position just to the north of us took some machine-gun fire. First time I'd seen the green enemy tracers. Some of the rounds hit pretty close to us. I could hear them ricocheting off rocks. When our guards returned fire, it was quite a show. Solid lines of red and green crisscrossing in the night."

Everett nodded. "It's an impressive sight, especially when you realize that only one round in ten is a tracer. Nine rounds between the tracers and you're still seeing solid lines burning powder." He paused. "So you experienced an exchange of fire with the enemy?"

"Yes, sir."

"So the war is becoming a little more real to you?"

"Yes, sir. And tomorrow, we'll be going outside the perimeter on a patrol. An instructor is assigned to each patrol of 11 or 12 men, the size of a squad. I'm more than a little apprehensive about it. We'll be out there where the enemy was last night."

"That's good, Bill. Fear is your friend as long as you control it. It keeps you sharp."

"That will be the culminating lesson in Jungle School. After that, we go to our units. Lieutenant Lowery is going to 1st Battalion. Lieutenant McKnight and I go to the 2nd Battalion at LZ English." Then he added, "Somewhere up north."

"It's outside the city of Bong Son in the northeast corner of Binh Dinh Province near the coast. The Area of Operations reaches well into the mountains. So you'll be getting sand in your boots as well as walking through triple-canopy rainforests."

"Sounds like a real challenge."

"More than a challenge. Historically, Binh Dinh Province has been the most difficult to pacify. And now, the North Vietnamese Army and the Viet Cong are moving out of the mountains and into the coastal plain. It's strategically important because capturing major cities and controlling the province would allow them to cut South Vietnam in half. Two spurs off the Ho Chi Minh Trail support that effort. You'll be leading men into the teeth of that force. Don't underestimate them."

Brandt whistled. "Like you said, sir, more than a challenge."

Again, Everett waived his hand. "But enough of that. Tell me a little about yourself. You sound like you're from Virginia, and you have an excellent military posture." He paused. "VMI?"

"Wow!" Brandt's eyes widened. "You're good, sir."

Everett smiled. "And a family tradition?"

"Yes, sir. My great-grandfather fought in the Battle of New Market."

"Ah, the battle in the Civil War the VMI cadets participated in. They kept the Union Army out of the Shenandoah Valley and secured the food supply for Lee's army."

"Right. And my grandfather and father also attended VMI."

"So, are you a career officer?"

"Yes, sir."

"Excellent."

Everett raised his arm and looked at his watch. "I've got a meeting with the Brigade Executive Officer now, so I've got to run. The brigade has four widely spread battalions. I'm informing him that I'll be establishing satellite offices in each base camp. I'll be damned if I get stuck in headquarters and only get filtered information from the field. It's unusual, but I want to be accessible to my soldiers."

Everett stood.

"You'll be getting in from the field periodically. Stop in and see me, Bill."

Outside the office, Brandt watched Everett stride down the road.

Interesting guy. Brandt took a deep breath. *So, Binh Dinh Province in a couple of days.*

CHAPTER 4

★ ★ ★

"Welcome to LZ English and the 2nd Battalion, lieutenant." The captain glanced down. "Brandt, I see. William F.?"

"Yes, sir."

"Great. I'm Captain Johnson, Personnel Officer. At ease."

Brandt snapped to parade rest.

Johnson smiled. "Stand easy, lieutenant. We're not on a parade ground."

Brandt stood at a relaxed version of attention.

"We've been expecting you for some time. As well as a Lieutenant McKnight."

"Yes, sir Lieutenant McKnight will be on the plane tomorrow. He had some paperwork to take care of."

Johnson sat back in his chair. "So you arrived at Long Binh, processed in-country, and they diverted you to An Khe and the 173rd Airborne. More processing at brigade headquarters and then a week at Jungle School."

He raised his arms, palms up, in an all-encompassing gesture. "Finally LZ English, your new home."

"Yes, sir. Every time I thought I was going to the war, it seemed to move farther away."

Johnson chuckled. "Well, I assure you the war has not moved again. It is here. In a moment, you'll meet the battalion commander, and he will give you your assignment. After that, come back here, and I'll take you to your company. You'll meet the executive officer and first sergeant, get your gear, and they will arrange for you to fly out on the next resupply chopper."

Johnson rose. "The commander is in the officer's mess. Shall we go?"

"Sounds good to me, sir."

Brandt walked alongside Johnson down a gentle slope flanked by the now familiar sandbagged, wooden-frame tents. Rows formed streets, and streets formed a town cast in olive drab. Individual soldiers strode here and there, but this town lacked the hustle and bustle Brandt experienced in the large installations of Long Binh and An Khe. He scanned left and right, back over his shoulder, and ahead down slope.

"I know what you're thinking," Johnson said. "LZ English is a forward operating base providing logistical, artillery, and air support for the battalion. Hence the designation, LZ—Landing Zone. Most of the residents are out in the field fighting a war."

Johnson stopped at a tent no different from all the others and gestured, "Such is the officer's mess in a forward area." He grabbed the screen-door handle. "Ready, lieutenant?"

Brandt took a deep breath. "Yes, sir."

Johnson led Brandt into the dining area, deserted save for the lone figure seated at the first table, stirring coffee, eyes fixed on the cup.

Johnson cleared his throat. "Sir."

The figure stopped stirring and looked up.

"Sir, this is Lieutenant William Brandt, our latest replacement." He looked to Brandt. "This is Lieutenant Colonel Dalton Alexander, 2nd Battalion Commander."

Brandt stepped forward. "Sir, Lieutenant Brandt, William F., reporting as ordered."

Alexander continued stirring coffee, eyes now fixed on Brandt.

"Thank you, captain. That will be all."

Johnson took a step back and hustled to the door.

Brandt remained at attention.

Alexander removed the spoon and placed it on a napkin beside the coffee mug. A long moment passed.

"Sit."

Brandt pulled a chair, sat at attention, hands folded in his lap.

Alexander sat back; his chair groaned. He held up a file folder and tossed it back on the table.

"I've read your file, Brandt. From what I see, there's no need for me to give you a rah-rah motivational speech or ask you about your training or qualifications for leading men in combat.

He tapped the file. "It's all in there. So I'm assigning you to Bravo Company. You'll be Third Platoon Commander."

Alexander rocked forward; the chair complained again.

"Did you see the sign above the entrance to our battalion area?"

"Yes, sir. 'SECOND TO NONE.'"

"I chose that motto because I have personally built this battalion into the finest fighting unit in the brigade. I hold that standard for myself, and I expect every officer to do likewise."

A thin smile creased Alexander's face.

"First Battalion's commander has taken the motto 'NONE' thinking he's topping me." Alexander snorted. "If that dumb shit wants to call himself 'NONE' he can do it all he wants. Doesn't make any difference to me."

Alexander sat erect.

"Brandt, I'm going to tell you one more thing, and don't you ever forget it." A pause. "Do you know what happens when you assume something?"

Rhetorical question. Keep your mouth shut, Brandt.

Alexander pulled a piece of paper and pen out of his shirt pocket, placed it on the table, and printed in all capitals, "ASSUME." Then he turned the paper around to Brandt and drew two vertical lines dividing the word on either side of the "U": ASS|U|ME

"When you assume something, you make an ASS," he said, pointing to the first three letters, "out of U," pointing to Brandt. Then he stabbed a thick finger into the last two letters—"ME."

Alexander leaned across the table, eyes boring into Brandt. "I don't care if you make an ass of yourself," he hissed, "but don't you ever make an ass out of me."

★ ★ ★

The helicopter banked sharply, circled a clearing below, and Brandt looked straight down at the ground through the open cargo bay door. Pressure built under his feet, an odd sensation, as if they were stuck to the floor. The boxes stacked around him remained in place, defying gravity.

Damn, this is weird. Instructors at Fort Benning said it was impossible to fall out of a turning helicopter. Something about centrifugal force. Right.

He tightened his grip on the doorjamb and leaned back on his haunches.

The crew chief shoved boxes labeled "AMMO," "GRENADE LAUNCHER," "40 MM," "HE AND AMMO," "7.62 MM," and "BALL" toward the cargo bay door just moving around as if he were working in a warehouse—not holding on to anything. More movement drew Brandt's attention. The door gunner hung outside the aircraft, safety harness taut, knuckles white against the handgrip, index finger on the trigger guard, and his head moved methodically from side to side.

Brandt followed the door gunner's gaze to the tree line surrounding the clearing. Foxholes dotted the circumference, a man in each hole leaned into sandbags, weapons at the ready. Men in jungle fatigues scurried back and forth from the foxholes to the center of the clearing, where several men stood around another large foxhole.

Like watching ants working.

The helicopter leveled out, slowed, stopped forward movement, and dropped altitude. The door gunner sat back and pointed his machine gun up at the sky, and the crew chief placed his hands on a stack of boxes. Treetops filled the view, then gave way to tree trunks, then grass, and then a cloud of dust. Brandt released his grip on the doorjamb. The chopper settled and soldiers converged. The crew chief tossed small boxes and shoved larger ones out the door. The soldiers carried or dragged them away, hunched over, muscling the weight. But the last items, rectangular metal containers with removable lids, the crew chief handled carefully. The man taking it moved slowly and deliberately away from the chopper.

The crew chief leaned toward Brandt and yelled over the engine's roar, "This is your stop, lieutenant."

Brandt stood uneasily, legs cramped after the 30 minute flight, grabbed his rucksack with his left hand, reached down to his hip with his right, gripped the .45 caliber pistol, took a deep breath, and lunged through the opening. He landed off-balance, stumbled as he tried to run in a crouch, and regained his balance, but then his steel helmet fell to the ground and he kicked it. He grabbed it and dashed forward through a maelstrom of dust. His eyes watered. Grit stung his face. The rotor blades pounded a palpable beat.

The roar changed to a distinct wop-wop-wop sound that receded rapidly. A hush enveloped him as the dust settled. Men moved quickly around him, splitting open boxes and handing the contents to others, and arranged the rectangular metal containers in a straight line, a few feet apart. No one paid any attention to him.

Like being in a dream.

He looked beyond the bustle. To the northeast, mountains rose above open fields and scattered trees; forest spread to the west, and mountains rose in the distance.

Huh? Not jungle. Forest.

He waited. There was no response, no greeting. A memory popped into his head. His plebe year at Virginia Military Institute. His first sergeant yelling, "Don't just stand around with your thumb up your ass."

Brandt took a deep breath and strode purposefully toward the center of the perimeter, the likely location of the company command post.

"Lieutenant Brandt," a gravelly voice called. "Over here."

Brandt pivoted and saw a dark, burly figure marching toward him. The man had captain's bars on his collar and carried a machete like a swagger stick.

No, more like a scepter.

A strange-looking rifle hung on his shoulder. Brandt jogged to him, stopped, and raised his right hand to salute but realized he still held his helmet.

"Put your steel pot on, lieutenant. You need to set an example for the troops." As he replaced his helmet, Brandt looked at the black curly hair on top of the captain's head.

"And don't salute me in the field. That makes me one hell of a target for snipers."

Damn, I know better.

He tucked the machete under his arm and stood as if reviewing troops in a parade.

"Captain Parker. I'm the company commander. Welcome to Bravo Company."

"Lieutenant Brandt. Reporting as ordered, sir."

Parker craned his neck to the side, looked at Brandt's left upper arm. "So you're my Ranger." He had a sarcastic tone.

Brandt stiffened.

I know how to play this military game. Don't speak until you're asked a question.

"I'm glad you're here," Parker continued. "Been short a platoon leader for a couple of weeks now. You'll be in charge of 3rd Platoon. Call sign: November 6."

Brandt nodded.

"We identify our three rifle platoons by the phonetic alphabet for radio security purposes; 1st Platoon is Lima and 2nd Platoon is Mike."

Brandt nodded again.

"There's no logic to it, no clever puns. The enemy can't attach any meaning to the names."

Brandt started to nod again, but stopped.

I must look like a bobblehead doll.

"And '6' designates the commander of the unit?"

The corners of Parker's mouth curled into a smile. "Right, lieutenant. And your Platoon Sergeant is November 5."

Parker raised his machete, pointed to a spot on the perimeter, and moved it in an arc. "Third Platoon's sector is 11 o'clock to 3 o'clock. Staff Sergeant Williams has been the acting platoon leader. Let's go meet him." Parker took a step, then stopped. "Oh, here's your weapon," he said taking the rifle off his shoulder. "It's a CAR-15. An experimental sub-machine gun version of the M-16 with a retractable stock. One of the first in Vietnam. It has some quirks. You'll need to practice shooting it—get used to the balance."

Brandt took the rifle and hefted it. "I've never seen one of these. I like the feel of it."

"Good. It belonged to Lieutenant Dugan, the man you're replacing. I hope you're not superstitious. See that nick in the carrying handle?"

Brandt looked down at a semi-circular hole on the top of the weapon's carrying handle.

"That was made by the bullet that killed him. Ricocheted off the handle and hit him in the stomach, tumbling as it entered." Parker shook his head slowly. "He was a good platoon leader."

Brandt started to respond, but Parker started walking again. He said over his shoulder, "Sergeant Williams has 16 years in the army. This is his second tour in Vietnam. He's good. Listen to him."

Brandt followed and saw a tall, willowy man climb out of a foxhole set about 20 meters back from the perimeter. He moved with a loping gait, shoulders hunched, as if self-conscious of his height. Brandt guessed about six feet four inches tall.

"Sergeant Williams," Parker said, "this is Lieutenant Brandt, your new platoon leader. Lieutenant, Staff Sergeant Williams."

Williams extended his hand. "Sure am glad to see you, sir."

Brandt laid his rucksack on the ground, placed the rifle on it and shook the hand. "Pleased to meet you, sergeant."

"Third Platoon is a little more than half strength," Parker said. "Twenty-five, to be exact. It's been a tough war lately."

"Got that right, sir," Williams agreed.

"But I expect a steady stream of replacements soon," Parker continued. "I'll leave you two alone for a while. Report to my command post at 1330, lieutenant. I'll brief you on Standard Operating Procedures and our next mission. You'll meet the other platoon leaders then, too."

"Yes, sir," Brandt said to Parker's back, the captain already marching to his command post, machete tucked under his arm.

"He ever cut himself with that?" Brandt muttered.

"What, sir?" Williams asked.

"Never mind. Why don't you fill me in on what's happening."

"Well, sir, this is our night laager position."

Brandt screwed up his face at the unfamiliar term.

"Oh." Williams noticed the questioning look. "Laager means a place you camp for the night, but more. Kind of like circling the wagons for protection. It seems to have caught on here in Nam."

"Thanks, sergeant." Another little fact to remember.

"Anyway, sir, we laagered up early today for resupply. I've got the squad leaders distributing ammo and C-Rations now. They'll be sending our men over for chow in a few minutes." He gestured to the center of the perimeter. Men holding large spoons stood behind each of the rectangular metal containers. A file of soldiers had formed in front of them.

Brandt smiled. "An army travels on its stomach. I saw how carefully they handled the Mermite containers."

"Yes, sir. We get one hot meal every three days or so. Whenever we get a major resupply. Most important thing on the chopper as far as the troops are concerned."

Brandt gestured with an arm toward the perimeter. "What's our responsibility?"

"We have the northeast section of the perimeter." He pointed. "Our first hole is that one, about 11 o'clock. First platoon, Lima, is on our left flank." He swept his arm in an arc. "That hole marks our right flank; 3 o'clock. Beyond that is 2nd Platoon, Mike."

Brandt followed his hand. "Equal spacing between positions, no gaps, good deep holes."

"Yes, sir. At first, you have to stay on the troops to dig them deep enough, but after the first enemy bullet cracks over their heads, you have to keep them from digging too deep."

Brandt chuckled along with Williams. "Anything else?"

"We have one OP out from 2nd Squad. No ambushes tonight. Nothing special."

"O.K., you can show me where the observation post is later. What about tomorrow?"

"Don't know yet. We come out of the jungle this morning, and the ocean is only a few klicks east. I figure we're in for a climb." Williams pointed northeast. "The Tiger Mountains. After your meeting with Captain Parker, I expect *you'll* tell *me* the mission."

Brandt took a deep breath, faced Williams, and looked him in the eye. "Sergeant, you've been the acting platoon leader for a while, but I'm the platoon leader now."

Furrows formed on Williams' forehead.

"But you've been in combat, and I haven't. I need to learn from your experience. Your advice and counsel is both expected and appreciated. So, whatever policies you have will stay in effect for now. If I think we need to change anything, I'll let you know. When a decision needs to be made, we'll discuss it, then make the decision together, if possible. But once the decision is made, the responsibility is mine."

Williams' brow smoothed. "I'm real glad to hear you say that, sir. I think we'll get along just fine."

"Sergeant Williams."

Williams looked over his shoulder. The voice sounded familiar to Brandt.

Williams stepped back and gestured to an approaching soldier. "This is your RTO, sir. Specialist Jenkins."

The radiotelephone operator stopped abruptly. His eyes widened.

Brandt placed the voice as their eyes met. His jaw dropped.

"Specialist Jenkins, meet Lieutenant Brandt, your new platoon leader."

Jenkins' mouth moved but no sound came out.

Williams glanced back and forth between Brandt and Jenkins. "Am I missing something?"

"Uh, Specialist Jenkins and I have already met, sergeant. In Long Binh, when he returned from R&R. I'm sure you'll hear the rest of the story later."

Jenkins curled and uncurled his fingers, looked around, as if he were searching for something he just had to do.

Williams smiled and leaned forward. "You're dismissed."

Jenkins stepped back and jogged to one of the foxholes on the perimeter and talked animatedly, gesticulating wildly. The two men in the hole leaned back, shaking their heads. Jenkins talked some more. They looked at Brandt, then back at Jenkins.

"I guess this would be a good time to meet the rest of the platoon," Brandt said. "How about we walk the line?"

"Yes, sir."

Williams led him to the foxhole on their far left. As they approached, the conversation stopped abruptly. The two men looked up expectantly.

"Gentlemen, meet your new platoon leader, Lieutenant Brandt. Sir, this is Specialist Evans, machine gunner, and Corporal Singleton, Alpha Team Leader, First Squad."

They stood, scanning Brandt from head to toe, darting piercing looks, their eyes filled with questions. Both of the men wore the Combat Infantryman's Badge. Brandt nodded acknowledgement, at a loss for words.

"As you were, gentlemen," Williams said before an awkward pause developed and led Brandt to the next foxhole.

Again, the conversation stopped cold. The same looks greeted him. And so it went, from foxhole to foxhole. Williams led Brandt away from the perimeter. Brandt let out a deep sigh, eyes downcast.

"Don't take it personal, sir. These men know that you're going to make decisions affecting their lives. They've survived combat. They've seen new men come and go. They're naturally guarded."

Brandt looked at Williams. "I guess so."

"It'll work out, lieutenant. Just give it time. Why don't you go to the platoon CP and get settled? I'll get the squad leaders and bring them over."

Brandt walked to his platoon command post, a five-foot-deep hole in the ground, sandbags stacked around the edge, two radios hissing static.

"Command post. Is that hyperbole or what?" Brandt muttered.

He sat down on the edge of the foxhole.

A 44-man platoon down to 25 men. Damn. Like I got a reinforced Ranger team here.

He scanned his section of the perimeter. Some men hustled back and forth carrying boxes. Others cleaned weapons, while some others conversed over trays of food. Even those who sat quietly seemed purposeful. They were on guard.

Well, I'm in charge. What the fuck do I do?

Brandt grabbed his rucksack and fidgeted with it. A moment later, he heard steps and looked up. A Specialist Fourth Class approached, shoulders squared and confident stride. Brandt stood and stepped forward.

The young man stopped and extended his hand, and Brandt noticed the white armband bearing a red cross.

"Sir, I'm Specialist Andrew Carson, your medic."

Brandt shook his hand.

"Glad to meet you, Specialist. I'd like to sit down with you soon and talk about the men—their physical condition, medical problems, your needs, and so forth."

"Glad to hear you say that, sir. There are a few things I could use some backup on."

Brandt nodded. "Go ahead."

"Well, sir, malaria tablets and iodine tablets for their water. It's an ongoing battle. The usual malaria tablet is no problem, but in this area, we need to take another one for a specific strain prevalent here. Some of the men don't take it because it makes them nauseous. Not a lot of fun, but it beats getting malaria.

"I've heard about that second tablet. We'll work on that right away." Brandt paused. "And the iodine tablets?"

"They just don't like the taste the pill gives the water." Carson shook his head. "But it's important. Last week, I had to send a man back to base camp to be treated for dysentery. That means we lost a fighting man, and one of my jobs is to keep the men in fighting condition."

"I'll emphasize that with the squad leaders to start and we'll see how it goes."

"Thank you, sir. I'm a few pounds lighter now after Captain Parker chewed my ass over it. Same for Sergeant Williams."

"Well, if it makes you feel any better, you're third in line now."

Carson chuckled, and then looked over Brandt's shoulder.

"Sir, here come Sergeant Williams and the squad leaders. I'd better get back to the resupply. I've got more supplies coming in."

"Sure. Get to it. And thanks for coming over and introducing yourself."

"Airborne, sir."

Brandt did an about-face.

"Well, sir," Williams said, "I see you met Doc. We're lucky. He's one of the best." Williams gestured with his hand. "Lieutenant Brandt, these men are your squad leaders."

Brandt looked at the three young men.

Damn. Can't be over twenty.

Their eyes drew his attention. Mature beyond their years.

Williams gestured. "Sergeant Hart, First Squad."

Hart stepped forward, sandy-haired, of medium build, about five feet eleven inches tall. He stood solidly on both feet, not at attention and not at ease.

"Sergeant Oseski, Second Squad."

Brandt looked at the name-tag. "Olszewski," he pronounced correctly. Brandt looked up from his own six-foot-one-inch frame to see a smile fill the round face. Broad shoulders rolled forward, leading the rest of the huge body as Olszewski planted one foot, then the other.

"Sergeant Martinez, Third Squad."

He moved quickly with a spring in his step. He stood about five feet nine inches tall and wiry.

Tough guy. Looks sharp even in wrinkled jungle fatigues.

"Glad to meet you, men," Brandt said. "From what I hear, you've got a damn good platoon. I'm depending on you to keep doing your jobs the way you have been. I'm the platoon leader, but if you have something to say, I want to hear it. We need to work like a team."

Brandt glanced at Williams.

"Sir, I already briefed them on our earlier conversation." Williams looked down at his watch. "If it's O.K. with you, Lieutenant, I'd like to finish up the rest of the resupply."

"Of course."

Williams dismissed the squad leaders. He looked over his shoulder and waited until the trio was out of earshot. "And I believe you have a meeting with Captain Parker, sir."

Brandt glanced at his watch. "Oh, shit." He grabbed his rifle and helmet.

"I expect we'll be meeting when you get back."

"Right," Brandt said. He slung his rifle over his shoulder and hurried to the company command post.

Captain Parker knelt on the ground with a map spread before him, a radio handset to his ear. Two lieutenants stood a few feet away, and Brandt veered toward them.

"You Brandt?"

"Yeah. Bill Brandt."

"Mike Merriweather, 1st Platoon."

"Bob Foster, 2nd Platoon. Good to have you here, Bill."

"How long you been in-country?" Merriweather asked.

"Almost two weeks. Couple days in Long Binh. A week in Jungle School at An Khe. Another day in LZ English. Thought I'd never get here."

Merriweather laughed. "I know, but it gives you a chance to get acclimatized. You'll be thankful for that tomorrow."

"How long you been here?"

"Three months."

Brandt looked at Foster.

"Two months."

Brandt's eyes widened.

The senior platoon leader has only been here for three months?

"Gentlemen," Parker called. "I see you've gotten acquainted. Good."

Three lieutenants squatted around the map, each took a small notebook and pen from his fatigue shirt pocket. Parker pointed to a circle on the map. "This is where we are now. Tomorrow we climb the Tiger Mountains. I plan to spend the night on top, here," Parker said, tapping the map with his machete. Three necks craned forward as each platoon leader jotted down map coordinates. "The next day we move down this finger," Parker traced the route. Again, the lieutenants jotted coordinates.

Parker looked up from the map. "We'll move out at 0700 tomorrow." He paused for emphasis. "I want everyone well rested. The next few days are going to be tough."

"Order of march tomorrow will be 3rd Platoon, 2nd Platoon, 1st Platoon. I will be with 2nd Platoon. Any questions?"

The three platoon leaders shook their heads.

"Good. Now for the following day's operation."

The lieutenants flipped pages in their notebooks. Each hurriedly scribbled "1. Situation," then beneath that, "a. Enemy Forces:" setting up an outline for the OPORD, the standard five-paragraph Operation Order that precedes every combat operation.

"As you know," Parker continued, "VC units have been moving down from the mountains into the coastal villages. Intelligence says that the headquarters element of the 135th VC Regiment is using Tan Loc as a base."

Brandt glanced at Foster and Merriweather. They were nodding as they wrote.

"The Battalion Commander wants to capture the 135th Headquarters element."

Brandt quickly wrote "b. Friendly Forces:"

"We will be coordinating with Charlie Company on this operation."

Brandt wrote, "2. Mission:"

"Our mission is to set up a blocking position south and west of Tan Loc the day after tomorrow. This will be a hammer and anvil operation."

Brandt wrote, "3. Execution:"

"Charlie Company, the hammer, will drive into the village from the north. We will be the anvil and seal off escape routes into the Tiger Mountains. Our responsibility extends from about 6 o'clock to 9 o'clock, the southwestern sector of the village. To get into position, we will march north across the Tigers. We'll make the climb tomorrow morning, spend the night on top, then move down into position the following day."

Parker took a breath.

"The terrain is 500 meters of open grassland between the mountains and the village, so we'll move into position along the base of the mountains using the brush for concealment. When we deploy, 1st Platoon will be on the left flank, 3rd Platoon in the middle and 2nd Platoon on the right flank. I want the platoon leaders to personally coordinate the links between platoons. Make sure there are no gaps in our line. Anybody coming out of the village should be easy to spot in that field. Try to take prisoners. If we need to fire, we need to be careful of Charlie Company in the village."

Parker paused as the lieutenants scribbled furiously. Brandt wrote "4. Service and Support:"

"We just got our resupply, and we're walking in, so nothing special for support."

Brandt crossed out paragraph four, glanced at Foster's notebook. Foster had written "5. Command and Signal:" and waited, pen poised.

"I will be in the center with 3rd Platoon. Company SOPs for signal will be in effect. Any questions?"

All three platoon leaders were still scribbling as Parker folded his map. He stood and dismissed Merriweather and Foster.

Brandt reviewed his four pages of notes.

"Lieutenant, I put your platoon in the lead tomorrow for a reason. The Tiger Mountains are a bitch. They kick everybody's butt, even the toughest who're used to the heat. I won't have to worry about you straggling behind."

Brandt glanced up at the Tiger Mountains. They did look steep and rugged.

Parker pulled a map out of his rucksack. "Here's your map. Notice the green cross. It's a reference point for giving your position. The reference point and the code change every day. Today the code is cars. Our position now is, from Ford, down three and right two. Use a different code name every time you use the reference point. Never give your position in the clear. Never use the code to give an enemy position."

Parker paused, then continued. "We open and close the radio net every day. Your RTO has a book of codes. We use strict radiotelephone procedure. The enemy might be a bunch of farmers, but they're good soldiers, and they do listen to our radio traffic. Units that don't use proper procedure get people killed needlessly."

"Got it, sir."

"Good. Any questions, lieutenant?"

Brandt flipped through his notes. "Uh, what's the tactical situation here?"

"We just started this operation. I expect it to last about three weeks. Then we'll rotate back to LZ English for a week of perimeter guard duty. It's a break. A chance to take a shower and eat hot food in the mess hall. The normal rotation for the four companies in the battalion is three weeks out in the field, a week in. However, we've been in the field for two weeks already."

"Enemy activity has increased steadily the last several months. VC are coming down out of the mountains from base camps, often accompanied by NVA advisors. We run Search and Destroy missions looking for them. When we find them, they try to break contact. They know this area and can disappear like ghosts. It's frustrating. You have to be patient and persistent."

"So, that's why we're coordinating with Charlie Company."

Parker smiled. "Exactly."

"If the VC run when we make contact, why is my platoon down to half strength?"

Parker raised his eyebrows. "In this area, the increase in enemy activity has taken the form of booby traps, snipers, and ambushes. About 80 percent of our casualties are from booby traps. The ambushes are large, set by the NVA. They try to trap a whole platoon or company in a kill zone. That's what happened to your predecessor. The snipers are harassment, trying to slow us down."

Brandt looked down at his map, then up at the mountains.

"I know what you're thinking, lieutenant. This isn't the First Cav. After we jump out of an aircraft, we're infantry. We walk. We're lucky if we get helicopters. Hopefully, that will change with all this enemy activity."

Brandt looked up and to his right.

What else? What else?

Parker glanced at his watch. "Why don't you head back to your platoon now. I'll be around in a little while. Be prepared to brief me on your platoon deployment and route of march for tomorrow."

Brandt started to turn, but Parker said, "By the way, lieutenant, get yourself something to eat. I know that stuff about making sure your men eat before you do sounds good, but I may need you at any time. I want you available immediately. Chances are, you won't have time to eat afterwards."

"Yes, sir," Brandt said to Parker's now familiar back.

Brandt headed to his command post.

To my platoon.

He stood a little taller; his pace quickened. Halfway there, he stopped.

How am I ever going to get everything done before tomorrow? Hell, before Captain Parker comes around this evening.

As Brandt approached the platoon CP, he saw Williams and Jenkins sitting on the foxhole edge, feet dangling inside. Each had a food tray across his lap. Brandt stopped and looked at the chow line.

"Sit down, lieutenant," Williams said. "Take a load off your feet."

Brandt dropped everything and plopped between the two men.

Williams reached behind himself, then held out a tray of food. "Have some chow, lieutenant."

"Thanks." Brandt looked down. "What is it?"

"As long as it's hot, you don't ask, sir."

Brandt laughed, then dug into the food. While he shoveled food, he opened his map and spread it on the ground beside him. "You were right, sergeant. We climb the mountains tomorrow and spend the night on top, here." Brandt pointed and Williams leaned forward. "The next day we set up a blocking position for Charlie Company west of Tan Loc along the base of the mountains."

Brandt looked up at Williams.

"We need to plan a route and decide what formation we'll use—who's on point. Let's see, uh, where the machine guns will be."

Williams finished eating, set his tray aside, and held up a hand. "That's a lot of work, lieutenant, and something you'll have to do every day. Let me run a few things by you."

"Go ahead."

"The right SOPs can make your job easier and make the troops feel, well not secure, but like they have something they can depend on. These are some of the Standard Operating Procedures I have for the platoon. We rotate point squad every day. That way, nobody feels like they're getting screwed and it doesn't dump on a guy just because he's good. And it forces more men to develop the skills for point. It's the squad leader's job to pick the point man."

Brandt stopped eating and put the tray aside, but held an intent gaze on Williams.

"As for order of march, I started with 1st Squad, 2nd Squad, 3rd Squad. Tomorrow, 2nd Squad would be on point, followed by 3rd Squad, then 1st Squad." Williams nodded toward Brandt. "If you want to continue it, sir."

"Sounds good to me, sergeant. Those policies will continue. Now, formations. In this open forest we should probably be in a column."

"O.K., sir. I usually pick a formation to start with, but I expect my squad leaders to think like the noncommissioned officers they are. If we're moving through open terrain in a column and it starts getting thick, the point squad should go into a file. Otherwise, it's like trying to walk through a fence instead of using the gate. If we're in a file and the terrain opens up, he should put his squad into a column so they don't look like ducks in a shooting gallery. They see the changes before we do. They'll call us and tell us what's happening. If you want to do something different when you get there and eyeball it, just tell 'em what you want."

"I like that," Brandt said. "You have that much confidence in our squad leaders?"

"If I don't, sir, it's my job to train 'em. Make them do their jobs. Let me do mine. Give yourself the time to do your job. Remember that, lieutenant."

Brandt let out a deep breath.

I just might be ready to brief Captain Parker.

"O.K., let's take a look at this map again. We need to get here." Brandt took a black grease pencil from his shirt pocket and started to draw a circle.

"Wait, sir." Jenkins reached into his rucksack and pulled out a large plastic bag, smiling from ear to ear. "I saved one for you when I changed radio batteries. It's for your map, sir."

Brandt slid the map inside, and the accordion fold opened to the next day's operating area. "Damn if it isn't the perfect size. The Army finally did something right. Thanks, Jenkins. I appreciate that."

Jenkins beamed. "Keeps it dry when you walk through a stream. Easier to wipe off the grease pencil, too."

Brandt circled the laager site on the map. "I was thinking of a route like this," he said, tracing a path with his finger.

Williams pursed his lips. "Tell me why you'd go that way."

"Well," Brandt said, "it stays off the trails and avoids being channeled into likely ambush sites by terrain features."

Williams looked up from the map, eyes wide. "I'm glad you already know about those things, lieutenant, but this is one of those times when you have to do what's not smart." He pointed. "I'd suggest we follow this trail."

"Why?"

Williams took a deep breath, a concerned look on his face. "The brush on the Tiger Mountains is thick. Small bushes, only three to six feet high, but hardwood. And the branches snake together. It'll beat you to death."

"But what about booby traps and ambushes?"

"We just have to be extra careful. Trust me on this, sir. It would take a week to cross the Tigers any other way."

"Well—" Brandt hesitated.

"Take another look at the map, sir. Why do you think Bravo 6 picked that laager site?"

Brandt traced the dotted line on the map with his finger. The trail led right into the laager site.

"Yeah, I see. Guess we're ready to meet with the squad leaders, sergeant."

Williams' face relaxed. "Jenkins, round up the squad leaders."

Jenkins jumped to his feet. "I'll take these trays back on the way. The last chopper should be here soon."

★ ★ ★

Brandt positioned his air mattress, as Williams and Jenkins had, on the ground near the foxhole edge. He settled back, yawned, and closed his eyes. A moment later, his eyes opened.

"Sergeant, is there anything else?"

"Well, sir, if Charlie attacks tonight, don't sit up. Roll over into the foxhole."

"Uh, yeah. Right."

"And don't let the Fuck-You Lizards get you, sir."

Brandt rolled to his side and propped himself on his elbow. "Sergeant Williams, they tried that new-guy bullshit on me in Jungle School."

Williams chuckled. "You college boys are just too smart to fool with that stuff."

Brandt thought he could make out a wry smile on Williams' face as night enveloped the last light of dusk. The verdant view of day faded into black treetops and mountain silhouettes. No glow of city lights on the horizon, even though villages dotted the map in his pocket. No traffic noise—just darkness and silence.

Who and what is out there?

The hush gave way to strange sounds, from animals and insects he'd never heard before. One sound rose above the others.

"Ooool. Uh oool. Uck ooo."

What the hell is that?

"Uckooo. Uckooo. Fuckooo. Fuckyooo."

No. It can't be.

It continued for another minute, clear and distinct, then faded into the night chorus. Brandt shook his head.

"Son of a bitch."

Williams' voice drifted across the foxhole. "Sleep tight, lieutenant."

Brandt rested his head on the air mattress and let out a deep sigh. *What would I do without Sergeant Williams?*

CHAPTER 5

★ ★ ★

Brandt gasped for air with each step, leaned into the steep slope, consciously lifted one foot, placed it a few inches higher, shifted his weight, willed the trailing foot to move, each step pushing him up through the sun's rays beating down on him. The increasingly thinner air cheated him of oxygen, and his rucksack straps cut into his shoulders. Sweat dripped from his nose onto the parched ground beneath him and left a trail of dark points in the red dust.

Hansel and Gretel—the trail of breadcrumbs.

He wiped sweat with his sleeve.

Where the hell did that come from?

Brandt craned his neck back, looked left and right, and saw only dusty, gray-green bushes on either side and a rucksack in front of him.

"Sir," Jenkins called from behind, "Bravo 6."

Brandt stopped and let gravity swing him around and down a step.

Jenkins, arm extended, offered the handset of the AN/PRC-25 radio used by higher-level commanders. The company commander wanted to talk to him.

Maybe that's why we call it the "Prick-25."

He reached for the handset and took a deep breath. "November 6. Over."

"This is Bravo 6. I'm calling a halt. Take a break." A deep breath. "Six out."

Jenkins smiled at the good news. He extended his arm again, this time holding the smaller AN/PRC-6 radio used within the platoon.

And the troops call it the "Prick-6." Huh. And I'm November 6.

Brandt sucked in another breath. "November, this is 6. Halt in place." Gasp. "Rest break. Six out."

Those near enough to hear him plopped to the ground immediately. Above and below him, the words rippled up and down the line. He returned the radio to Jenkins, already on the ground. The RTO leaned back against his rucksack and wiped his face with a drab olive-green towel draped around his neck. Most of the towel looked black, saturated with moisture.

Now that his field of vision wasn't filled by a rucksack, Brandt saw the lead element of 2nd Squad about 50 meters ahead on almost level ground.

That point marks the end of the steep climb. The trail follows the spine of the ridge, a gentle slope. The rest of the way should be much easier.

He pulled his shoulders back and took a deep breath.

I'm going to make this climb.

Brandt looked up and down his platoon's file, then took several steps up the path to Sergeant Martinez. The sergeant's eyes widened.

"Sergeant, I want these men facing out alternately."

Now Martinez's eyes were filled with disbelief. "Sir, no way in hell anybody could fire on us here. Look around."

"I don't care. I want that to become automatic. So they don't have to even think about it."

As far up the path as he could see, eyes stared down at him. He'd never seen so much white in men's eyes before.

Martinez looked up at the soldiers above him. "You heard what the man said. Do it and pass it on. Now, troops."

Movement spread through the file like a ripple in a pond. Some men only managed to turn a couple of inches, the result of digging their rifle butts into the ground and pushing with their heels to swivel the 70-pound rucksacks on the ground. Brandt nodded and walked down into 1st Squad. The same astonished looks greeted his command, followed by the same efforts at compliance. He trudged back up the trail to Jenkins.

"Sit down, sir."

Brandt stopped. "Good idea." He collapsed on his butt, leaned back against his rucksack and kicked his legs out straight. He opened a canteen, tipped it up to his mouth. Brandt yanked the canteen away and spat. "Damn. I burned my lips."

"Swish it around before you drink," Jenkins said. "Pour some into your palm and put it against your lips. Then drink."

Brandt tried that hesitantly. It was hot, but it was wet and drinkable. "Thanks."

"Next resupply," Jenkins continued, "get yourself a plastic canteen. They don't get as hot as the metal ones."

"I'll do that." Brandt put the canteen away and examined the vegetation around them. Small, oval, dusty-green leaves that looked like an Army version of confetti hung deceptively in a widely dispersed pattern. Reddish-brown branches snaked together from bush to bush. The main branches and trunks seemed like thick, curved bars of steel, smooth and hard. The bushes rose about three to four feet above his head.

"I see what Sergeant Williams meant when he talked about walking on the trail. We'd never be able to walk through this."

Jenkins was about to answer when they both heard the ever-present hiss of the radio stop. Their eyes met. Brandt knew what that meant.

"November 6, Bravo 6. Over."

Brandt reached for the handset. "This is November 6."

"Let's move out." Parker added, "We're ahead of schedule. I think we can slow the pace down a bit."

"Roger that, 6." An involuntary, self-satisfied snort escaped Brandt.

I guess Bravo 6 won't worry about me straggling behind anymore.

Brandt picked up the platoon radio and relayed the command. He noticed that those in earshot had not moved. They waited for their sergeant's command and captured a minute more of rest.

Brandt tried to get up, but remained rooted to the ground. He struggled again, but still could not get up.

"Roll to the side like this," Jenkins said, "onto one knee. Then push up with your arm. It's the only way to lift the ruck, sir."

Brandt tried it and stood upright. Men up and down the line performed the same movement, a strange dance. The file picked up momentum and resumed a steady rhythm. Minutes later, Brandt crested the slope and walked erect. The dense brush of the slopes gave way to dwarf versions of the same shrubs, about 18 inches high, sparsely scattered through dry grass on the 20-meter-wide ridge. A breeze blew across the crest, hot, but it evaporated sweat and cooled Brandt's body.

An incredible vista opened on both sides of him. He looked down, found the spot where they spent the night, and surveyed the surrounding area, a patchwork quilt of greens and browns, open areas, rice paddies, and thick bands of interlocking vegetation around villages. As Brandt's gaze traveled eastward, the brown tones gained ascendancy, and the greens contracted to isolated islands. The browns paled into a strand of pure white that stretched to the southern horizon. A sparkling blue nestled into the beach, and the South China Sea spread seamlessly into the sky. To his left, Brandt saw a mirror image of the same breathtaking scene stretching north as far as he could see.

"Uh," Brandt grunted. He pitched forward and the parched dirt of the trail replaced the scenic view. His back arched, arms flailed, and helmet flew. He swung his legs under, regained his balance, and landed on his feet.

"Shit," Brandt blurted. "Stumbled on a damn rock."

"Good move, sir," Jenkins called.

Brandt turned to his smiling RTO, and a flush spread up Brandt's neck and across his cheeks. An image flashed through his mind of a college football game. He was getting up off the ground very slowly. A 230-pound offensive guard had just cross-body blocked him from the blind side. His coach stood over him. "Damn it, Brandt. Keep your head in the game. You can't be thinking about anything else."

Yeah, breathtaking view alright. Especially if that had been a mine.

Brandt focused on the men ahead. Because of the gentle slope up to the peak, he could see everyone, including the point man. Small trees and clusters of bushes crowded the trail.

Spacing looks good, but can't see much to the side.

The point man froze. Everyone behind him stopped but forward momentum closed ranks like an accordion. Brandt held his hand high above his head, signaling those behind to halt.

As he accelerated his pace and continued forward to the point, he heard Sergeant Martinez behind him. "Face out alternately, right and left. Your *other* right, troop."

I only said it once.

Sergeant Olszewski called to him. "Booby trap, sir."

"Let's go take a look," Brandt said.

Olszewski pointed to slack monofilament fishing line hung across the trail from a small tree on the right side of the trail into a bush on the left side.

Brandt squatted. His eyes followed the line into the bush. Hidden beneath the leaves, Brandt discovered a hand grenade tied to the base of the thick stem, the line knotted to the straightened pin.

He stood and looked at Olszewski. "Who's the point man?"

"Shaw, sir."

"Good work, Private Shaw."

A surprised look covered Shaw's face. "Uh, thank you, sir."

Brandt squatted again and studied the booby trap.

Olszewski leaned over his shoulder. "That's one of our grenades. Can't we just bend the pin back and take it?"

Brandt shook his head. "The first thing I learned about these things is don't mess with 'em unless you absolutely have to." He pointed. "See the ground under the grenade? It's been disturbed. Maybe there's another grenade underneath it. A double booby trap. Or maybe they just did that to keep us from taking it." Brandt shook his head. "Clever little fuckers." He stood.

Olszewski held a small grappling hook in the palm of his hand, a thick bundle of twine tied to it. "We can blow it in place, sir."

"Blow it, sergeant."

Jenkins was beside him in a now familiar pose, arm extended. Brandt took the handset. "Bravo 6, November 6. Over."

"This is Bravo 6. We're bunched up behind you on the trail. Why are you stopped? Over."

"Found a booby trap across the trail. Hand grenade. One of ours. We can blow it in place."

"Roger that. Make sure your men are well clear of the area. Six out."

Sergeant Williams joined the group. "I hear we outsmarted Charlie again. Good work, point." He looked down, shook his head. "Nasty little things. We gonna blow it?"

Olszewski held up the grappling hook. "We're ready."

"O.K.," Williams said. "Everybody get back with 3rd Squad. Keep your heads down."

The men needed no further encouragement, and the area cleared quickly. Olszewski carefully lowered the grappling hook to the ground on other side of the fishing line, then gingerly looped the cord over a branch above the grenade and backed away, playing out the cord. Brandt and Williams accompanied him to a shallow depression in the ground 50 meters from the booby trap. They scrunched down into it.

Olszewski looked at Brandt. "Ready."

"Blow it," Brandt said.

Olszewski yelled over his shoulder. "Fire in the hole. Fire in the hole. Fire in the hole." He took up slack in the cord, then yanked.

A sharp explosion shattered the silence, followed immediately by a second explosion. Thunder echoed through the valleys around them. A brief hail of dirt and rocks hit the ground. A hush settled around them and Brandt stood. Black smoke and dust billowed, leaves and splinters fluttered to the ground, and the thick cloud expanded and diffused, then drifted with the breeze. Brandt gazed through a curtain of charcoal-gray gauze, transfixed. The beautiful view he saw only moments ago had transmuted.

Like looking outside through a screen door.

Sergeant Williams stood. "Show's over, troops. We got ground to cover. On your feet."

Olszewski positioned his squad along the trail. Brandt took the ever-ready handset from Jenkins. "Bravo 6, this is November 6. The trail is clear. We are ready to move out. Over."

"Roger, November 6. Let's get moving."

As they climbed, the ridge widened and the vegetation thickened. A few minutes later, the trail leveled and the peak flattened and spread into a broad, flat oval. Olszewski turned and faced Brandt. "This it?"

"This is it," Brandt said.

Olszewski motioned to his team leaders. The rest of Brandt's platoon moved past him. The squad leaders seemed to know where to go and placed men in position.

Sergeant Williams joined him. Brandt looked up. "Another Standard Operating Procedure?"

"Yes," Williams said. "When we pull into a laager site, the lead squad sets up in the direction of march. The next squad moves to the left of them, last squad to the right. That way, we have hasty security.

Gives us time to link up with the other platoons, decide where the foxholes should be."

The 1st and 3rd Platoons filled in behind them. Captain Parker approached, followed by Foster and Merriweather.

"I'll set up our platoon CP, sir." Williams hurried away.

"Change in plans," Parker said. "Delta Company made contact, and Big 6 diverted Charlie Company to support them. Tomorrow we'll search that village ourselves."

"Who?" Brandt asked.

Parker chuckled. "Big 6. It's the battalion commander's call sign. By the way, lieutenant, I hear you did real well on the hump up the mountain."

Brandt started to respond, but Parker cut him off.

"But then, I'd expect that of a Ranger."

Brandt stiffened.

He glanced at Foster and Merriweather standing behind Parker. Foster rolled his eyes. Merriweather shook his head.

"Apparently," Parker continued, "you know a lot about booby traps."

"Well, I guess I had some good classes. That was the first time for real."

"Good. I need that. It's going to come in handy around here."

Parker pulled out his map, "Anyway, it's early. We'll rest and eat here, then move down to this broad, gently sloping finger to spend the night. That will get us into the village at sunrise."

★ ★ ★

The finger Bravo Company descended pointed directly north and terminated in a round hill. Brandt stood beside Parker 50 meters below the crown on a broad, grassy slope. He scanned the area. To the east and west were thick stands of trees, broad-leafed undergrowth, and bright-blossomed vines. At the base of the slope, a trail ran east–west. Beyond the trail, narrow rice paddies spread into the distance, walled by dark green bands of vegetation. A red sun dipped below the trees to the left, casting a soft glow over the scene.

Brandt did not see beauty. Thick undergrowth to the east and west would allow an enemy force to approach on the trail unseen, making it a likely ambush site and the rice paddy, a gauntlet of bullets.

Parker pointed with his machete. "I want to cover that trail tonight in case Charlie's using it at night. But on the other hand, this hill makes a good laager site. Where would you set up the company, lieutenant ?"

"Well, uh."

"Relax, lieutenant. Just think out loud."

Brandt looked over his shoulder at the top of the hill and then down at the trail.

"If we set up on the trail we'll definitely block any traffic on it. But our only fields of fire would be down the trail and out into the rice paddy. Not likely that anybody would come at us from the paddy. We could put Claymores and machine guns on the trail in both directions and take out anybody that bumps into us." Brandt paused, peered into the shadows of the thicket on his right, then up at the hilltop again.

"If it's anything larger than a squad coming down the trail, we'll only get the lead element in the first exchange of fire. They could maneuver through the trees and get on top of the hill before we knew it. Then they'd be shooting down on us."

Brandt glanced at Parker. His face impassive, he slapped the side of his leg with his machete.

"If we set up on the hill," Brandt continued, "we can see all approaches. It's a more secure position."

"But somebody could sneak by on the trail. We'd never know it."

"Well, we could put an OP down on the trail. Make the observation post large enough and it can double as an ambush. We can support them from here without even moving." Brandt took a deep breath. "That's what I'd do. Set up on the hill and put an ambush on the trail."

Parker held his machete in front of him as if he were studying the edge. His poker face revealed nothing.

Brandt realized that his hands were drawn up into tight balls. He forced the fingers open and wiggled them.

"O.K., lieutenant. That's what we'll do."

Parker smiled, tucked the machete under his arm and marched to the company CP.

Brandt let out a long, slow breath.

Parker called back over his shoulder, "Rest well tonight, lieutenant. You're going to need it tomorrow."

CHAPTER 6

★ ★ ★

Bravo Company left the laager site after breakfast on a Search and Destroy mission, marched all morning and afternoon under a withering sun, and found only empty huts and root cellars in hamlets scattered among parched fields, red dirt, and sparse dry grass. They found no weapons caches, no tunnels, no documents. Then Parker sent Brandt to recon the area for an ambush site. A kilometer from the company, Brandt stopped and halted the platoon. He took a deep breath and shrugged his shoulders.

Why am I so tired? I'm in better shape than this.

He scanned the terrain and shook his head.

Not jungle. Where's the jungle I always saw on TV?

He walked forward to the point squad and Sergeant Hart.

"Frustrating day. Haven't found a thing. Where are the VC, anyway?"

"Nothing new, sir. They know how to hide and cover their tracks. We just need to keep at it and we'll find them."

"I didn't expect this kind of terrain."

"Yeah. It changes a lot in II Corps area. A little ways to the east is the ocean—sandy soil, palm trees, and beach." Hart pointed. "Little ways to the west are rice paddies, then hills and forest. A little further west is jungle and mountains."

"Interesting. Thanks."

Brandt pointed in the direction of march. "Is that a mirage?"

"What?"

"There. Trees and green, broad-leafed bushes."

"Right, sir. Like little islands in this area. Probably water near the surface, maybe an underground spring."

Brandt wiped sweat.

Hart's eyes narrowed. "You O.K., sir?"

"Yeah, I'm fine."

"Drink some water, sir."

"Soon as we get into that oasis ahead. Let's take a break."

"Sounds good to me, sir."

Brandt signaled the platoon forward, and Hart guided the platoon into the cluster of vegetation. The men circled into a perimeter and sought concealment in shade. Brandt sat down, rubbed a cramp in his leg, and leaned back against a tree.

Tree. A poem about a tree. English class. The words? The author was, well, wasn't he a soldier, too?

Brandt's brow knitted, and he rubbed his eyes, but the words trailed off. At least he had relief from the rays of the mid-afternoon sun.

Rays. Physics class. Was light pure energy or was it a particle with mass?

Brandt shook his head. "What was it I needed to do?"

He rested his head against the tree, wiped sweat with his hand. His face felt hot.

He heard that now familiar voice in his head. "Water, dummy. Water."

Oh, shit. Heat exhaustion.

Brandt sat up straight, pulled out his canteen, raised it, stopped, poured water into his hand, and sipped. Then he splashed some on his face, poured some over his head, and drank half the canteen.

Damn, that was close.

He looked up and smiled. Shade. Not that it was any cooler in the shade. The canopy of leaves just kept the sun from beating down on you.

I guess I proved the particle theory of light today. Light definitely has mass, at least here. Beats down like relentless, hot hail.

Brandt took another sip of water, inhaled, and let out a huge breath. *I have to drink more water.*

Brandt pulled his map out of the left leg pocket of his fatigue pants. He needed to find an ambush site. Intelligence said trails were heavily used.

Intelligence? I haven't even seen an enemy.

He lifted his canteen and took another sip. *The enemy.* He shook his head.

Where the hell are they, anyway? Haven't even seen tracks on the trails.

He studied the map. He found only one likely ambush site—a trail intersection that connected four villages a few kilometers apart. The trails ran north–south and east–west beyond the villages.

O.K., let's go see what Sergeant Williams thinks.

Brandt stood slowly, tested his legs, and picked up his helmet and rifle. After a few faltering steps, he strode forward. Williams sat with Sergeant Olszewski and two riflemen from 2nd Squad. As he approached, the conversation stopped. The soldiers looked up expectantly.

★ ★ ★

Brandt stood in the northeast quadrant formed by the trail intersection. Bare ground stretched in all directions. Sparsely scattered trees and bushes dotted an otherwise featureless landscape. Williams and Jenkins stood next to him.

"No good ambush sites anywhere around here, sergeant."

"I agree, but this is the most likely place for enemy traffic."

"Right. I guess this is it."

Brandt took the radio handset from Jenkins. "Bravo 6, November 6. Are you prepared to copy? Over."

"This is Bravo 6. Affirmative. Over."

"I have a position to report." Brandt placed his finger on the map reference point labeled "tools." "I will be at, from Screwdriver, up three and a half, right one."

"Will be? Aren't you there now?"

"Affirmative, but I will move on and circle back after dark."

"Negative, November 6. I don't want you stumbling around in the dark. Stay put and set up now."

Brandt's jaw dropped and he stared at Williams. The sergeant shrugged his shoulders, held his palms up in a gesture of resignation.

Brandt took a deep breath and exhaled slowly. "But 6, the sun's just setting now. It's still light. There's no concealment around here, let alone cover."

"I don't expect an argument when I give an order, November 6." Brandt yanked the handset away from his ear.

"No, sir. But—"

"End of discussion, November 6. Set up now. That is an order. Do you understand?"

Brandt pulled the handset away again and looked around. No protection from enemy fire. Not even a place to hide.

Set up positions before dark in a spot like this? Bad move, but what more can I say? Only one response to a direct order.

"Roger. Wilco. Over."

"Six out."

Brandt remained motionless and stared at the ground, his mouth drawn into a tight, thin line across his face, the color draining from his lips.

"Sir?" Jenkins reached up and gingerly took the handset from Brandt.

A MATTER OF SEMANTICS

Williams shook his head. "Bravo do get excited."

"This sucks."

"This is the Army." Williams placed a hand on Brandt's arm. "You got no choice, lieutenant." He removed his helmet, wiped the top of his bald head, and scratched the fringe of curly, salt-and-pepper hair. "So, how we going to set this up?"

Brandt let out a long sigh. "O.K., let's set up three positions in a triangle—one point at the intersection, the other positions out along each trail. That way, we cover all approaches and still have rear security. Each position covers the back of the others. "Let's put 2nd Squad at the intersection."

Brandt pointed with his rifle. "Third Squad over there, on the trail to the left."

He gestured in the opposite direction. "Put 1st Squad over there, on the trail on our right."

Brandt turned back to Williams. "What do you think, sergeant?"

Williams gazed at the trail intersection, then spun in a circle. "Sounds good, lieutenant. Where we going to be, sir?"

"With Second Squad, the middle position. We will control both trails from that spot. Anything else, sergeant?"

"Well, since we got nothing to hide behind, let's make sure the positions are far enough back from the trails so that they can't reach us with grenades."

"Yeah," Brandt said. "Good idea. If we position our Claymores right, we won't have to use our grenades."

Brandt faced the orange sun. "Won't be long before dark. Haven't seen any locals for quite a while. Hopefully, nobody's seen us."

"Right. Let's get settled in." Williams put his helmet on and raised his voice. "Squad leaders, on me."

★ ★ ★

Brandt lay on the bare ground between Jenkins and Williams. His head nodded then snapped up again. He rubbed his eyes.

Damn it. I've gone without sleep before.

He looked at the luminous dial on his watch. 0218. The night deepened, the darkness thick. No glow from city lights, no moon. Bright stars sparkled overhead, but their light was no help. *If only there were some way to use their light,* thought Brandt. A hush permeated the blackness.

Huh. No insect noises. Not even those damn lizards. No sound at all.

Jenkins rolled close to Brandt and whispered, "Sergeant Hart reports movement near his position. It's not on the trail. He—"

Brilliant light ripped the dark, and a sharp thundering shattered the silence. Brandt jerked as if in spasm. Ominous stillness reclaimed the night. Williams leaned close to Brandt. "That was a grenade. Hart said they're not on the trail?"

"Right."

"Means they know where we are, but not exactly. They want us to fire our rifles so the muzzle flashes mark our positions. Pass me the radio."

Brandt took the handset from Jenkins and passed it to Williams.

"November, this is 5. Do not fire rifles without permission. I repeat, do not fire rifles. Break squelch twice to acknowledge."

Brandt heard the ever-present hiss of the radio stop, return, stop, and return again. Each squad leader, in turn, silently acknowledged the order. All they had to do was depress the push-to-talk button on the radio handset. He'd have to remember that.

Silence and darkness became his allies. Time passed in a way that he had not experienced before. As the night moved inexorably toward the event, the minutes swelled and became heavy with dread. He had not found the enemy. They had found him. Brandt's heartbeat pounded, and his grip on his rifle tightened.

A grenade exploded, but nowhere near his positions. Another quickly followed, not far from Sergeant Hart's position on the right. Brandt looked at his watch. 0244.

How long can this go on?

Brandt took a deep breath and exhaled slowly. So loud was the rush of air that he wondered whether they could hear it.

"Be cool, lieutenant." Williams' calm voice reassured. "They're probing. Throw a grenade, move to another spot, and throw another one. They're hoping they hit one of our positions or we get impatient and shoot."

Every 10 to 15 minutes, a grenade exploded in seemingly random locations. Sometimes, a second explosion followed immediately. They waited in silence—listened and waited. Smoke drifted. Brandt blinked his eyes and wrinkled his nose. He rolled his shoulders, rubbed the back of his neck, and shifted his legs and arms.

Williams leaned in close. "Be patient, lieutenant."

"Are we throwing any of those?"

"Can't tell, sir. Sure as hell, our squad leaders won't want to be talking on the radio now."

An image formed in Brandt's mind of his last minutes in Ranger School. A sergeant was giving final words of advice. "Don't die because you laid on the ground and did nothing. Your best chance of survival is to do something."

Another explosion broke a long silence, this time very close to Hart's position. Brandt's watch showed 0300.

Damn. How could they be so patient? What's going on over there? I have to know.

"Jenkins, call Sergeant Hart. Tell him I'm coming over there."

Williams grabbed Brandt's arm. "Sir."

"I need to find out what's happening over there."

Williams let go. "Be careful."

Brandt crawled up alongside Hart and checked his watch. 0316. "What's happening?"

"They're crawling around all over the place. Seems more than one group. I've thrown grenades at noise, but no—"

A heavy thump came from their right, followed by lighter bumps and then a skidding sound behind them. Hart lunged to the ground. Brandt hesitated. Bright flash and thunder erupted. Dirt and rocks stung Brandt's back.

"Damn. That was close," Hart whispered. "Good thing they threw it too soon. Hear that fucker roll?"

Brandt breathed rapidly, his fingernails dug into his palms. "Yeah." The word came out in a gasp.

"Throw one, sir. It'll make you feel better." Hart handed him a grenade and pointed.

Brandt pulled the pin and heaved the grenade. Silence followed the explosion.

"Damn, sir. You got one hell of an arm."

"You're right. I do feel better."

The exchange continued, punctuated by periods of silence, listening, and waiting. Brandt checked his watch again. 0415.

Thunk.

He leaned close to Hart. "Sounds like somebody dropped a heavy object. Directly in front."

"Yeah. They flinched first."

"Alright," Brandt said, "you, me, and Singleton, we all throw grenades at the same time."

"Fuckin' A, sir." Hart whispered to Singleton, then said to Brandt, "When you pull the pin, don't let the handle fly. Pull it open slowly. It won't make noise that way. Ready?"

Brandt took a grenade from his ammo pouch, inserted a finger through the ring. "Yeah. Pull rings." Brandt pulled the safety ring on his grenade and squeezed the handle tight. "Now," he whispered, and slowly lifted the handle on the grenade. When it disengaged, he counted to himself, as he knew the others were doing, "One thousand, two thousand, three thousand."

Brandt rose up with the other men, heaved the grenade as hard as he could, and then hit the dirt.

A second later, three almost simultaneous explosions ripped the night. Screams and moaning pierced the hush that followed. Scuffling and dragging noises continued to mark the spot. Hart had another grenade ready and heaved it. Stillness followed the explosion. No noise. No movement.

Hart leaned close to Brandt. "Got those motherfuckers."

Again, they waited in silence. Listened and waited. Brandt glanced down at his watch. 0422.

Such patience.

A twig snapped to their front. Brandt froze. A moment later, scuffling came toward them. A pause. The soft scrape of feet on dirt and gravel continued. Closer and closer. Gradually, an apparition formed, approached closer, and stopped. A crouched, ghostlike figure faced them, only three feet away.

Hart started to raise his M-16 rifle. Brandt slowly put a hand on it and shook his head. Not for just one man.

Brandt laid his rifle on the ground in front of him, reached back to his right thigh, and gripped the hilt of his Gerber double-edged dagger, eyes locked on the figure in front of him still unaware of his presence. He gingerly twisted the knife out from under the safety strap instead of unsnapping it and slowly pulled the blade.

The man looked over his shoulder. Brandt heard a whisper, strange sounds he never heard before, followed by more scuffling. Two crouched figures materialized, one on either side of the first. They moved forward a step, then hesitated.

Oh, shit.

Brandt slid the knife back into its sheath, released his grip, brought his hand slowly back to his rifle, and turned his head in slow motion toward Hart. Their eyes met, inches apart in the darkness. Again in slow motion, they nodded and raised their rifles. Brandt pulled his trigger. Fire jumped from his rifle barrel and spewed 18 rounds. Hart's rifle spit flames and roared in Brandt's ears.

Quiet and dark again. Three bodies lay on the ground in front of them. Brandt sucked in a deep breath and stared, then whispered, "Gotcha mother—"

Fire erupted in a semicircle around their triangle, and fire spewed out of Brandt's three positions—deafening noise and blinding light. Bullets kicked up dirt behind him, alongside of him, and in front of him. Brandt changed magazines and began firing again.

The rapid report of M-16s and the slower firing of AK-47s rose and fell in an uneven rhythm. His M-60 machine guns growled continuously over the smaller weapons. A new sound dominated the din; a slow, relentless pounding from a machine gun Brandt had never heard before raked bullets back and forth across their triangle. Flashes of yellow flames leaped from gun barrels all around Brandt; green tracers clawed into his positions, and red tracers darted out; and searing bursts of light and blasts of grenades assaulted Brandt's senses. Brandt looked around and shouted orders to gain some control over what was happening. He fumbled with a new magazine and dropped it. Chaos reigned.

Shit. I can't even hear my own voice.

Brandt took a deep breath, unhurriedly inserted the new magazine, and matched Hart's rhythm of disciplined three-round bursts and well-aimed shots.

Crack. Crack. Crack. Brandt dove face down, hugging the dirt. The enemy machine gun fixed on his position. Bullets flew over his head, kicking up dirt around him. He pressed himself to the ground.

Somebody is trying to kill me. I could die now. All of my men could die. Oh, God. If we could just get out of here alive, I'll never miss church again.

A grenade exploded close behind Brandt. He bounced on the ground, changed magazines again, and looked up to fire. The pre-dawn sky revealed tops of trees and outlines of bushes, and he focused his fire more accurately. Only sporadic enemy fire came in from farther and farther away. The din subsided and gradually died away. Silence hung heavily in the air. For a moment, no one moved.

Brandt glanced around and felt the eyes of his men on him. He swallowed hard, took a deep breath, and stood. The final shots echoed in his ears. Sergeant Hart stood, followed by men in the other positions. Brandt looked down at the enemy soldier he killed. Eighteen holes in his chest oozed blood, and his eyes and mouth were wide open in a hysterical silent scream.

I got you first.

Brandt squared his shoulders and breathed deeply. He scanned the area and saw lumps of flesh and cloth scattered about him, pools of blood, and carnage.

And stillness. Such violent tranquility.

"Sir!" Jenkins ran toward Brandt, his face contorted. "Sergeant Williams got hit."

Brandt sprinted to his command post. Williams lay on a poncho, grimaced, and bit back a scream. Olszewski ripped open Williams' pant leg and wrapped a bandage around it, then looked up. "It ain't too bad. He'll be alright."

Brandt's jaw dropped; his eyes widened. One of his men lay on the ground in pain. Blood darkened the center of the bandage, the stain spread outward. Williams writhed. Brandt's shoulders sagged.

The pounding pulse of a helicopter drew his attention.

"I called medevac," Jenkins said. "Here it comes." Jenkins took a deep breath. "Uh, Bravo 6 wants you to call him right away. He sounds pissed, sir."

Brandt gazed at the bodies on the ground, the pools of blood, and Sergeant Williams, then stared at the handset Jenkins extended.

Set up on open ground in broad daylight? Shit.

"Sir?" Jenkins said.

Brandt straightened up, clenched fists raised, nostrils flared. He spun on his heel. "Later."

He knelt beside Williams and placed a hand on his shoulder. Tears welled up in his eyes. "I'm sorry."

Williams rose up, shook his head, and opened his mouth but squeezed his eyes shut and gasped. He took a deep breath and said, "Not your—" and clenched his jaws.

Olszewski eased him back on the poncho, and four men from 2nd Squad carried Williams, cradled in the poncho, to medics aboard the helicopter. The men of November Platoon clustered around in silent tribute.

Lieutenant Bill Brandt stood apart and watched the medevac helicopter recede, shrink to a small dot in the sky, and disappear.

★ ★ ★

After a somber march back to the company perimeter, Brandt stood at attention. Captain Parker leaned into Brandt's face.

"When your platoon is in contact, I want to talk to you. Not your platoon sergeant, not your RTO." He jabbed a finger into Brandt's chest. "You."

Brandt braced against the blast, focused on a point between them, pierced the wrath, and allowed it to break over him like a wave and trickle off his back. Brandt kept his mouth shut—an open mouth was a magnet for a foot—the "No excuse, sir" implied.

Parker leaned back.

Good. This is over. I can regroup now.

"Lieutenant," Parker's voice came an octave lower and in a more even tone. "Just what were you thinking at that time, anyway? I hope to hell you weren't trying to win a medal."

Aw, shit. Another wrinkle in the military discipline game. When a superior asks you for an explanation, "No excuse, sir" doesn't work.

Brandt took a deep breath. "I couldn't tell what was happening from where I was. I needed to know so I could decide what to do. The only way to find out was to go to that position." He hesitated, then continued, "And I can move more quietly by myself." He took another deep breath. "Especially at night."

Brandt looked into Parker's inscrutable face. The lull seemed to last an eternity. Brandt finally saw a barely perceptible nod. His shoulders relaxed.

"Lieutenant," Parker said, "a combat commander fights with his finger on the push-to-talk button of a radio, not on the trigger of his rifle. You'll kill more enemy soldiers with your radio than you ever will with your rifle."

A quiet exhale. "I understand, sir."

"You got three choices, lieutenant." Parker held up his index finger. "Don't go anywhere your RTO can't go." He held up two fingers. "You hump your own Prick-25." Three fingers. Brandt gulped. "I handcuff you and Jenkins together." Parker paused. "Which is it going to be, lieutenant?"

Brandt let out a sigh. "Number one, sir."

Parker placed his hands on his hips. "You lost a good man last night. Now what are you going to do without Sergeant Williams?"

A rhetorical question.

Brandt waited. Parker shook his head. "It's not likely that we'll get a replacement very soon. Your squad leaders are good, but they're not ready to be platoon sergeants. And there's no one in the squads ready to replace them. Think about it and we'll talk after dinner."

"Yes, sir."

"Dismissed."

CHAPTER 7

★ ★ ★

"Dear Mom and Dad," Brandt wrote. Pen poised beneath the salutation, he sighed.

That's the easy part. But, they already know the daily routine. The weather's always the same. What else can I say without adding to their worry? So far, Mom, none of my men have been killed. Just five wounded in the last few weeks. Four to booby traps, one to a sniper. They're on their way home now, and they'll be fine. I'm doing fine, too, because I don't have feelings anymore.

Brandt pounded his fist on his left knee, looked away from the pad balanced on his right knee, and searched for a topic. His eyes rested on the mountains to the west and he wrote, "The sun's dipping behind the mountains in a wash of pinks and oranges. Sunset after an easy day and a relaxed supper."

Relaxed? Huh. I guess so. How'd that happen?

Brandt paused and shook his head. After a moment, he ripped the page off the pad, crumpled it, and then pulled a letter from his shirt pocket. He scanned it quickly and wrote, "Hi Jim."

Brandt looked up and around, then continued writing.

"I hope all is well with you. Still selling lots of mutual funds? That one you put me into in college is doing well. I got your letter yesterday. Sometimes it takes a while to get out to us, so pardon the slow reply.

Thanks so much for thinking of me. It means a lot to get something from home, back in The World, as the men say here."

"You asked what it was like over here. I've been out in the field, what some guys call 'Indian Country,' for about a month now."

Brandt paused another moment.

"I no longer consciously fight the fear of tripping a booby trap with every step, of walking into the sights of a sniper's rifle in every tree, of blundering into an ambush in every valley. Those possibilities, the fear, are still there. All of that has become commonplace, like sleeping with my rifle, round in the chamber, brushing my teeth using a canteen cup, or just taking a leak anywhere I happen to be."

Brandt paused.

How do I communicate the everydayness of danger without getting grisly. Something back in The World that's the same.

Brandt stared at the ground for a moment. "Yeah," he said and resumed writing.

"It's like fishing, Jim. That's about the only thing that comes close. Fishing and snakes. Remember in high school when we'd drive up into the mountains to fish for trout? We knew the rattlesnakes, moccasins, and copperheads were there. It's their natural habitat, but we never saw them very often. We wanted to fish, so we accepted the risk and were careful. Just like the enemy here.

"I guess I've become used to the prospect of death. My death. It seems weird to write that, but we read Castaneda's *Journey to Ixtlan* in college. Remember how Don Juan talked about death following him around? He got used to it. It's like that."

Interesting analogy. I'm still walking along streams, watching where I step, wondering what's around the bend, searching for quarry. The only difference is that the stakes are higher.

"Yeah, Jim, I've settled into a groove. Since that first firefight, my men respond differently. When I approach a foxhole, the conversation stops, but I no longer endure those piercing, questioning looks I got at first. They even bitched out loud when I told them no cooking fires this evening. A good sign."

Brandt sat a little taller and smiled.

"Yeah, Jim, things are going well."

Brandt heard soft footfalls and looked up. Jenkins stood in front of him, shifting weight from foot to foot, eyes cast down and away.

"Sir, I'm going over to Singleton's position for a while. O.K.?"

That's the first time in a couple of hours that he's said anything. Unusual for him.

"O.K." Brandt watched as Jenkins darted off to the left.

"Got a minute, sir?" Sergeant Hart stood to his right.

"Sure. Have a seat."

"That's O.K, sir." Hart remained standing. He looked up and to the left, as if searching for something. The fingers of his hands opened and closed.

Brandt placed the letter and the pen on the ground beside him and leaned back against his rucksack. "You got something to say, sergeant?"

Hart took a deep breath. "It's about the operation tonight."

"Yeah?"

"Well, sir, the other squad leaders and I were talking." Hart looked away.

Brandt made an exaggerated move, leaning to his side and craning his neck as if looking around behind Hart. "And you've been elected platoon sergeant."

"No, sir." Hart stiffened.

"At ease, sergeant. It's not hard to see why men look to you for leadership."

"It's not like that."

"What's it like?" Brandt dropped his voice and spoke slowly. "I need to know."

Hart took a deep breath. "We're going to be moving at night. That ain't smart. Not around here. The men are scared shitless, sir."

Brandt pulled his legs up, crossed his arms and rested his elbows on his knees.

So that's why Jenkins was so quiet. Why he took off like a jackrabbit.

Brandt opened his mouth and shook his head. Then his nostrils flared and eyes narrowed.

"Get the other squad leaders. Now."

Brandt watched Hart jog away, then placed his face in his hands, elbows still resting on his knees.

Oh, shit.

He heard footsteps and looked up. His three squad leaders stood in front of him. "Sit down."

They hesitated.

"I said," Brandt raised his voice, "sit down."

They plopped onto their butts, sitting Indian style, silent. Olszewski fiddled with his boot laces. Martinez adjusted the sweat band in his helmet. Hart glared at the other two.

"I've heard what Sergeant Hart has to say." Brandt waited. More silence.

"O.K., I'll start. What's our mission? We separated from the company this morning and crossed over a low ridge. Now we stay hidden until dark, then move about 500 meters tonight and set up a blocking position to cut off a likely escape route into the mountains. Captain Parker will loop around the end of the ridge at first light and drive through the village. What's so hard about that?"

Brandt waited. Silence.

Brandt leaned toward Martinez. "Sergeant Martinez, I was thinking of putting your squad on point tonight."

A MATTER OF SEMANTICS

Martinez looked up at that, eyes wide, then over to Hart. Hart held his gaze, silent.

Martinez leaned toward Brandt. "O.K., sir. You want to know? You got it. This is crazy. This whole battalion, 80 percent of the casualties are from booby traps. During the day. We walk at night, sure as hell we'll get our best shit blown away." Martinez sat back and held his breath.

"So, you never move at night?"

Martinez shook his head. "Only thing we do at night is ambushes. But move from point A to point B? No way, sir."

"I can't believe that."

Hart nodded. "That's right, sir."

"So, Charlie owns the night. He walks where he fucking pleases and you hide, right?"

Hart pounded his fist on the ground. "No fuckin' way, sir." Hart's eyes showed trepidation. But his nostrils flared, and he held the forward lean, fist on the ground.

Brandt held up his hand, palm outward. "Sorry. I didn't mean it that way. But that's the way it looks, doesn't it? When do you think they set those fucking booby traps, anyway? In broad daylight, when our choppers are flying around all over the place?" Brandt shook his head. "No. We have to challenge him. Take the night away from his scrawny ass." He paused to let that sink in. "We're here to help Vietnam defend itself against Communism. Same way France helped 13 colonies become the United States." He paused again. "The mission of the Infantry is to close with and destroy the enemy. We bust our asses humping the hills looking for Charlie. He hides and runs when we find him. Disappears like a ghost." Another pause. "Night is our best shot at nailing him."

They sat back, eyes narrowed, jaws clenched.

Brandt could not doubt their courage, their willingness to follow his orders. He tried a different tack. "Then why did Bravo 6 give us this mission?"

Three sets of eyes fell to the ground.

"Sergeant Hart?"

Hart looked to his right, placed his hands on his hips. "Ski, what was that you said to me earlier?"

Olszewski raised his head slowly, glared at Hart, then faced Brandt. "Well, sir, I was just wondering. How come we don't move with the rest of the company anymore? I mean, we been going off on our own more and more. Know what I mean, sir?"

Brandt shrugged. "How's that different?"

"Well, " Olszewski glanced at Hart and Martinez. They both nodded. "Used to be, all three platoons moved together. The whole company. Now, well, we been going off on our own a lot."

Brandt leaned back and pursed his lips.

The past three weeks we've done independent platoon missions— recon and fix the enemy—and Bravo rushes in to throw a knockout punch. Move with stealth to seal off escape routes, ambushing well-used trails. Parker is using us like, oh shit, like a Ranger team. Now the night move. And he's moving at first light.

"Look." Brandt paused. He waited until he held their gaze. "Next time Bravo 6 gives me a mission order, I tell him to shove it, right?"

They all smiled and chuckled at that thought.

"With his machete. Sideways."

That got all-out laughter.

Oh, thank God.

Brandt seized the opening. "It is possible to move at night. You just have to use the right techniques and be careful."

Hart looked at Brandt out of the corner of his eye. "You know how to do that?"

Brandt nodded.

"Where did you learn that?"

Brandt looked down, took a breath and looked up. "Same place I learned about booby traps."

Martinez forced the issue. "Ranger School?"

Brandt nodded.

"Sounds like a bad-ass school."

"I had a lot of sergeants run my ass into the ground and teach me how to tell the difference between shit and Shinola."

That got another laugh.

Brandt looked over his shoulder. The sun had already disappeared, and nothing had been settled. He'd only succeeded in reestablishing rapport. He needed to break the impasse and accomplish the mission but also preserve their relationship.

What was it Sergeant Williams said? If the squad leaders don't know, it's my job to train them.

"I'll walk point tonight."

Three jaws dropped.

"But, if I don't," Brandt nodded toward Martinez, "get my best shit blown away, it's the last time I do it." He looked at each one of them. "It's not my job. My job is to train you and the men how to do it. I expect everyone to do his job."

Brandt paused to let that sink in.

"Do we have a deal?" Brandt held his breath.

The three sergeants looked at each other. "Yes, sir."

Brandt let out his breath slowly.

Thank you, Sergeant Williams.

"O.K. We'll be moving out at midnight. It'll take a few hours to cover 500 meters. Brief your squads and be back in 30 minutes. I have some SOPs for night moves."

They all stood. Hart and Olszewski headed off to their men. Martinez remained.

"Something else, sergeant?"

"Sir, my squad will take the lead. And I will be right behind you." He smiled. "I want to learn that bad-ass shit."

"Thanks. I'll see you in a little while."

Brandt watched Martinez walk away. He picked up the pen and letter and wrote, "Got to go now, Jim. To be continued."

★ ★ ★

Brandt adjusted the sling on his rifle, taped the metal fittings to silence rattles and clinks, slipped it over his head and shoulder, and cinched it tight. The CAR-15, with the collapsible stock, fit snugly across his back. Brandt's equipment had been distributed among members of 3rd Squad, including his rucksack and helmet—hands free, no extra weight.

Brandt shrugged, settled the rifle, then slapped at his neck.

Damn mosquitos.

Brandt faced Martinez. Behind the sergeant, his platoon stretched back into the darkness, each man an arm's length behind the other in a long single file, exactly as he'd briefed his sergeants earlier. He leaned close to Martinez.

"Remember, it's important that the men each stay within arm's length of the man in front of them so that they don't lose contact. They must follow directly behind. We'll be walking on the trail—just the opposite of what we do in daytime."

Martinez nodded as Brandt's spoke, the sergeant's gaze intense.

"Walking off the trail, we make too much noise in the brush. It's harder for the men to follow my exact path. And it's harder to find the traps. You'll see. Bare dirt and sand reflect light. If there's something in your way, you know it's not a branch or vine. If they stay on the trail, the men know they're walking on ground that I've cleared."

He paused. "Pass it back to send up a count."

Martinez looked back over his shoulder. "Pass up a count."

Brandt heard a murmur recede into the stillness of the night. A moment later the murmur returned like a soft echo. The man behind Martinez put a hand on his shoulder, placed his lips near the sergeant's ear. Martinez leaned close to Brandt. "Twenty-four."

"And I'm twenty-five", Brandt said. "All accounted for." He took a deep breath and exhaled slowly. "Let's go."

Brandt turned but felt a strong hand grab his arm. Then he heard a soft voice, "*Vaya con Diós,* Lieutenant."

Brandt looked down and found the marker he had set at the edge of the trail, a spot he had checked before dark. More than once. Brandt took a deep breath, stepped forward, and began the process of clearing the trail in front of him. He raised his right hand out and above his head, his left hand out and down to his knee. Slowly, he bent his knees and descended, the fingers of his left hand probing the air in front of him. When his left hand touched the ground, he placed his palm on the dirt, drew it across the trail, barely touching the surface. He slowly lowered his right hand. When his left and right hand met, he reached out further and swept his hands back across the trail. Brandt stood erect, left hand high and right hand low. He raised his right leg until his thigh was parallel to the ground. Then he swung his foot under his knee, lowered it until the toe of his boot touched the ground and gradually rolled his foot down on the trail. His hands passed up and down, and he raised his left leg, placed his foot down as carefully as the right.

Not a sound had been made. The Night Walk.

Always felt foolish practicing this in daylight. So comical to someone watching. I don't feel foolish now.

Brandt settled into a smooth rhythm, attention focused, and time slowed. He probed the dark easily at first. Then the exaggerated, repetitive motions took a toll on his muscles. How many deep knee bends can you do? How long can you hold your arms out? Sweat stung the corners of his eyes. An ache cramped the small of his back. He started to raise his right leg but froze.

Did I clear the trail?

He turned to Martinez. "Rest break. Remind the men to sit down on the trail." Again, the murmur receded into darkness.

Brandt eased himself down on the trail and wiped his forehead. He checked his watch. 0205. Halfway there. He gazed down the trail. It virtually glowed in the moonlight. His muscles relaxed, and his strength returned.

Time to move.

He stood. Martinez stood, and movement rippled up the trail. The count came back. "Twenty-four."

Brandt resumed his Night Walk, settled into the rhythm, and sifted air swept dirt, but weariness tugged at his muscles sooner this time. In the distance, a lighter sky silhouetted the black, scalloped line of treetops.

Almost there.

Brandt increased the speed of his movements.

The voice inside his head said, "Patience. Patience." Brandt froze. For once, the voice was soft. A whisper. "Speed kills. Automatic, unthinking flow of arms and legs is hypnotic. It numbs the senses."

Brandt resumed deliberate, conscious motions. Down, sweep dirt, up slowly, step. Down, sweep dirt, up slowly, step. Down, sweep dirt, up slowly—the soft sensation on his fingertip registered like an electric shock.

The jolt stopped him. He felt Martinez's hand on his back, heard him grunt. Brandt's right hand descended to meet his left and clasped the thin filament, his hands joined as if in prayer. His right hand followed the invisible fishing line to a small tree off the trail, his left hand, to a bush hugging the trail's left edge.

He released the line, stood, and faced Martinez. "Booby trap."

"No shit? Where?"

Brandt grasped Martinez's hand, guided it down to the trail.

A MATTER OF SEMANTICS

"Bring your hand up slowly because the line is slack across the trail. If you bring it down, you might trip the trap."

Brandt felt him shudder at the touch of the limp, delicate line. Martinez experienced the electricity too.

Martinez shook his head. "Damn. Never would've believed it."

Brandt moved to the edge of the trail. Martinez followed.

"Remember what to do?" Brandt asked.

"We post a man right here." Martinez replied. "He directs everybody behind him around the bush. After the last man passes him, he comes around and passes up a count."

Brandt nodded. Martinez turned to the man behind him, tugged on his sleeve and gestured for him to follow.

Brandt carefully moved off the trail, sweeping the ground and air around the bush until he was again standing on the trail, Martinez close behind. Brandt continued his Night Walk until he cleared enough trail for the rest of the platoon. He stopped, took a deep breath, waited, and listened. It seemed an eternity before Martinez said, "Twenty-four."

A simple message, but it brought profound relief.

Brandt continued down the trail and deployed the platoon along the base of the hills cradling the village against the beach as stars faded and gave way to predawn colors. He gazed back down the trail he had traversed, chin up, shoulders back, chest thrust out, weary muscles charged with renewed energy.

Point man. What a rush.

He took a deep breath.

Why did I ever become an officer?

CHAPTER 8

★ ★ ★

Brandt scraped the last smidgeon of peanut butter out of the small, round tin with the remaining morsel of cracker.

Cracker? More like a rigid disk of cardboard.

He licked the tip of his forefinger.

At least the peanut butter tastes like peanuts. Another great C-Ration lunch.

He washed it down with a swig of water from his canteen, a grimace on his face.

"Ah, I've acquired a taste for iodine."

Jenkins smiled, dug into his rucksack, and pulled out a small foil packet. "Here, sir. Pour some Kool-Aid into your canteen. It kills the taste of the iodine."

Brandt took the offering. "Grape. It doesn't say what vintage."

"Huh?"

"How much?"

"Try half the package. Shake the canteen real good."

Brandt followed the instructions and took a sip. "Hey, that's better. Just a light tang of iodine on the palate."

"What?"

"Thanks. I'll have to ask my mom to send me some in the next CARE package."

Jenkins beamed.

Sergeant Olszewski approached and knelt down. Brandt pointed to the map beside him.

"We're about five kilometers away from the valley we're supposed to recon."

Brandt tapped the map with his finger. "Looks like there's a village directly in our path halfway there."

Olszewski picked up the map and studied it. "We gonna search the village?"

Brandt looked up, raised his hand to shield his eyes, and checked the sun's position.

"Don't think we'll have time to search the village. Not smart to just cruise through it." Brandt paused, then continued with exaggerated sincerity. "Shouldn't disturb the people for no reason. It's designated a friendly village."

"Shit. Somebody in Saigon decide that?"

"Hell, I don't know." Brandt snorted. "Maybe somebody in Washington."

"Left or right around it. Which way, sir?"

Brandt peered into the distance.

"Vince Lombardi told his backs to run to daylight."

Olszewski looked at him sideways. "Uh-huh."

"Well, can't see much from here. I'll make a decision when I can eyeball it. I'll walk near your point. I want to check out the terrain before we get too far into it."

Olszewski stood. "O.K., sir. Wilkins is point man today."

Jenkins rose with the PRC-6 radio in hand.

Brandt folded the map, scrambled to his feet, slipped the map into his pocket, shouldered his rucksack, and checked the safety on his rifle.

"Jenkins, tell the other squad leaders to form up into a column. Time to move out."

"O.K., sergeant, let's go." Brandt jogged forward, caught up with the lead element, and blended in as just one of the soldiers. The brisk pace over flat, grassy terrain covered ground quickly.

Brandt called a halt 50 meters from the village. Small, maybe 15 huts and some palm trees. A thick band of tall plants with long, broad leaves and dense undergrowth bordered the left edge. Widely spaced palm trees and low, scrub vegetation encircled the right.

Olszewski joined him. "Watcha think, sir?"

Brandt surveyed the terrain on both sides of the village. He pointed to the left. "Wide, barren field over there. Looks volcanic. Red, cinder-like dirt. Nothing growing. Not even scrub grass. We could travel fast and make good time. On the other hand, there's no cover, no concealment. We'd be ducks in a shooting gallery."

"Yeah."

"To the right," Brandt said, gesturing with his rifle, "is a grassy field ringed with small trees and bushes. The ground rises gently above the village. Concealment and high ground is good, but we can't see very far ahead. It also provides concealment for snipers and ambushes. We'll have to move carefully, more slowly."

"No good choices. So what's new, sir?"

Brandt scanned the area again.

A fork in the road. Quo vadis? Which way? Read a book in high school by that title. Didn't work out too well for the Romans.

He strode toward the volcanic field, paused, and studied the expanse. He paced toward the grassy field, stopped, and placed his hands on his hips.

Yogi Berra said that if you come to a fork in the road, take it, and people laughed. I think I know what he meant.

Brandt noticed a quizzical expression on Olszewski's face.

I'm taking too long. Need to pick a direction and go.

"Sergeant, we're going through the field on the right. Let's get moving."

Brandt let 2nd Squad move forward, waited for 3rd Squad, and assumed his usual position in the middle of the formation. As they entered the field, he scanned the terrain. About two football fields long and one football field wide and not as grassy as it looked from a distance. Just scattered patches of dry grass and a few scattered shrubs, but mostly parched soil. He glanced downslope into the village, about 80 meters to his left. A low band of vegetation 30 meters wide separated it from the field. Nobody working, no kids playing. Halfway into the field, he spun 180 degrees and checked the formation behind him. All platoon elements had entered the field. He turned again to move forward but stopped and inspected the village. Something didn't seem right here, too quiet. He shook his head.

Brandt checked flank security, out 40 meters toward the village. Garcia, one of the new replacements, shuffled along adjusting web-gear suspenders, eyes focused on fumbling fingers. He started to say something to Martinez about training the new men.

An explosion shattered the silence. Brandt hit the ground, then bounced up and searched in the direction of the sound. Garcia lay sprawled on the ground, helmet rolling away, dark stains spreading into his pants. Carson sprinted to the man, followed closely by Martinez. Brandt spun around to check the rest of the platoon. Everyone else looked O.K., facing outward, alert. He hustled over to Carson. The medic cut open Garcia's pant legs and wrapped gauze around the wounds.

"How is he?"

"Just shrapnel puncture wounds. No arteries severed, nothing broken. Most of this might be just pieces of rock and dirt. Hit his head on the ground pretty hard, so he's in and out of consciousness. He'll be O.K." Carson brushed dirt off a bruise on the man's head. "You hear that, buddy? You're going to be O.K."

Jenkins appeared next to Brandt. He took the handset but paused, took a few deep breaths, and then raised it to his head.

"Dustoff, Dustoff. This is November 6, over."

"November 6, what is your situation?"

"We are in an open field. One wounded. Tripped a booby trap. Multiple shrapnel wounds in his legs."

"What is your location?"

"From Green, down one-half, left one-half."

"We just happen to be in your neighborhood. Be there in 10 minutes."

Carson looked at Brandt expectantly.

"Ten minutes."

Carson gave a thumbs-up.

Martinez rummaged in Garcia's rucksack, pulled out a poncho, unfolded it, laid it on the ground, and helped Carson move Garcia onto the poncho.

Brandt spotted a small crater not far away. He sidestepped around Carson to the bowl-shaped depression, studied it, and called Martinez over.

Brandt pointed. "That hole in the ground used to be a bush." He swept his hand toward another bush a few feet away. "Garcia must have walked between them."

"Yeah," Martinez said, "right into a tripwire."

Brandt nodded. "They buried the explosive device under the bush to hide it."

"Judging from the size of the hole," Martinez said, "probably a grenade. Dumb shits buried it too deep. That's why he just had puncture wounds. Mostly rock and dirt, like Doc said."

"And look at the ground before and after." Brandt said. "Looks like a path along the edge of the field."

"Uh-huh. But faint. Not used lately." Martinez looked at the village, a sneer on his face. "Wonder why?"

Brandt looked along the path. "So Garcia was following the easiest way through the clumps of grass. And he was adjusting his suspenders, not looking where he was stepping."

Martinez let out a long sigh. "He should have known better. Why aren't they training these guys?"

"Probably are," Brandt said. "But training is one thing. Most people need to hear it over and over again to learn it." He remembered something Sergeant Williams had said. "And that's our job."

"You got that right, sir. Let's get started when we laager up tonight. Make time for it."

"Yeah." The beating of helicopter blades drowned out Brandt's voice. He watched the chopper settle about 20 meters from them. It didn't land but hovered a couple of feet above the ground.

Right. Booby trap. Mine. They don't want to set off another one with their skids.

Brandt watched as Martinez and Carson lifted the poncho cradling Garcia. They carefully sidestepped to the chopper through dust and grit whipped up by the rotor wash. The crew chief and onboard medic transferred Garcia to a stretcher.

The crew chief spoke into his headset, and the chopper rose, made a sharp turn, and receded rapidly. In the silence, everyone stood still for a long moment.

Brandt shook his head, fists clenched. Garcia. But he couldn't think about the casualty. He needed to get the platoon focused. He raised his chin and bellowed, "O.K., let's get moving."

He took a few strides, but a much larger explosion jolted him. Another man lay on the ground about 30 meters ahead and to his right. Carson sprinted to him. Brandt broke into a run, stopped, moved deliberately, and checked the ground in front of him. Olszewski joined Carson beside the man. A lot more blood pooled onto the ground this time.

Carson looked up, stepped toward Brandt, and spoke softly. "It's Satterlee. Bad, sir. His left foot is mangled. Most of the bleeding is coming out of the ankle area. Don't want to take the boot off. Not sure how much of a connection remains with the foot. Right calf is torn up, too. I tried to stop the bleeding with pressure bandages and a tourniquet. I'm worried about him going into shock. You'd better get that medevac back here fast."

Jenkins extended the handset.

"Dustoff, Dustoff. This is November 6. We have another WIA. Serious foot wound, lots of bleeding. May be going into shock."

"This is Dustoff. Be there in a couple of minutes."

Brandt inspected the ground around Satterlee. A bare patch of dirt. No bushes. Not even grass.

"Must have been some kind of mine," Olszewski said.

"Right, a pressure trigger on the mine."

"How do you know?"

"Well, if it were a pressure-release device, it would have exploded behind him as he stepped off it. Wounds would be on the back of his legs."

The return of the helicopter drew their attention. Time and motion blurred. Brandt watched as four men transferred Satterlee to medevac.

Satterlee. Damn. He only had three months left on his tour. A machine gunner. Have to pick a new man to carry it. Olszewski will take care of that for now.

The helicopter lifted off and the engine noise diminished. Brandt took a deep breath.

"They're going to be O.K." He raised his hand and propelled it forward. "Move out. We got a job to do."

The men moved slower, cautiously placing their steps. The point man reached the far end of the field 50 meters ahead of the platoon and veered toward a break in the vegetation, a natural gate at the crest of the rise. He stepped through it and his head disappeared below the crest followed by another explosion. Rock and dust mushroomed into the air. Everyone froze. The noise subsided, dust dissipated, and silence settled.

Brandt and Carson started forward. A head and shoulders popped above the crest, and the face displayed the biggest smile Brandt had ever seen.

"Dumb fuckers set the delay too long." Wilkins yelled, his voice euphoric. "I dove downslope below the explosion."

Brandt took a deep breath and let it out slowly.

"Everyone, listen up. Turn around and head back. We're getting out of here the way we came in. Try to retrace your steps."

Heads nodded enthusiastically.

Brandt made his way back to the platoon's rear guard before he gave the order to move and assumed the role of point man. He passed by Corelli, an M-79 gunner in 1st Squad. Brandt nodded to him and attempted an encouraging smile. Time slowed. Corelli took a stride and shifted his weight forward. The ground under Corelli's foot erupted, dirt and rocks flying with shrapnel in all directions. Brandt heard no sound. His only sensation, a sudden pressure on his right side, as if slammed on the blind side by a defensive end.

Darkness.

Brandt blinked his eyes, and saw blue sky and Hart's face above.

"You O.K., lieutenant?"

Why is he whispering?

Carson appeared next to Hart. "Don't see any blood, Doc."

Brandt felt the medic's hands palpating his chest, arms, legs.

Carson turned to Hart. "He's fine. No injuries."

Hart shook his head. "Fucking amazing. Look at the size of that hole. They probably buried an artillery round. Maybe a 105."

Carson nodded. "You never know how shrapnel is going to disperse. Especially when it's buried like that." He looked down at Brandt. "You feel any pain?"

Carson's voice sounded almost normal volume. Brandt hesitated. "Uh, I don't think so." He felt his own arms, trunk, legs. "No. Everything feels O.K."

"You're fine, sir. Just a little disoriented from hitting the ground so hard. You need to get up and moving. We need you now."

Carson stood and faced Hart. "Help him up and hang on until he's steady. I'm going back to Corelli."

"Can you get up, sir?" Hart grabbed Brandt's arm and placed a hand behind his shoulders. Brandt sat up, pulled his legs under himself and stood, unsteadily at first. Hart supported him.

"What happened?"

"Corelli stepped on a mine. You were right next to him." Hart pointed to the crater five meters away.

"How the hell?"

"Yeah, you really sailed through the air, sir."

He saw the radio lying on the ground.

"Jenkins?"

"He's O.K. He's helping put Corelli on the chopper. He called for medevac right away. You've been out for a few minutes."

"Corelli?"

"He's going to be O.K. Big piece of shrapnel punched a hole in his left hand. Nothing else."

The hiss of the radio stopped and Parker screamed, "November 6, Bravo 6."

Brandt picked up the handset. "November 6, over."

"I monitored your requests for medevac. What the hell is going on? Are you O.K.?"

"Affirmative. We walked into a minefield. Three wounded."

"Get the hell out of there. Move to a location where your platoon can rest. We're a long hump away, but we'll get to you as soon as we can."

"Roger. Wilco. We're going to back out the way we came in."

"You be careful. Six out."

Jenkins approached slowly, his face flushed from effort, eyes filled with fear. He took the radio but remained silent.

Brandt scanned the field. His men frozen in place, eyes on him, pleading.

"Sir?" Hart's voice filled with the unspoken question on everyone's face.

Yeah. What next? Can't just stand here. Have to do something. Backing out didn't work.

A determined look came over his face. The men needed leadership. He nodded.

"Everyone move to the center of the field. Form a single file behind me."

The men hesitated, reluctance to step apparent on their faces.

"Look for disturbed ground, like digging covered up. Darker patches of dirt. Anything sticking up out of the ground. A trip wire."

No one moved.

Olszewski raised a deep, forceful voice and stepped confidently. "You heard the man. Get moving."

Martinez and Hart repeated the command. The men took deliberate, carefully placed steps and converged.

Brandt examined the gap between danger and safety.

Forty meters. An easy pass to a receiver; less than five seconds to run. Now a gauntlet to traverse.

He knelt on both knees, reached down to his right hip and drew his Gerber double-edged dagger from its scabbard.

In a barely audible voice he said, "Please God, help me."

With the blade poised above the ground, thoughts and images swirled in his head. He was back in high school. Friday afternoon homeroom. A nun entered.

"Before dismissal, let's say a prayer that our football team wins tonight."

Brandt raised his hand. "Aren't the nuns at Cathedral having their students pray for their team?"

"Of course they are, William."

"Then how does God decide whom he's going to help?"

The image dissolved in the nun's frown.

Does God get involved in football games? What if the people in the village are praying to God? Does God take sides in wars?

Brandt shook his head, but another image intruded. He was back in Ranger School, on his knees, bayonet in hand. The grizzled sergeant loomed over him.

"Don't just stab your knife into the ground. If the mine is designed to go off when pressure is applied, it could explode in your face."

The image faded. Brandt took a deep breath, studied the ground in front of him. He leaned forward and to his left and slid the knife into the ground at a shallow angle, withdrew it, moved the insertion point to his right, probed and moved again until he completed a 180 degree arc. He inched forward and repeated the actions. Lean, probe, crawl. Lean, probe, crawl. Sweat formed on his brow, dripped off his nose. Lean, probe, crawl.

Brandt paused, sat back on his heels, wiped his face, reached behind, and rubbed his lower back.

Hart grabbed his shoulder. "You got us half way there. Not much further."

Encouraged, Brandt attacked the ground with renewed vigor and accelerated his pace. Lean, probe, crawl.

The grizzled sergeant intruded again. "Speed kills, Ranger. Slow and sure is safe."

Brandt nodded, took a deep breath, and resumed deliberate motions. Lean, probe crawl. Lean, probe, crawl.

Clink.

Brandt froze.

"Oh, shit."

Gingerly, he probed around the source of the sound, confirmed the location of the mine, sat back and looked over his shoulder at Hart.

"I see it. Dirt right over it is darker, even though they tried to smooth it. Just like you said."

Brandt leaned forward, carved a big X in front of the mine, then an arrow pointing to the left. He faced Hart and said, "Pass it back. Mine. Go to the left of the X. Point it out to the man behind you."

Hart brought the man behind him him forward and relayed the instructions.

Brandt concentrated on the ground and resumed the measured pace through a wide detour. Lean, probe, crawl. With heightened caution. As if in a trance, he shut out all thought, obsessed on dirt, rhythm, touch. Lean, probe, crawl. Time slowed, his breath marked each harrowing probe. Lean, probe, crawl.

Again, pain in his back intruded. He sat back on his heels.

Hart tapped his shoulder. "I think we're there. You did it. You got us out."

★ ★ ★

Brandt sat on the edge of his foxhole and gazed around the company perimeter. Everyone bustled with purposeful activity. Captain Parker talked on the radio, his map spread on the ground. The other platoon leaders conferred with their platoon sergeants. His squad leaders checked fields of fire in their sectors.

Everyone avoided him. He let out a deep sigh. Images and sounds churned in his mind: echoes of explosions; the medevac hovering; blood-stained dirt; the faces of each wounded man wracked with pain; three of his men wounded in less than 15 minutes, on the ground, bleeding; and the knowledge that he'd led them into a minefield.

Brandt slid down into the foxhole, crossed his arms over his knees, and rested his head on them. He began to shake, deep sobs rising from his chest.

Brandt heard a voice and looked up.

"Sir, you O.K.?"

Hart's voice.

Hart leaned over the foxhole. "Sir? Sir?"

The concern in Hart's voice brought on another wave of tears and sobs. He laid his head on his arms.

The emotion subsided. Brandt took a few deep breaths. He sensed another presence and looked up. A pair of boots dangled into the foxhole, then dropped to the bottom. Captain Parker sat in front of him. Brandt wiped his eyes.

"Tough day, lieutenant."

Brandt gulped air and nodded.

"This is war. Soldiers are wounded in war."

"But I led them into that field."

"Yes, you did. But on the way over here, we went through that bare field of dirt on the other side of the village. I walked with Mike and sent Lima around on the flank to clear the vegetation. The advantage of a larger force. I wouldn't have gone that way with just one platoon."

Brandt nodded and sighed.

" Like I said, this is war."

"But I lost three men in less than 15 minutes."

"Bill, 80 percent of our battalion's casualties come from mines, booby traps, and snipers, the rest from ambushes. The enemy won't stand and fight us. That's why we're out here looking for them. The mission of the Infantry is to close with and destroy the enemy. We can't help but take casualties doing that. It might help you to know that Alpha Company had 15 men wounded last month and five killed in action."

Parker paused to let that sink in, then held out his canteen. Brandt took a long draft and returned it.

"O.K., lieutenant, your men have had a tough day, too. They need strong leadership now. You're an officer, and that's your job."

They stood, climbed out of the foxhole, and Parker headed back to the company CP. Brandt stood alone, surveying his sector of the perimeter. The men seemed subdued. Jenkins sat with Carson, but only a word or two passed between them. Martinez and Hart conferred on the link between their squads. Olszewski handed the new machine gunner his weapon. Satterlee's gun.

A surge of emotion rose with the image of Satterlee's face.

Brandt shook his head. "No."

An image of a footlocker formed and his emotions flowed into it. Brandt slammed the lid down and closed the lock.

"Sir," Jenkins approached hesitantly, "you want me to call the squad leaders?"

Brandt took a deep breath. "No. I'm going to walk the line and talk to the men."

CHAPTER 9

★ ★ ★

Brandt took notes as Parker pointed to a cluster of villages on his map. "It would take too long to search them, so skirt the villages and search this valley to the west of them. There may be some tunnels there. This stream," Parker traced the thin blue line on the map, "flows down the mountains into the plain and eventually to the An Lao River. This map doesn't show them, but intel says two mountain trails, possibly infiltration routes off the Ho Chi Minh Trail, intersect here at the head of the valley." He pointed with his machete. "It's likely a trail comes off that intersection, follows the stream, and leads into the villages." Parker looked up again. "Of course, these maps might be off by a couple hundred meters."

"Yeah," Brandt said. "I've noticed that."

Parker looked up. "It's too far for you to come back in tonight, so if you don't find anything, I want you to set up an ambush based on signs of enemy movement. Call in the coordinates when you've chosen your site."

Brandt jotted more notes. "Yes, sir. Anything else?"

"What route do you plan to take into this area?"

"Well, sir, if they're hiding in the foothills, they probably want to be near water. I think I'll find the stream south of the villages and follow it up the valley. I'll run cloverleaf patterns. Send a squad to the left to search in a circle and another to the right in a circle while the other one searches forward. It takes longer, but gives more thorough coverage of the area. If nothing else, I'll find the trail and that intersection."

"How far out will you send the squads?"

"No further than I can maintain eye contact with them. No more than 100 meters. I want to be able to react quickly to reinforce if one makes contact."

"Fine. Good hunting, lieutenant."

★ ★ ★

The platoon climbed a low hill. Brandt raised his left arm high.

"Jenkins, tell the squad leaders to halt in place."

He turned 360 degrees and scanned the terrain. Grassy valley cut by the stream, forested ridges to the north and south, and to the west, a steep wall rising to the peaks of the Central Highlands.

"Sir." Ski appeared beside him. "You want me to set up hasty security?"

"Yeah. Good idea."

Ski gave a few hand signals to his fire team leaders.

"Uh, sir." Ski hesitated.

"What is it?"

"Well, sir, I was just wondering."

Brandt cut in. "I don't want you to wonder, sergeant. I want you to think."

"Yes, sir. I was just thinking." Ski cleared his throat. "We followed that stream, found the trail, and searched the ground from wall to wall of this valley and haven't found anything. And we're almost at the head of the valley."

"Yeah. I noticed that."

"Well, if this place is so deserted, no signs, then why isn't the trail overgrown?"

"Could be they're disciplined about cleaning up signs. You wondering if this is a good place to set up an ambush?"

Ski smiled. "That's what I was thinking, sir."

"Well, that trail intersection at the base of the mountains should only be about 200 meters to the west. NVA patrols might be coming down those trails from the Ho Chi Minh Trail. That's the best place for us to set up an ambush."

Ski nodded. "Yes, sir. But the VC around here know that, too. They might've seen us snooping around."

Brandt took a sip from his canteen. Something nagged at him. He shrugged his shoulders.

"I agree. Jenkins, call the other squad leaders."

"O.K.," Ski said, "I'll check security while they come up here."

Brandt took another sip. The nag returned with an image of a medevac helicopter receding into the distance.

If we set up before dark, it could be a repeat of the last ambush.

Brandt took another sip and replaced the canteen. The little voice in his head said, "What are your Standing Orders, Ranger?"

Brandt looked over his shoulder as if he expected to see someone. "O.K.," he muttered. "Standing Orders, Roger's Rangers. Major Robert Rogers, the French and Indian War. What the hell does that have to do with anything?"

"What, sir?" Jenkins asked.

"Uh, nothing." Brandt turned and stepped away.

Brandt called up a visual image of the first page of his Ranger Handbook.

Yeah. Order number 8. When we march, we keep moving until dark so as to give the enemy the least possible chance at us.

"Correct, Ranger," said the little voice. "It's worked since 1759."

A MATTER OF SEMANTICS

A minute later, Hart walked up to Brandt, followed by Ski and Martinez.

"So, this where we're going to set up the ambush tonight, sir?" Hart asked.

Brandt squinted at the sun as it descended toward the hills, then faced the three squad leaders.

"This low hill affords a good view of the terrain. Actually, it's more of a bump on the valley floor than a hill. And it's just large enough for us to spread out and set up a good ambush."

Brandt knelt and laid his map on the ground. The others crouched.

"Any thoughts?"

"Well," Martinez pointed to the map. "We're farther away from that trail than usual. Maybe fifty meters. Too far to throw grenades."

Ski chuckled. "Even for you, sir."

Brandt ignored the banter, but couldn't conceal a smile at the sign of growing acceptance. "I know, but as Ski pointed out, Charlie would expect us to ambush the intersection of the trails." He pointed toward the mountains. "Over there. If we set up here, we have a longer kill zone and this bump in the ground has such a slow rise that we still have grazing fire on the trail with our rifles and machine guns."

Brandt paused. "Any suggestions?"

"We could put extra Claymores on the kill zone," Martinez said. "One at each end like usual and two more to cover the middle. That just might finish the job without shooting."

"And we can put a trip flare in the center of the kill zone," Hart suggested. "In case it's too dark or foggy to see when they come calling."

"O.K.," Brandt nodded. "I like both of those ideas. We'll do it that way. I will initiate the ambush with a Claymore."

He pointed to the radio handset on Jenkins' suspenders.

"Bravo 6, November 6. Are you prepared to copy? Over."

"This is Bravo 6. Affirmative. Over."

"I have a position to report." Brandt glanced down at his map. "I am at, from Dodgers, up two and a half, right three. Over."

"Is that your ambush site?"

"Affirmative."

"That looks good. Proceed as planned. Six out."

Brandt gave the handset back to Jenkins and said to the squad leaders, "I want you to put your men in position now. Have them eat some dinner in place. Then we'll form up in order of march and take a look at that area around the trail intersection. Just as the sun disappears behind the hills, we'll head back here. Dusk. The most difficult time of the day to see. By the time we get back here, it will be dark. Put markers in the ground now so it will be easier to get into position smoothly."

"But, sir," Hart said, "Bravo 6 always wants us to set up before dark."

Brandt took a deep breath and let it out slowly. "He said, 'Call in the coordinates when you've chosen the site.' I did that. Just as ordered. But I'll be damned if I lose any more good men because I let the enemy see where I set up an ambush in broad daylight." He looked at each of them. "Anything else?"

They looked at each other. "No, sir," came a chorus in reply.

"Do I have to walk point tonight?"

Martinez stepped forward. "No sir."

★ ★ ★

A distant bloom of light followed by an explosion shattered a silent night.

Brandt looked at his watch. 0306. A self-satisfied smirk spread across Brandt's face.

It's near the trail intersection.

Ski leaned toward Brandt. "They think we're over there."

"Yeah," Brandt said.

The VC probed for almost two hours, the flashes and explosions punctuating the silence and darkness every 15 to 20 minutes. Brandt visualized men in black pajama-like clothing or loin cloths throw a grenade and listen, then furtively crawl to another spot and repeat the procedure. Throw, listen, crawl. Throw, listen, crawl. Such patience. Such determination.

Ski tapped Brandt's shoulder. "This is like watching a thunderstorm from your bedroom window."

"Yeah, like when we were kids."

"But they're late," Ski continued. "When they don't find us, I'll bet they boogie down the trail to get out of here before it starts getting light."

"You're probably right. I'm going to alert Hart and Martinez. We need to be ready." Brandt took the radio handset from Jenkins. "November, this is November 6. Dawn's coming soon. Victor Charlie will have to head home fast. Be ready. Acknowledge."

Each squad leader responded.

"Six out."

★ ★ ★

The trip flare burst on the trail and illuminated an eerie tableau—five silhouettes frozen for an instant, soon to become an eternity. Startled, Brandt hesitated with his thumb on the trigger of the Claymore.

"Now." A whispered shout from Ski triggered Brandt's thumb. One pound of C-4 plastic explosive and thousands of ball bearings in the Claymore, followed immediately by the other three, exploded with such sudden force, the silhouettes vanished, chased by a fusillade from machine guns and M-16s.

"Cease fire." Brandt shouted.

Brandt blinked away colored balls as his night vision returned. His jaw worked, but no sound came out.

Ski filled in the word. "Go," he shouted.

The momentum of his men charging to the kill zone pulled Brandt forward. Five bodies sprawled at awkward angles, blown a few yards beyond the trail. He stood, motionless, absorbing a scene he'd never seen before. The bodies looked like paper targets at a rifle range, perforated by thousands of steel ball bearings from the Claymores, larger holes punched by the bullets. Veins emptied onto the ground, arteries spurted, faces ripped and distorted.

Unhurried, purposeful movement around him broke his fixation, and the deliberate work of his men registered. First and 3rd Squads set up security. Second Squad searched bodies, grabbed at satchels and pockets and picked up weapons. The stocks of the enemy's AK-47s glinted like jewelry, studded with ball bearings, splintered by bullets.

Ski strode calmly to Brandt.

"Five dead VC. No documents or maps. We got five AKs. Ready to move out, sir. We better hustle."

Brandt blinked. "Uh, Yeah. Let's head for the rally point."

Brandt jogged away. A few strides later, he looked over his shoulder into the last glimmer of the dying flare. Darkness claimed the bodies. He settled into a fast-paced march, and his breathing returned to normal.

As dawn colored the eastern horizon, Brandt thrust his chest forward and smiled.

Five dead VC. No friendly casualties. Just like we planned it.

CHAPTER 10

★ ★ ★

Brandt looked over his right shoulder and said, "Jenkins, call the squad leaders and tell them to halt in place."

He turned, raised his hand high above his head and signaled a halt to those in sight while he scanned the thinning vegetation of the jungle fringe. He turned again and continued scanning in their direction of march. *Open forest. Widely spaced trees and small bushes. Good visibility out to 100 meters ahead. More room to maneuver. Less likely to stumble into an ambush. But snipers could see you coming from farther away.*

A clump of bushes formed a nook to his right, and Brandt headed for the concealment. He knelt, spread his map on the ground, and tapped a finger on it. "We should be here," he said to no one in particular. He pulled his compass, sighted on a hill to the west, then located another hill to the northeast, sighted on it, and marked the map. "Well, pretty close." He studied the map. "Forest ends 250 meters ahead. Open fields for a kilometer past that, then rice paddies. Level terrain all the way. Less than two kilometers to the company laager site."

Brandt sighted his compass on the company's location, lowered the compass, but held his gaze. "Straight line through forest, then into the open fields. No cover, no concealment."

Captain Parker told us to cut short our recon and come in. Wonder why? He said he had a surprise for me.

Brandt sensed a presence and looked up. Jenkins stood a few feet away. The RTO stepped forward, knelt, and offered the radio handset. Brandt shook his head. "How do you know?"

Jenkins smiled. "Just doing my job, sir."

"Bravo 6, November 6. Over."

"Bravo 6."

"We are inbound your position, from Ford, right two, up one. Be there shortly."

"Roger that. Six out."

Jenkins took the handset and moved a few meters away.

Brandt stood. "Tell the squad leaders to move out."

The platoon marched through the forest at a brisk pace. As they approached the edge of the forest, Brandt called another halt but continued walking toward the point. Sergeant Martinez fell in step beside him.

"What's up, sir?"

"We're approaching the edge of the forest. I want to eyeball what's ahead of us. Let's get your point man and take a walk."

"Airborne, sir."

The three men, Jenkins in tow, walked cautiously through the transition zone of forest into field, widely scattered trees and clumps of small bushes. They low-crawled the final ten meters and rested in the shade of a broad-leafed sapling.

Brandt pulled his binoculars, surveyed the grassy expanse, and then scrutinized the tree lines, right and left, that curved like arms embracing the field. He handed the binoculars to Martinez. "Take a look."

Martinez repeated the scan. "Looks O.K. to me." He returned the binoculars. "Uh." Martinez hesitated.

"What is it?"

"Well, why have we been stopping so much. Coming out of that jungle, it's an easy walk. Straight shot into Bravo."

"You in a hurry?"

Martinez took a deep breath. "I'm just wondering if it's more stuff you learned in that Bad-ass School."

Brandt chuckled. "Yeah. Mostly, I keep hearing those sergeants talking to me."

"No shit?"

Brandt nodded. "I remembered one instructor telling us that it's more dangerous entering a friendly position than it is leaving a perimeter into enemy territory."

"How's that?"

"He said that sometimes not everybody gets the word you're coming in. Somebody might be half-asleep on guard duty. Somebody with an itchy trigger finger might be surprised when you burst through brush."

Martinez nodded thoughtfully.

"He said it's important to make sure people know when you're coming in and which direction you're coming from."

"No surprises. Makes sense."

"In the jungle, you can't see terrain features for navigation. Can't walk in a straight line, so distance is hard to estimate, direction difficult to control."

"That's for sure."

"So," Brandt continued, "I stopped when we came out of the jungle to verify our position and then direction of march to Bravo. At the edge of the jungle, I could see a hill to the west and another to the northeast. I sighted on them with my compass and drew lines back from them on the map. Where they met marked our exact position. It's called triangulation."

Martinez took a notepad out of his pocket and started writing.

Brandt waited.

"Then I used the compass to set the direction from that point to Bravo. I called in our position and told them we were on our way. So now they know which direction we're coming from and about when we'll get there." Brandt paused while Martinez wrote. "And I wanted to recon this spot because walking out into an open field, especially with tree lines surrounding, is a perfect spot for an ambush. Sometimes, the instructor said, you can see reflections off glass or metal, maybe tree limbs or bushes that have been cut to create lines of fire, stuff like that."

"I like that Bad-ass School."

★ ★ ★

After an uneventful passage into the company laager site, the platoon filled in a sector of the perimeter while Brandt proceeded directly to the company CP. Parker waited, a big smile on his face. Behind Parker, a sergeant first class rose from the ground, an M-16 clutched in his left hand, a rucksack slung over the same shoulder. He stood six feet four inches tall, weighed about 250 pounds and had a narrow waist.

Did they draft this guy from the NFL?

"As I said, lieutenant, I have a surprise for you." He half turned and gestured. "Meet Sergeant First Class Ferguson, your new platoon sergeant."

The man strode forward, right hand extended. Brandt's hand disappeared into it.

Firm, confident grip, but not trying to crush my hand.

"I sure am glad to see you, sergeant."

"Milton Ferguson. Glad to meet you, lieutenant."

"Sergeant Ferguson," Parker continued, "just arrived in-country. He was originally slated to go to the 101st. We're lucky to get him. This is his third tour in Nam."

"That's right," Ferguson chimed in. "But in Long Binh, they told me there was a lieutenant in the 173rd doing the platoon leader's job and the platoon sergeant's job all by himself." He paused. "And doing a damn fine job of it."

A MATTER OF SEMANTICS

Oh, a diplomat too.

"Well," Brandt responded, "I've got three squad leaders who've performed above and beyond their years and experience. They've kept my butt out of trouble."

"Most of the time," Parker interjected with a chuckle and a smile. "And I know you two have a lot to discuss. Dismissed."

Brandt headed for the platoon CP, Ferguson striding alongside.

"Like I said, sergeant, I'm glad you're here because it's been a rough several weeks."

"I can imagine, sir. But I hear we got a real good platoon."

"The troops are good soldiers. Not a bad apple in the bunch. We've been getting a steady stream of replacements lately. Forty now, almost full strength, up from the 25 when I took over the platoon. The squad leaders and veterans work hard to bring them up to speed, and I'm pleased. However, I'm concerned about a couple of them."

"Sounds familiar."

"Like I said, the squad leaders have been great, but they still have a lot to learn."

"To be expected."

Brandt stopped and faced Ferguson. The sergeant squared his shoulders to Brandt, face blank, unreadable. "And there's still a lot I need to learn. You've got more experience. I want to draw on it. Help me train the men. Whenever possible, I want decisions to come from our collaboration. I will appreciate your counsel."

No change in expression. Brandt took a deep breath. "However, I'm the platoon leader. The decisions and the responsibility for them are mine."

A big smile creased Ferguson's face. "I'm glad to hear you say all that, sir. That's exactly how I see my job. I think we'll get along just fine."

Relief. "We've got some platoon SOPs that I'll run by you while we eat dinner. You can let me know what you think."

"A good way to get started, sir. I got a good overview of the Area of Operations here from First Sergeant Klein and a little more from Captain Parker." He looked away, then back again and seemed to be choosing words. "But I'd like to hear your thoughts on our platoon operations, tactics, and so forth."

Yeah, I wonder what he's heard about that.

"We can do that while we dine over C-Rations. Finest delicacies in cans. I got pork slices. Date on the box says," Brandt paused and smiled, "1945. Year before I was born."

Ferguson shook his head and laughed. "Well, sir, I brought us some of those new Beef with Rice Lurps."

"Those new freeze-dried LRP rations? How'd you manage that? We never get them. They only send them to the Long Range Patrols."

Ferguson gave him a sly grin. "Got some old friends in Supply."

"O.K., let's get to the CP, and I'll introduce you to the squad leaders and the men."

"Good. I'd like to meet the squad leaders right away, but then I'll have my own meeting with them later. As for the troops, I'll take care of that myself." He shook his head. "Take too long." A pause. "And I expect Captain Parker will call in the platoon leaders for a briefing on our next mission soon."

"Fine with me. We'd better get over there."

They continued to the platoon CP. Jenkins looked up, dropped a half-filled sand bag, and laid down his entrenching tool.

"Specialist Jenkins, this is Sergeant First Class Ferguson, our new platoon sergeant. Call the squad leaders and tell them to come to the CP."

"I saw you talking with the sergeant. I already called them. They're on the way."

"Outstanding, Specialist," Ferguson boomed. "I like a man who knows his job and takes initiative."

Jenkins stood a little taller, a smile fighting through his serious expression.

★ ★ ★

Brandt walked back to the platoon CP after the meeting with Captain Parker and the other platoon leaders, notebook and pen in his left hand, rifle slung over his right shoulder. Ferguson approached from the opposite direction, the setting sun blocked out by his formidable physique. Brandt watched as he closed the distance. Ferguson's chiseled features slowly emerged from the silhouette.

"Just finished walking the line, lieutenant, and introduced myself to the troops. I know you didn't have time to check the line after you got in this afternoon. Spacing between the foxholes is good, and they're deep enough, but I made some adjustments in the Final Protective Lines of Fire. The OP is on its way out. The link-ups with the other platoons are good. Overall, I'm impressed, sir."

Brandt blinked, and his jaw dropped. Stunned silence.

Damn. Forgot what it was like to have a platoon sergeant.

"Thank you, sergeant."

"Just the way it's supposed to work, sir."

Brandt stood silent. After a moment, Ferguson smiled. "So, what we gonna do tomorrow?"

Brandt blinked. "Right." He laid his rifle against sandbags in front of the foxhole, spread his map on the ground, and flipped pages in his notebook. The three squad leaders joined them, formed a semicircle and sat Indian style, expectant looks on their faces.

"Let me guess," Ski said, "we're gonna search for something to destroy."

Brandt shook his head slowly.

A quizzical look clouded Ski's face. "No? Then what?"

"We don't Search and Destroy anymore. The Army thinks it's bad for the image of the war and our operations are now called *Reconnaissance in Force*."

Ferguson grunted.

Martinez said, "Sir, the mission of the Infantry is to close with and destroy the enemy."

Brandt nodded. "And that has not changed. You ever hear of a guy by the name of Clausewitz?"

Blank faces stared back at him.

"He said that war is a continuation of politics by other means."

Hart chimed in. "So another guy in Washington decided that? *Sounds like same shit, different day to me.*"

Ferguson cleared his throat. "You gentlemen have a problem with improving your vocabularies?" He scanned each face.

The three squad leaders remained silent.

Ferguson continued. "I've seen this kind of thing many times. Let the politicians do their jobs. We will continue to do our jobs to the best of our abilities."

He held their attention for a moment and then looked at Brandt. "Lieutenant, what's our mission."

Brandt placed his notebook and a grease pencil on the map and began the operation order.

★ ★ ★

The next morning, Brandt followed 1st Squad out of the company perimeter. On his left and right, soldiers in foxholes leaned into sandbags, methodically scanning their sectors of responsibility, rifles at the ready. His next step carried him across an imaginary line called the perimeter. Beyond the perimeter lay potential danger. Enemy territory. His heart beat faster, his breathing became more rapid, and his stride lengthened.

Brandt took a few deep breaths, settled into a smooth stride, checked the formation and spacing of his men, and began the rhythmic scanning of the ground ahead, his left and right flanks, up in the trees, and forward out to the horizon.

As he covered ground, Brandt recalled a military training class. The instructor said that in previous wars it was called going over the top into no man's land, or crossing the front line, a line extending for miles in either direction, formed by troops in regimental or division strength, thousands of men facing a similar front line formed by the enemy. Current military terminology called it the Forward Edge of the Battle Area or the FEBA.

However, the instructor said, in Vietnam, the FEBA was anywhere outside the few large cities along the coast. Anywhere you could track down the enemy and engage him. The FEBA in Vietnam consisted of base camps and company-sized perimeters scattered throughout the countryside. An operational map at headquarters looked like a checkerboard. Officers moved round game pieces from grid square to grid square.

Brandt did an about face and continued walking backwards. He could no longer see the company perimeter. The squads behind him formed two snaking lines about 40 meters apart. No soldier directly behind another. Each, no closer than 20 meters to the man in front of and behind him, the classic column formation. He marched just off center behind the lead squad. He had most control over the formation there, ideal for this open forest—flat ground with visibility out to 100 meters in any direction. No single line of fire could hit more than one target. Satisfied, he spun another 180 degrees and repeated the scan.

Brandt then recalled a meeting at Fort Bragg with the company commander mentoring his lieutenants.

"Vietnam is being called the platoon leader's war, gentlemen. When you take your platoon across a perimeter, it means more than just reduced safety. You will be on your own. No one higher in rank. You will be in charge, responsible for the lives of your men. You make all decisions. Added responsibility to the sense of danger."

But Brandt welcomed the opportunity to work independently. His platoon, at one-third the size of a company, could move with more stealth. He liked being on his own.

Brandt heard Jenkins jog up beside him, breaking his train of thought. "Except for that damn radio," he said.

"What, sir?" Jenkins asked as he offered the radio handset.

Brandt grabbed it. "Already?"

Jenkins smiled. "Nothing new, sir."

Brandt pressed the push-to-talk button. "November 6."

"Let me know when you get to the blue line on your funny paper," Parker said tersely.

"Roger. Wilco. Over."

"Six out."

"Well, not completely on your own," Brandt mumbled, continuing the conversation with himself.

"What, sir?" Jenkins asked again.

"Bravo wants to know when we reach that stream on the map. Call Sergeant Hart and tell him to let us know when he first sees it. Hold in place until I can eyeball the area with him." Jenkins nodded and drifted away.

The undergrowth grew thicker, the trees more dense, and visibility decreased. His men closed the distances between them. He called up an image of his map and route of march. When they emerged from the forest, they should see the river directly ahead of them. Downstream, it flowed into a wide plain that spread to the ocean. Upstream, it cut through a narrow valley framed by two steep ridges. The map showed no villages, no trails.

"Sir."

Brandt looked to his right rear, and Jenkins said, "Sergeant Hart reports that the forest is denser and he's moved into a file formation. He expects to see the river soon." He offered Brandt the PRC-6.

"November 5, did you monitor that last transmission?"

"Affirmative, 6. Will coordinate with November 2 and 3."

"Six out."

He gave the radio back and Jenkins moved away. Brandt took a sip from his canteen and watched the squad leaders giving hand signals. Men cheated inward as they walked, narrowed the gap in the column, and blended into a single line that passed more easily and quietly through dense forest.

Brandt quickened his pace, passed troopers, and closed on the platoon's point. He heard Jenkins breathing heavily as the RTO worked to keep up. Soon, branches slapped at his face, and vines yanked his ankles and forced a slower pace. The men of 1st Squad knelt on the ground, rifles at the ready.

Brandt said to Jenkins, "Tell the other squad leaders to halt in place. We're at the edge of the forest."

He moved forward cautiously and stopped when he saw Hart and his point man lying beneath a bush just inside the tree line carving the forest border.

Ferguson walked up beside him.

"Ready for a look at the valley, sergeant?"

He smiled. "Can't wait, sir. Let's do it."

They crawled the last 10 meters, easing up beside Hart.

"See anything?" Brandt asked.

"No, sir. Wiggins," Hart nodded towards the man lying next to him, "and I have been watching for about 15 minutes. No villages in sight. No signs of Charlie. Birds have been flying around. A deer came down to the river on the other side, got a drink, and headed up the valley. Seems like nobody's home."

Brandt scanned the valley. About two kilometers wide at the mouth but narrowed sharply, pinched between steep ridges. Thick vegetation covered the slopes. Lush green grass carpeted the valley floor. The river meandered down the center. Small knolls only 1–2 meters high and maybe twice as long popped up from the valley floor like islands. Unusual. Not hills, just bumps covered with thick bushes and small, broad-leafed trees. About half a kilometer up the valley, near its western wall, rose another knoll much larger than the others. Brandt pulled his binoculars, but they revealed no more detail, only a larger version of the hillocks scattered about the valley floor. Brandt motioned for Jenkins to move up.

"Bravo 6, November 6. Over."

"Bravo 6. Over."

"On my funny paper, my position is, from Dog, up four, right three-and-a-half. I see the blue line. Proceeding as planned."

"That's good. Keep me informed. Six out."

He handed the receiver back to Jenkins. "Tell the other squad leaders to come up for a look."

After Ski and Martinez viewed the valley, they all crawled back into the concealment of the forest. Well back from the tree line, Brandt found a clearing about 30 meters across and huddled with Ferguson and the squad leaders, map spread on the ground. "Well, you've all had a chance to eyeball this." Brandt pointed at the map with his grease pencil. "What do you think?"

The squad leaders exchanged glances and looked to Ferguson. He remained silent, face deadpan, and nodded toward them.

Martinez shook his head. "Quiet. Natural. Peaceful."

"Looks funny to me." Ski pointed to the map. "Map doesn't show any of those bumps in the valley floor. They're weird."

"We're supposed to set up an ambush tonight, right?" Hart asked.

"Our mission," Brandt stated, "is to recon the area and see if there's any evidence of traffic passing through the valley. If so, set up an ambush. Reason is, Intelligence says the valley is used as an infiltration route."

Hart snorted.

"Shit," Martinez said under his breath.

"Fuckin' A." Ski said out loud, followed by, "Sorry, sir."

Brandt smiled at the frankness of his squad leaders. "I know. Army Intelligence is an oxymoron."

Ski screwed up his face. "Huh?"

Brandt chuckled. "You gentlemen have a better reason for walking up the middle of this deserted valley?"

They all shook their heads in resignation.

"Gentlemen," Ferguson interjected, "Intelligence is your friend." He looked back to Brandt.

Brandt continued. "O.K. Supposedly, the NVA and VC come down from mountain base camps into villages on the coastal plain. Small groups of five to seven. Probably for re-supply, operational plans, advisors."

"How far up we got to go?" Hart asked.

"Well, our mission," Brandt paused and looked at each of them, "is to recon, look for signs of traffic. So let's look at how we'll do that first. As soon as we find so much as a footprint, I want to look for an ambush site with concealment and hunker down."

"Sounds good to me. But why?" Martinez asked. "You don't like to set up an ambush in daylight."

Ferguson looked back and forth between Brandt and the squad leaders, still poker-faced.

Brandt looked down for a long moment and remembered something Sergeant Williams said to him his first day with the platoon. Brandt cleared his throat. "Sometimes you have to do what's not smart. If they're using this valley regularly, they probably have lookouts on those ridges keeping an eye on it during the day. The longer we walk around, the farther up the valley we go, the more likely we are to compromise ourselves. If they do spot us, they'll either not send anybody through tonight or come down on us like Sitting Bull on Custer."

Three heads nodded. "So how we gonna do it?" Ski asked.

"They're coming out of the west." Brandt pointed to the map. "Here. We'll stay on this side of the river for now. It's not likely they'd cross the river at night if they don't have to. The valley floor is flat, grass no more than a foot high. We can stay in sight of each other at all times."

"I like that," Hart said.

"Our axis of march," Brandt continued as he traced a line on the map with his finger, "will follow a line midway between the river on our right and the western wall on our left, moving in a column. We'll run a modified cloverleaf every 100 meters, only sending out two squads. Since the order of march today is 1st, 2nd, 3rd, 2nd squad will loop to the left, 3rd to the right to search our flanks. I want 1st squad to stay in and set up security." He looked up, anticipating questions.

"Sir," Hart interjected. "Why don't you want me to loop forward as the third leaf in the clover pattern?"

Brandt said, "Well, we have no idea what's out there. They could have a gatekeeper force near the mouth of the valley. Maybe a sniper on the ridge."

Brandt saw questioning looks and continued. "If each squad is at the peak of its loop, say 100 meters out from the center and one draws fire, we're too spread out to reinforce. This way, we'll have a quick reaction force ready to go."

Their faces brightened. "I like that, too," Ski chimed in.

"We're going into a hot area. No cover or concealment. Long lines of sight. And we're on our own. I just think it's prudent."

They responded in chorus. "Airborne."

"O.K. When we get to that big knoll, I'll go over the top of it with 1st squad while 2nd and 3rd do their clover. I want to see what's there, see if they've been using it." He paused, not needing to say, "And make sure there's nobody there now." Instead, he said, "That's it. Any questions?"

Three heads shook slowly. Brandt looked to Ferguson.

Ferguson said, "I like the plan. Clovers are an efficient way to search a large area. Tell your men to take their time searching. Be thorough. Don't have to hurry. We got all day."

"Right." Brandt said. "We'll decide on an ambush site if we find anything. This clearing will be our rally point if we make contact or get separated. Make sure your men know where this spot is in relation to the valley. Let's get moving."

The squads worked methodically, covering wide swaths of ground. Ferguson alternately accompanied each search team. So far, they found only an undisturbed, idyllic valley. Brandt knelt on the ground, his attention divided, alternately watching 2nd and 3rd squads search in circles. Intermittently, his gaze scanned the crest of the ridges looking for something he hoped was not there, a glint of sun off gun barrels or a reflection off binoculars.

Brandt sighed at the tedium, the waiting and watching. They were 500 meters up the valley, had done four cloverleaf searches, and still no sign of enemy traffic. First Squad formed up, ready to move forward. "Sergeant," Brandt called. Hart turned. "The next clover will bring us to the base of the big knoll. I want to go over the top with your lead team."

"You sure you want to do that, sir?"

Brandt smiled. "Got to do something to earn my pay."

Hart shook his head, then pointed. Ski and Martinez signaled their readiness to move. Brandt returned the hand signal, shouldered his rucksack, and picked up the pace.

He studied the big knoll. The indistinct bulk resolved as he drew closer, details coming more into focus with each stride. Oval shape, 20 meters wide and 10 meters high. The long axis extended 35 meters up the valley. Thick undergrowth at the base thinned up the steep sides and gave way to small trees and grass.

Martinez led his squad toward the river, Ski toward the western ridge. Brandt followed Hart's Alpha Team, led by Corporal Singleton, up the narrow point of the oval. They started in single file but soon fanned out into a line as the vegetation thinned. Brandt sensed a presence behind him and looked over his shoulder. Ferguson followed him stride for stride. Brandt crested the knoll and saw a grassy plateau spiked with young trees spaced six to eight feet apart, leaves a gossamer canopy filtering light, a natural gazebo. He could see through the foliage a commanding view of the valley. While Hart hustled his men into a hasty perimeter around the crest, Brandt watched 3rd Squad move along the riverbank about 200 meters away. He turned to look for 2nd Squad. They had already completed the search, the western wall of the valley only 120 meters from the knoll.

"Sir." Jenkins handed him the PRC-6. "Third Squad found something."

Brandt put the radio to his ear and stepped to the eastern edge of the crest. He could see Martinez and his men on the riverbank. "November 6, over."

"We found some footprints in the mud here. It's a small marshy area. Looks like somebody took a few steps into it and backed out. A few feet away, we found a broken branch on one of these bushes and matted grass. Like the guy stumbled to get out of the marsh, maybe stomped his feet to get mud off his Ho Chi Minh Sandals."

"Sounds like Victor Charlie screwed up. Good work," Brandt said. "Head back in and approach from the south. I don't want to disturb anything in front of us. Act like you're leaving the valley. Over."

"Roger that, 6."

"One more thing. You know where we are. Can you see us?"

"Negative."

"Good. Come on in."

A few minutes later, Brandt again huddled with Ferguson and his squad leaders. Ski spoke first. "So how we gonna do this?"

Brandt looked at him. Funny how routines broke tension, got things moving along.

"Before we decide what we're going to do, we need to think like the enemy. What's he going to do?"

They nodded.

"To the east, it's about 200 meters from here to the river, then another 500 to the eastern wall of the valley. To the west, it's only about 100 meters to the western wall. I figure they'll take the wide-open super highway between this knoll and the river. However, if that's been used a lot, a cagey patrol leader might take the narrow country road to the west, just to mix things up. Maybe sneak behind this knoll and any trouble. We need to cover both."

"How can we cover both at the same time?" Martinez asked. "If we divide, we only have half the firepower."

"True," Brandt said. He looked at Ferguson. "Sergeant, any suggestions?"

"There is a way to cover both sides. You set up two ambush positions, mirror images of each other, on both sides of the hill. Part of the force occupies one; the rest take the other one. When the enemy chooses one of the routes, you fill in that position and spring the ambush with full strength." Ferguson paused. "Make sense?"

"Good plan, but it sounds tricky," Martinez said, "changing positions like that at night."

"It could be," Ferguson said. "But here we only need to move a few meters and there are no obstacles in between. We'll get the positions set up and rehearse moving from one position to the other."

"That's good for two reasons," Martinez said. "Communication and control will be easy when we move. When we fire it will be like a solid wall of lead hitting anything in the kill zone."

"I like it," Brandt said. "Let's do it."

"Then we better get started," Hart said. "Got twice as much work to do."

"Right," Brandt said. "Since you've got your squad providing security, you maintain that while we set up the kill zones. Ski, you set up the kill zone to the west, Martinez, to the east. I want Claymores at the north and south ends of this knoll on each side. That will give us kill zones 35 meters long. Should be enough to completely contain the small groups that are supposed to be moving through. Angle them in so it's a crossfire of a couple thousand ball bearings."

"What if it's a larger force?" asked Martinez.

"If we get surprised, if it's a platoon or more, I'll call in artillery so we don't give away our position. That could be coming from anywhere."

"How about our firing positions?" Hart asked.

"I want 3rd Squad at the north end, 2nd Squad in the middle, and 1st Squad at the south end. That way, we can use today's order of march when we head out of here."

Hart nodded. "Makes sense."

Brandt continued. "Position your men on the edge of this flat area where it drops off. Selectively remove any branches or bushes in the way, but don't distort the natural look of the plants. In this small area, we'll be tight, maybe an arm's length apart. Make sure the firing lanes are clear."

"Right. Initially, 2nd Squad will occupy its position to the west, 1st and 3rd, to the east. If I'm right about which way they go, we'll have minimal movement. I'll be at the north end," Brandt continued, "with 3rd squad so I can see what's coming.

"O.K.," Ferguson said, "I'll anchor the middle."

Brandt continued, "If they're going to the east, I'll break squelch twice on the radio. If they go west, I'll break squelch three times." Brandt paused to let that sink in.

"To the east, twice; west, three times," Hart repeated.

"Yes. I will initiate the ambush by blowing the Claymore at the north end. Fire at will after that. After we spring the ambush, 1st Squad set up security to the south, 3rd Squad to the north, and 2nd Squad will do the search."

Brandt looked at Ferguson. "Anything else?"

"Ski," Ferguson said, "when your men do the search, work in two-man teams, one doing the search, the other holding a flashlight and a rifle. Disarm the enemy first. We don't want any surprises. Be thorough, but work quickly. Let's get out of here as soon as we can." He paused. "Lieutenant?"

"Remember, the rally point is that clearing in the dense part of the forest, well back from the tree line. Be sure your men know. Sergeant Hart, when we head out, I will be with your lead element."

"Fine, sir," Hart said, "but we can handle the point at night."

Brandt paused and rocked back on his heels. "Airborne." He took a deep breath. "Any questions?"

Each man, face filled with the gravity of the conversation, shook his head slowly.

Brandt stood. "O.K. Let's get to work."

★ ★ ★

Brandt checked the luminous dial on his watch. The green hands and dots marking the hours and minutes glowed 0112.

Is that all?

He shifted his weight, but could find no comfortable position. He had long since exhausted the limited possibilities in lying prone on hard ground with a rifle at your shoulder. He eventually settled for rotating the discomfort from one spot on his body to another. So it went, hour after uneventful hour. Such were the nights in the boonies of Nam, devoid of city bustle, bright lights, or even distant traffic noise.

He remembered a class in Ranger School. The instructor summing up, "Rangers, in the absence of physical activity, of sensory stimulation, the mind works to fill the void in consciousness. It flits like a grasshopper on a summer day, images and thoughts bursting briefly and randomly. Lying in ambush is an exercise in patience and self-discipline, a challenge to stay alert, to keep your mind focused. You can scan the darkness, sort the sounds and silence only so long. You can review your preparation, your planning, your orders only so many times before crossing a line into paranoia, itself a distraction."

Like now. Like this shit.

Brandt shook his head, but the tap on his shoulder jerked his thoughts back to the task at hand.

Sergeant Martinez pointed northward. "I heard something," his voice not a rasping whisper but a trained, barely audible normal tone. "Maybe a clink of metal on metal. Definitely not a natural sound. I haven't seen anything yet."

"So we have company. If somebody screwed up and made a metallic noise, they'll all have frozen immediately. We might not be able to locate them until they start moving again," Brandt said. "And don't look directly at the source of sound. Scan from one side to the other. Use your peripheral vision. You're more likely to see movement before shape."

"I'll bet somebody's getting a very silent ass-chewing right now." Martinez released a breath, almost a laugh. "I couldn't tell how far away, but it must be close."

"Uh-uh," Brandt said. "Even soft, sharp, unnatural sounds travel a long way at night."

"How far?"

"We had a class in Ranger School. Sat in bleachers at dusk and waited until full darkness. We couldn't see a thing, but an instructor lit a cigarette lighter and a brilliant point of light flared briefly. Then the instructor chambered a round into his rifle. I heard the sound of the bolt retract, then slide back into place, sharp and clear. I guessed the instructor must be about 20 meters in front of us." Brandt shook his head. "Guessed wrong."

"How far?"

"Hundred meters away."

"No shit? That's amazing."

They resumed a silent watch and Brandt focused on the likely route to the east.

Martinez tapped his shoulder again and pointed. Brandt scanned to the north and a shadowy figure materialized, backlit by a half moon and a clear, star-filled sky. It moved hesitantly from left to right and back to the left. Brandt guessed about 70 meters away. He leaned toward Martinez, but kept his eyes focused forward. "That must be the patrol leader. Looks like he's trying to decide which way to go."

Martinez nodded. "I'll bet he goes left."

"How do you know?"

"He's spending more time on that side. And it's darker there, too."

The patrol leader turned and six figures rose from the grass and resumed their journey, the leader in the middle. They headed to Brandt's left between the knoll and the western valley wall.

Brandt tilted his head to the side. "Good call, sergeant."

He took the radio from Jenkins and pressed and released the push-to-talk button three times. First and 3rd Squads moved across the knoll into their alternate positions deliberately and silently. Satisfied that they were settled, Brandt said to Jenkins, "Pass up a count."

When the count came back confirming everyone in position, Brandt looked up the valley to relocate the enemy patrol. Martinez, anticipating his need, pointed. "They've been moving slowly, stopping a lot. Still about 30 meters out."

"You see any movement farther up the valley, a trailing force?"

"Nothing. This must be it."

"Sure as hell hope so."

The shadowy figures grew indistinct as they entered the shadow of the ridge, no longer backlit by moonlight. Eyes fixed on movement, Brandt held his breath as he gauged distance. Time slowed, tension mounted.

The enemy patrol crossed the imaginary line marking the kill zone—seven faceless figures, walking single file, arm's length apart, stepping into eternity.

With the enemy patrol fully inside the kill zone, Brandt picked up the trigger of the Claymore with his left hand. With his right, he felt for his rifle on the ground in front of him. Brandt looked down and closed his eyes. He released half the breath he held as if firing his rifle, and pressed down on the Claymore trigger. Light seared through his eyelids, and thunder assaulted his ears. Another burst of light and thunder erupted. Controlled small-arms fire and machine guns rose to a crescendo.

Brandt opened his eyes, night vision intact, and raised his rifle, but the seven targets slumped to the ground before he could fire. Total surprise, over in a matter of seconds—no chance for the enemy to fight back.

"Cease fire," Brandt yelled into the radio. "Cease fire." The squad leaders repeated the order, and the crescendo diminished into silence.

"Go," Brandt yelled as he charged down, leading the platoon like a falcon diving on prey.

CHAPTER 11

★ ★ ★

Captain Parker finished briefing the platoon leaders after the evening meal.

"That's it, gentlemen. Make me proud. Dismissed."

Brandt returned to his CP and assembled his leadership team.

Ferguson spoke first. "Well, sir, what the captain say is our job for tomorrow?"

Brandt faced him, grimaced, and said, "We've got a long hump tomorrow." He marked two circles on the map and turned it around so Ferguson and the squad leaders could see it better. "We're here," Brandt pointed with the grease pencil, "and this is where we're going. About 14 kilometers."

Ski leaned over the map. "At least it looks flat," he said. "Should be a piece of cake."

"Well, you might not like the flavor of this cake. We're coordinating with Charlie Company and a company of Korean infantry to cordon off a village. The captain wants to get there first. Like a welcoming committee for the Koreans. We're point for the company and he said to set a fast pace."

Ferguson grunted.

Ski sat back. "A race through Booby Trap Alley in this heat? Just so we can beat the ROKs there?"

Martinez raised his chin. "What's so important about getting there first?"

"That question is above my pay grade, sergeant."

"What's important?" Ferguson paused. All eyes shifted toward him. "The intel. What's so important about this place?"

"Intel says," Brandt hesitated, but no one cracked the usual jokes about the value of Army Intelligence. "This village is a VC headquarters. Supposed to be a big meeting going on with NVA advisors. That makes it a prime target."

Ferguson leaned toward the map, drew back, and pursed his lips. "Then it's likely to be well defended."

"Right," Brandt said. "That's why three infantry companies are headed there."

"For a meeting like that," Ferguson added, "they probably sent out some patrols for early warning. We need to be extra careful moving fast."

"Yeah," Hart said. "It's my rotation for point squad tomorrow." He tilted his head back and rolled his eyes. "Fast and careful is my middle name."

Brandt ignored his tone of voice.

"This village," Brandt pointed to the map, "sits at the base of the foothills. Bravo seals off the southern perimeter with Lima and Mike. Charlie, the northern perimeter. The ROKs will enter the village from the east and do the search. Our job is to get behind the village and cut off escape routes into the mountains."

"Well, if we have to get behind the village, why do we have to travel with Bravo?" Ski asked. "Why can't we go off on our own like usual?"

Brandt stole a glance at Ferguson. Deadpan.

"Sergeant Olszewski, a while back you complained about having to go off on our own."

Ski looked down at the ground and back up and took a deep breath. "Well, I like it now."

Brandt pointed to the map again. "At this village, Sergeant Olszewski, about seven kilometers from the objective, we break off from the rest of the company and head west into the foothills." They all leaned into the map. He traced a path with his finger. "We'll loop behind this ridge south of the objective to screen our approach and sneak into position here." He pointed to a small rectangle on the map, then looked at Ski. "Happy, now?"

Ski grumbled something unintelligible.

Brandt completed the operation order and dismissed the squad leaders, and Jenkins moved away to prepare for sleep.

Brandt sat down and leaned against his rucksack. Ferguson sat Indian style in front of him.

"Well, sergeant, your thoughts?"

"Booby Trap Alley?"

Brandt chuckled. "Yeah, Ski always looks on the bright side of things. Actually, it applies to this whole area."

"So we get the tough job again. Well, sir, I'm not worried about that. What concerns me is the possibility of ambushes or snipers as we get close to the target. Especially moving fast."

"Right. I'm glad you pointed that out. I think I'll walk with the point squad tomorrow instead of in the center of the column. I'll be able to keep a tight rein on direction, be able to react more quickly."

"Good idea. How about putting flank security up front, too, alongside the point squad. With the point man and two men on each side, it's like hunting dogs flushing game."

Brandt leaned forward, and his eyes glowed. "At a fast pace, it's more like blitzing linebackers forcing the quarterback's hand before he's ready. I like it. Let's do it."

"O.K. I'll be in the usual position, back of the column. If the point squad makes contact, I'll be able to maneuver the rear squad while you direct fire in front."

Brandt let out a slow deep breath. "I think we're ready for tomorrow. No surprises, right?"

Ferguson shook his head. "Nam always has a surprise for you, lieutenant."

★ ★ ★

Brandt turned in a full circle as he walked forward and checked the spacing of his men. *Twenty meters between each man. Just right.* The squad leaders maintained the intervals even at the fast pace set by the company commander. Forty men covered an area the size of a football field, a much bigger task to direct and control. Behind his platoon stretched the other two platoons, the weapons platoon and the company command group.

So much forward momentum. Like a race car speeding through S-curves on a track. Moving this fast is dangerous. No, crazy.

Brandt stopped and dragged a sleeve across his forehead but only succeeded in smearing dust with sweat. Saturated jungle fatigues stuck to his skin. He breathed heavily.

How long can the men endure this pace?

He reached up and scratched a small circular scab on the side of his neck.

Fucking leeches.

The medic told him not to scratch it. Right. Crossing a river cooled you off, but it had its drawbacks. A week had gone by and the scab was still there.

Familiar feelings in Brandt's legs told him to get moving or they'd cramp. No time to take salt tablets. He hunched over and twisted, shifting the weight of his rucksack, then winced as the straps slipped back into the grooves on his shoulders. He leaned forward to get the seventy pounds on his back moving in the right direction and resumed the breakneck pace.

His eyes moved in the automatic, rhythmic scanning motion of a combat soldier, constantly gathering information, looking for something he hoped wasn't there. Snipers in tops of trees, booby traps in clumps of grass, trip wires across trails. Never seeing just for the pure enjoyment of it.

The trail they followed through the wide coastal plain entered a village on the far side, the one on the map he memorized after breakfast. Memorizing a map was just one of the little things that boosted your chances of staying alive—for a little longer anyway.

A map marks a good target. Dad said, "A Purple Heart is just an enemy marksmanship medal."

"Damn it, Brandt, keep your head in the game," he muttered.

The village loomed close, roughly circular in shape, maybe twenty-five or thirty huts, a few palm trees above the thatched roofs, and a trail intersection dividing it neatly into quadrants.

Don't like the looks of this village. But why? Looks like a hundred other hamlets north of Bong Son between the Central Highlands and the South China Sea.

"Sergeant Hart," he yelled. A flushed and grimy face snapped around. "Slow down when we go through this village. And be careful. Remind the men to stay off the trail. Watch for booby traps."

A quick wave of the squad leader's arm acknowledged his order.

As the platoon entered the village, residents scattered and disappeared into huts.

"Corporal Singleton," Brandt called, "they seem jumpy to you?"

The Alpha Team leader of 1st Squad turned toward Brandt. "Yes, Sir. Ain't nobody running up begging food." Singleton raised a compact, muscular arm and pointed. "But look at those gooks up at the trail crossing. Just standing there like watching a parade."

Brandt's eyes followed Singleton's finger. A family of Vietnamese clustered in front of a hut, two children, a young mother, a grandmother, and a grandfather. They stood side by side, arms around each other, wearing traditional black pajama-like clothing and conical straw hats. Ostensibly, one member of the family missing. Fighting with the Army of the Republic of Vietnam, his ally? Hiding in the jungle with the Viet Cong, his enemy? Or just dead, in which case it didn't matter. You just never knew. Never.

Brandt scrutinized the intersection. Sandy trails about three feet wide. Trails? A major highway intersection in this part of the world.

This is where we separate from the rest of the company.

"Lieutenant." Jenkins extended his arm across the trail. "Bravo 6 wants to talk to you."

"What the hell are you doing over there? You should be on this side of the trail with me."

"Sorry, sir, but Walsh is having trouble keeping up. I went over to help lighten his load."

Sweat streamed down Jenkins' face—a nineteen-year-old kid, 5 feet 10 inches tall, maybe 150 pounds, carrying two radios besides his own equipment—and he was helping carry someone else's stuff. Brandt shook his head.

Walsh, the new replacement. Need to talk to him but it'll have to wait.

Brandt took the receiver and continued walking, Jenkins on one side of the trail, Brandt on the other. "Bravo 6, this is November 6. Over."

"November 6, what's slowing you down?"

"Just moving through a village, 6. Be on the other side of it in a few minutes."

"Forget the village and get your butt moving. Do you roger that?"

The little voice in his head said, "What does the Ranger Handbook say about tired troops?"

Brandt subvocalized, "Do not expect tired troops to be effective. They cannot walk all day and stay alert at night."

He tried again. "Roger that, 6. We're almost at a double time now. It must be 115 degrees. I want to be able to fight when we get there."

"I didn't ask for an excuse. Get moving. Six out."

The coiled cord connecting the radio to the receiver stretched to its limit during the conversation, and Brandt drifted to the center of the trail easing the tension on the cord. He handed the receiver back to Jenkins.

When he reached the intersection, the family of onlookers drew his attention. They seemed rigid, impassive, almost blank. His eyes locked with those of the young mother. Brandt frowned; his brow furrowed. Something behind the emptiness in her eyes beckoned, distant and opaque, down a long, dark tunnel. Pressure pushed on his chest like a huge hand. Time slowed. He felt suspended between two forces, the pull of the tunnel and the push of the hand.

"What is it, sir?" Jenkins' voice called him back.

Brandt looked down. He'd stopped in mid-stride, his left foot a few inches above the ground. He pulled back, squatted, and examined the intersection. A faint, barely perceptible crisscross pattern laced the sand.

He raised his left hand high. "Halt."

An image flashed through Brandt's mind. Ranger School. Fort Benning. A burly, bear-like sergeant towering over attentive faces. "Rangers, listen well. Charlie has ingenious ways of neutralizing our advantage in firepower. You will have to see the glint of sunlight on seemingly invisible fishing line, read warnings of patterns in the sand." Then with a sweeping gesture of his hand, the sergeant shifted attention to the models. "Primitive, but effective."

Brandt knelt down and scrutinized the pattern, beginning at the center and working outward in quadrants.

Hart appeared across from him. "Booby trap, sir?"

"You see any wires, anything sticking out of the ground?"

"Nope. Nothing," Hart replied after a moment.

"Neither do I. See that pattern in the sand?"

"What pattern? I don't see anything," Hart said as he leaned closer.

Brandt pointed.

"No shit, sir. How the hell did you see that?"

"Watch," Brandt said as he gingerly brushed sand aside with the heel of his hand. He moved slowly, careful not to use any downward pressure. Gradually, a paper-thin, woven bamboo mat materialized.

"What's that?"

"Mantrap," boomed Ferguson. He strode to the intersection, glared at the family, then surveyed the center of the village. "I'll start a search of the village, lieutenant."

"Right," Brandt agreed. "But make it fast. Captain Parker'll have a shit-fit."

"Fuck him. He's been reaming Lima Platoon up our ass all morning." Ferguson spun around and shouted orders before Brandt could respond.

Brandt refocused his attention on the mat. "It's too light to be holding anything down."

Brandt searched for an edge, found it, and began to lift the mat. Then he paused and looked at Hart. "You can back away if you want."

"It's O.K., sir." But Hart did rock back on his heels.

Brandt peeled back the delicate cover. Rushing sand hissed as it tumbled down under the mat, while dank, fetid air escaped in the opposite direction. Brandt wrinkled his nose. The mat curled open like the jaws of a demon, allowed sunlight to fill its depths, and revealed deadly fangs.

Hart leaned forward. "Holy shit," he whispered.

Jenkins and Singleton joined them, all transfixed. Sharpened bamboo stakes filled the 6-foot-deep pit. Sword-like points awaited prey, impaled and writhing.

"Damn, sir." Jenkins broke the spell. "You almost stepped into that."

Brandt stood, eyes riveted on the family. He stepped toward them, eyes narrowed, nostrils flared. He held his rifle at waist level, the knuckles of his right hand white against the dull black metal of the trigger guard. The family cowered.

"Lieutenant." A thunderous voice drew his attention. Ferguson trudged toward him, his left hand clamped around the neck of a young man wearing a black loincloth and a red headband. The man struggled, feet kicking and arms flailing. Ferguson lifted his arm a little higher, not even breaking stride, half carrying, half dragging his captive.

"Found him hiding in a root cellar," Ferguson said as he stopped and shoved him toward Brandt. "I expect this is our local VC engineer."

Soldiers aimed their rifles at the new target, anxious eyes looking to Brandt for an order to fire. The man stood as if frozen. Fear and uncertainty filled his face.

Brandt exploded with rage, grabbed the man by the arm with his left hand, shoved him to the edge of the pit, suspended above the bamboo stakes. The man arched his back and strained against gravity, his toes clawed desperately at the crumbling edge of the pit, and his eyes bulged with hysterical gleam.

"Taste it." Brandt screamed. "Taste the fear, you son of a bitch. You dug your own grave."

The young mother bolted from her position, clutched Brandt's sleeve and collar, and yanked wildly. High-pitched wailing assaulted Brandt's ears. She pierced his frenzy with alien, meaningless sounds—which he understood perfectly.

Ferguson grabbed her by the shoulders and ripped her away from Brandt. Immobilized by massive hands, she gasped for air, her chest heaved, and tears streamed down her cheeks. Her lips trembled, devoid of sound.

Brandt pulled the man back from the edge, but did not release his grip. Brandt felt strangely aware of his hand on the man's arm, a tangible connection to his enemy. Such an unusual sensation, to actually touch your enemy. Like American Indians used to "count coup," earn prestige by touching an enemy in battle. The man in his grip had a face. A face filled with fear.

Again, his eyes locked with those of the mother. The tunnel reappeared. His rage emptied into it, while images and sounds rushed out. A montage swirled in his mind: bright flashes and thunder over battlefields; lifeless friends and lifeless enemies rising to a single body count; a bugle played Taps; an altar boy climbed out of a foxhole; addiction sated in the violent tranquility after a firefight; anthems clashed with hymns; political slogans; precious lives traded for medals; a solitary soldier held a compass with no needle. Banished feelings returned to the vacuum of his soldier's soul. Conviction shared its perch with doubt.

Brandt's shoulders relaxed, the grip on his rifle eased. He glowered at his enemy, then at the pit, and back into the face of his enemy. The man's eyes widened. His lips moved but the only sound, a choked cry. Brandt dropped his rifle, lunged forward and grabbed the man by the neck and loincloth. A long growl escaped from the depths of Brandt's being as he lifted the man above his head, paused, then heaved him over the pit. The man landed on his shoulder, dust flew, his head bounced, and he rolled to a rest at Hart's feet. He stared at Brandt, trembling, gasping.

"Tie him up, sergeant. We'll give him to Bravo and they can send him back for questioning next chance they have to set up an LZ."

Singleton strode toward the family and growled, "Let me blow them away for you, sir." He raised his rifle. "Let's waste this place. Torch the gooks and the village."

Metallic clicks clattered around Brandt. His men flipped safeties to full automatic, constricted on the family. Hate spewed like an implosion, so much force moving inward to one spot. Brandt stopped in midstride, his jaw dropped, and his eyes widened. They raised rifles, fingers poised on triggers. Brandt blinked. They looked like hunting falcons, their hoods removed and eyes locked, craving prey blood, awaiting the release command.

Brandt blinked again. He glanced at the mother, back at the man-trap, and then at Singleton and the trail leading out of the village.

"Get back in formation," Brandt yelled. "We've got a job to do."

Unbelieving stares greeted his command.

Brandt raised both arms, hands shoulder high. "Don't you understand? The VC come through here, set booby traps, tell them not to help us. We come in and expect them to help us. If they do, the VC come back and slit their throats. These people don't give a shit about this war. They just want to be left alone."

"But, LT—" Singleton started.

Brandt cut him off. "Who the hell are we? We're the 173rd Airborne. Best fucking soldiers in the world. We take on the best the enemy has to offer." He paused and looked from man to man. "We don't make war on women and children."

Eyes fell to the ground, the silence deafening. Brandt picked up his rifle.

"Sergeant Hart, get your squad ready to move out."

Ferguson released the mother, stepped alongside Brandt, and bellowed, "You heard the man. Get moving."

The soldiers spun on their heels and jogged into formation.

"Singleton," Brandt called and motioned him over.

Singleton plodded to Brandt and stood, shoulders slumped, eyes downcast.

Brandt grasped the corporal's arm. "Drop a grenade in the motherfucker. Mark it so the platoons behind us see it."

Singleton drew his shoulders back, lifted his chin and a big smile spread across his face. He drew in a deep breath. "Yes, sir."

Brandt stepped away.

Ferguson gave Brandt a crisp nod. "I'll head to the rear of the platoon now and hand the prisoner over to Bravo." He grabbed the VC soldier and led him away.

Brandt watched them recede. The prisoner slouched; he seemed docile and resigned to his fate.

Jenkins approached, arm extended. "Bravo 6 again, sir."

Brandt took a deep breath. "Bravo 6, this is November 6. Over."

"November 6, why are you stopped? Lima and Mike are stacking up behind you."

"Found a mantrap, 6. At the intersection of the red lines on your funny paper. Also found one Victor Charlie hiding in a root cellar. Be careful when you move through. Over."

"Nice work, November 6. Drop a grenade in it and mark it. Have your rear squad hold Victor Charlie at the intersection and pass him on to the lead squad of Lima. We'll send Victor back for questioning when we get a chance to set up a landing zone. Now get moving, and pick up the pace. We've got time to make up now. Six out."

Brandt and Singleton exchanged glances, shook their heads, and moved apart.

Brandt raised his voice, "Platoon," then lifted his arm high, thrust it forward. "Move out."

At the far edge of the village, Brandt looked back over his shoulder. His rear squad just passed the intersection and Singleton, one grenade lighter, jogged past him. A cloud of dust and bamboo splinters rose from the pit and shrouded the scene. The young woman stood alone, chin raised, eyes riveted on Brandt.

Brandt reached up and felt the small circular scab on his neck.

"Fucking war. Like a goddamn leech."

CHAPTER 12

★ ★ ★

Brandt halted the platoon after a kilometer's march past the village. Sergeant Hart knelt against a wall of trees and vegetation that screened a rice paddy. He stood as Brandt approached.

"It's a big sucker, sir. That ridge we loop behind is on the other side."

"O.K. Let's take a look."

Brandt crawled through undergrowth smoothly as a snake, cautiously as a panther, spotted a natural window in the foliage, angled toward it, and stopped at the edge of the rice paddy, still concealed in shadows. He removed his helmet, placed it on the ground and wiped a sleeve across his sweaty forehead. As he gazed through the foliage, a grin spread across his face.

If I do a real thorough job of checking out the terrain, the troops will get a little rest.

He pulled his canteen from its pouch, raised it to his lips, took a long drink, and replaced the canteen. Then he drew his binoculars from their case and studied the terrain in front of him. Like Hart said, a rectangular paddy, unusually large for this area of Binh Dinh Province, the ridge on the other side about a kilometer away. First, he searched the tree line at the base of the ridge, then he scanned south, and finally, he probed the shadows of the northern edge. Lush vegetation partially masked a village. Quiet. Peaceful. Everything looked as it should.

Brandt listened for that little voice inside that he'd come to rely upon during his time in Nam. He heard nothing. Perhaps the still-pounding pulse in his ears drowned it out. He needed to check the village before crossing the paddy, but that mantrap put them behind schedule. Captain Parker's schedule.

He said, "Forget the village."

Brandt drew in a deep breath and let it out slowly.

Duty. Accomplish the mission. But what about responsibility to my men?

Brandt shook his head.

Like being a pawn in a multi-layered chess game. Players move me. I move my pieces. Except that my pieces have names and faces. If we don't make it there, we won't be any help at all.

Sweat trickled around the scab on his neck. He reached up to scratch it but stopped and rubbed his forehead instead.

Get your head back in the game, Brandt.

Brandt sensed a presence behind him, rolled onto his side, and looked over his shoulder. Sergeant Ferguson loomed over him. Ferguson knelt down, stretched into a prone position, and crawled alongside Brandt.

"How's it look, sir?"

"Beautiful, sergeant. Quiet country village on our right. Picturesque rice paddy. Foothills rising on the far side." Brandt paused. "Which amounts to a long walk with no cover or concealment." He paused again. "Just fuckin' beautiful."

Ferguson chuckled softly.

Brandt extended his arm, offering the binoculars. "Take a look."

Ferguson scanned the terrain. "Perfect description, sir."

"I'd like to clear the village, but Captain Parker said not to waste time with villages."

Brandt replaced the binoculars. "We could send one squad across at a time. The unit crossing would have cover fire. But that would take three times as long. And Captain Parker's inflexible."

Ferguson took a long moment before responding. "Well, sir, I say we make a beeline straight across this paddy. Get on the other side lickety split."

"O.K. Let's get to it."

Brandt stood and moved to his left, framed by a 20–meter break in the tangle of trees and bushes that ringed the rice paddy. He looked up. A pair of curved palm trees arced over the opening like an entryway.

Dante's Inferno. Over the gates of Hell, the inscription, "Abandon all hope, ye who enter."

Brandt frowned.

Where did that come from? Why can't I stay focused?

He knew that his next action would carry his men into battle. Brandt took a deep breath, raised his arm, hesitated, and then propelled his hand forward.

First Squad charged into the paddy and spread into a column formation followed by 2nd Squad. Ski moved past him and nodded his head. "Air—fucking—borne, sir." The paratrooper's salutation lacked the usual enthusiasm, conveying only willingness to obey an order. Brandt looked down into the murky water, wrinkled his nose, and then plunged his right foot down searching for the bottom. It was only knee deep. A few mud-sucking steps later, he heard Jenkins splash in behind him. The sloshing moved off to his right.

Well into the paddy, Brandt glanced over at the village 100 meters to his right. There were about twenty huts with thatched roofs. Copses of trees cast deep shadows. A stone wall circled a well in the center.

Quiet. Nothing moving.

Brandt's eyes narrowed.

Then why the foreboding?

Brandt slogged forward, leaning into each stride to pull his heels out of ankle-deep mud. Familiar wavy lines in the water ahead radiated away from him.

"Damn snakes," he grumbled, "I sure as hell hope nobody starts shooting."

He examined the snakes closely. Skinny bodies blended smoothly into oval-shaped heads.

They're harmless, but I still don't like the idea of diving in with them.

Brandt noticed Jenkins looking intently at the water and heard him muttering something to himself.

"At least it's not deep," Brandt called to him.

Jenkins looked up. "Do they really use their own shit for fertilizer, sir?"

"I don't know. Don't think I want to know either," Brandt answered.

He turned 180 degrees, but continued walking backwards.

Third Squad is completely in the paddy, now. Good spacing, no gap between 2nd and 3rd Squads.

He performed another scan of the village to the north.

No kids running around, no old ladies sweeping dirt in front of huts. Too quiet.

His brow darkened.

Something familiar about this. Not good. But what?

Brandt spun around and looked directly ahead. The long axis of the platoon aimed at the southern tip of the ridge; another 200 meters and 1st Squad would be out of the paddy. He passed the halfway point, stepped over another dike onto dry ground, and stomped his feet and shed mud. His first few steps squished water through the nylon mesh of his jungle boots.

"Lieutenant."

Jenkins slogged toward him, stepped over the dike, accelerated his pace, and held the radio receiver close to his chest, not extending his arm as usual. He didn't want to wave it around in the middle of a rice paddy.

"Bravo 6 wants to talk to you."

"Tell him you can't get to me right now, that it'll only be a couple of minutes."

"Right, sir," Jenkins said as he fell back.

"Just what I need now," Brandt groused. Then he heard Jenkins' footsteps again.

"Sir, Captain Parker says he's gonna staple my ass to yours if I don't learn how to stick with you. He says he means now, not two minutes from now."

Brandt stopped, let out a deep breath, and held out his hand. Jenkins gave him the handset, and they both resumed a quick pace on the dry ground.

Damn bulls eye growing on me.

Brandt took a deep breath before he spoke in a controlled voice. "Bravo 6, this is November 6. Over."

"When I want to talk to you, I don't want to be kept waiting. Do you roger that?" Brandt held the receiver away from his ear.

"Roger, 6," Brandt replied.

Parker's voice boomed again. "I need to know your position. Now."

Brandt stopped.

Oh, shit. Not now. That son of a bitch.

He dropped to his right knee, slowly pulled the map out of his pants pocket, and slid it onto his left thigh.

That bulls eye is flashing neon.

Brandt scanned the map, located his position, and then found one of the coded reference points.

"My position is, from Schlitz, right two, down one. Do you copy?"

"I copy, from Schlitz, right two, down one." Parker's voice softened, perhaps a little congratulatory, in tone. "That's good. Keep it up. Six out."

Brandt put the map away, handed the receiver back to Jenkins, and stepped over a dike.

Crack. Crack. Crack. A hail of brass tore the air around him.

Brandt dove into a corner formed by two dikes, slammed into dry ground, crushed by seventy pounds of equipment on his back, and dust flew up into his eyes and mouth. He spit and blinked as he pulled the quick release on his rucksack and shrugged it off. To his left front, he heard the rapid report of an automatic weapon firing from the village and three close, almost simultaneous, explosions. A pain-filled scream rose as the din subsided. Like an echo, the same refrain sounded to his right. The cacophony rose again as small-arms fire filled the gap. He blinked to clear his eyes and spit dust. Sensory information assaulted his ears.

Ambush.

Brandt rose up and peered over the dike. Crack. Crack. Crack. Bullets raked over his head and thudded into the dike in front of him, sending him ducking for cover.

The volume of noise rose again as he heard his platoon return fire.

Once more, Brandt rose up to assess the situation. Crack. Crack. Crack. Again he dove into the corner.

Damn, I guess they know who I am. That son of a bitch.

"Jenkins," Brandt called. "Where are you?"

"Over here," came the reply from the other side of the dike. "Every time I try to climb over, they shoot right at me."

Brandt rolled onto his left side and faced the dike separating him from Jenkins.

"Shit. How the hell?" Brandt's brow knitted. "Jenkins, toss the Prick-6 over."

A second later, the PRC-6 radio landed in front of him.

"November, this is November 6. Status report. Over."

Hart reported first. "One shoulder wound, small arms. One serious grenade wound; lost a foot. Bleeding bad. Must have been an RPG." He took a breath. "We can't move; can only maintain return fire."

"No casualties," reported Olszewski. "We can't move either."

"One casualty, small arms," reported Martinez. "Every time we try to get over these dikes, all hell breaks loose."

Casualties in lead and rear squads, none in the middle. Classic ambush tactics. Platoon Sergeant is with rear squad.

"Jenkins," Brandt yelled, "get me a medevac on the Prick-25."

"Already on the way, sir."

"November 5, are you monitoring? Over."

"Six." Gasp. "This." Gasp. "Is 5." Ferguson paused. "Just made it over to November 3." A deep breath. "I copy. Over."

"Five, take 3rd Squad and bust out on the right, then roll up their flank. First Squad and 2nd Squad will cover. On my command. Do you roger? Over."

"You got it," Ferguson said, "let's get out of this fucking place."

"November 1 and 2, aim your grenade launchers on the machine guns in front of 3rd Squad. Are you ready?"

"Ready," came the reply from both squad leaders.

"November, this is 6. Go."

Thunder erupted all around Brandt, matched by an echoing volley coming from the village and aimed at 3rd Squad. Brandt rose up and peered over the dike. No shots fired at him. He stayed up just long enough to see one of his men in 3rd Squad drop.

"Six," reported Ferguson, "it's no good. We still can't move."

"I got a good look," Brandt said. "It's at least a reinforced squad in there. Maybe a platoon. I'm going to get some artillery. Maintain return fire, but don't waste it."

"November 6," Martinez reported. "I have another casualty; leg; small arms."

"Dustoff is on the way. Hang in there."

"Sir, Bravo 6 is on the horn," Jenkins called.

Brandt tried to climb over the dike. Crack. Crack. Crack.

Not again.

But the bullets came from his left this time.

Where did those guys come from? Maneuver from the village? Reinforcements from somewhere else? Shit.

Crack. Crack. Crack. Thud. Thud. Thud. The bullets slammed into the dike on his right.

He picked up the Prick-6. "November 1," he yelled. "Did you see where those last shots came from? Our left flank?"

Crack. Crack. Thud. Thud. Brandt jumped, as if in spasm. He sensed something pass over the calves of his legs.

Damn. Did I actually feel those without getting shot?

"Now I see 'em," Hart said.

"Get that son of a bitch off my ass," Brandt yelled. "I'm wide open here."

Before he even finished the first sentence, Brandt heard Hart's machine gun and M-79 grenade launcher firing.

Jenkins yelled, "I'm tossing over the handset for the Prick-25. It's Bravo 6."

A moment later, the handset dangled over the dike. Brandt pulled on it, stretching the cord to its limit.

"Bravo 6, November 6. Over."

"I heard your request for a medevac. What's your situation?"

"Position same as last report. Pinned down in this rice paddy. Four casualties; one serious. Seems like a reinforced squad, maybe platoon. Can't maneuver; calling in redleg."

"Roger that. We're too far away to support you. Gunships are all committed elsewhere. Hope redleg does the job. Keep me informed. Six out."

Brandt had not been shot at since Hart went to work on the left flank. He rose up slowly and peeked over the dike—no shots fired at him. The situation had stabilized into a stalemate. He eased back down.

"Jenkins," he called. "I'm coming over." He tossed the handset back, then the PRC-6.

Brandt heard Jenkins scuffling, dragging his radio.

"O.K., sir," he called back.

Brandt took a deep breath, gathered his legs under him, and then scrambled up over the dike and dropped down next to Jenkins and listened. Again, no shots fired directly at him.

"Damn. It's good to see you, sir."

"Same here. Give me that radio."

Brandt pulled out his map, spread it on the ground, and found an artillery registration point.

Not too far away. Good. That'll speed things up.

"Kingpin, this is November 6. Fire mission. Over."

"This is Kingpin. Send your mission." The voice sounded mechanical, almost bored.

"Kingpin, adjust fire. Shift from registration George. Direction, North, right 450. Over."

"November 6, I copy. From George, right 450. Over."

"Kingpin, enemy troops dug in."

"November 6, one round smoke on the way."

"Kingpin, roger. One round smoke on the way."

A few seconds later, the artillery smoke round hit about one kilometer from the far side of the village, 1,100 meters from his position and 700 meters from the village, lined up perfectly.

We're too close to the target to bracket it. Just need to walk it in.

"Kingpin, drop 400. One round HE."

"On the way," said the aloof voice.

The high explosive round slammed into the ground 400 meters closer than the smoke round.

"Kingpin, drop 200. One round HE."

"On the way."

The artillery round struck 700 meters north of his position and 500 meters north of the village. Brandt glanced down at his map, up at the point of impact, then at his map again. He paused, a page of his Ranger Handbook in his mind.

Next round will be 600 meters from our position. Danger Close protocol. Maximum range adjustment 100 meters, creeping method of adjustment. All guns will fire. If one or two guns are erratic, I can figure that into the adjustments.

"Kingpin, drop 100. Be advised, Danger Close. I say again, Danger Close."

"November 6, I copy. Drop 100, Danger Close. All guns will fire."

Brandt waited, eyes focused on the expected point of impact. The ground erupted 600 meters in front of him, 400 meters from the village, and a second later, the thunderclap hit Brandt.

He nodded slowly. *Tight group. Long, narrow oval. No erratic rounds. Just what I need.*

Brandt dropped the point of impact 100 meters three more times, then 50 meters placing the rounds 50 meters from the village.

All right. One more adjustment and we've got those bastards.

"Kingpin, drop 50. Fire for Effect."

"November 6, drop 50, Fire for Effect. Battery four. HE. On the way."

Ferguson called on the PRC-6. "November 6, their level of fire is dropping. Those sons o' bitches are burying their heads already. Sock it to 'em."

Brandt nodded. First good news today. "Jenkins, that medevac should be getting here soon. Call the squad leaders and tell them to get their wounded over here. With covering fire."

"Right, sir."

Brandt rose up and assessed the situation. They did have fire superiority, but the enemy maintaining disciplined AK-47 fire, kept them pinned down.

"Sir," Jenkins offered him the PRC-25 receiver. "Dustoff wants to talk to you."

Brandt took the receiver, looked south, and saw the medevac chopper, a black dot in the sky.

"Dustoff, this is November 6. Over."

"This is Dustoff Two-Niner. What is your situation? Over."

"Have fire superiority, but still taking some fire. Four wounded, one serious."

"How serious?"

"Lost a foot."

"I'm coming in. Let's make this fast. Two-Niner out."

Brandt looked north toward the village. "Where the fuck's that artillery?" Brandt complained to nobody in particular. "It should be here by now."

"Here come the wounded," Jenkins said.

Brant shifted his gaze: two men ambulatory, each helped along by a buddy. They made no sounds, but pain and fear filled their faces. One stumbled, his whole body contracted, and the man helping him struggled to keep going. He saw a third casualty draped over the shoulders of another man. Behind them, four men carried somebody in a poncho, the medic matching pace alongside. The wounded man writhed, his face hidden, his voice distorted in screams. Brandt's stomach tightened; his breathing quickened.

Behind Brandt, the familiar wop-wop-wop of rotor blades rose above the sporadic small-arms fire. Brandt spun around and saw the big red cross on the chopper's nose. The machine guns in the village came to life again, raking the air above him. He watched as the bottom of the chopper swung toward him like a pendulum as it cut a tight turn in the air and sped south. So much for the Geneva Convention.

Brandt picked up the Prick-6. "Goddammit! Give 'em some cover."

Noise erupted all around him. His platoon fired with a vengeance.

A calm, business-like voice broke the hiss of the radio in Brandt's ear. "This is Dustoff Two-Niner. Tried to come in, but took too much fire. Will circle 'til you cool it down."

"Roger, Two-Niner," Brandt replied. "Sorry about that. We have redleg on the way."

Brandt shifted the Prick-6 to his right ear, the handset for the Prick-25 at his left ear and his rifle in his lap. He had not yet fired a shot. He had spent the entire firefight talking on the radio, directing fire, maneuvering squads, reporting to higher command, requesting artillery, and talking to a helicopter.

The hiss of the radio stopped.

"November 6, this is Kingpin 6."

The battery commander? What the fuck? Brandt keyed the PRC-25 handset. "Where's my artillery?"

"Be advised, November 6. That's a friendly village. We can't fire your mission. Do you roger? Over."

"What?" Brandt screamed in disbelief.

"November 6. I repeat. That is designated a friendly village. New rules of engagement. Cannot fire your mission."

Brandt gasped and his eyes widened.

What in hell is going on? Never been refused a fire mission.

A MATTER OF SEMANTICS

A scream rose from the wounded and pulled Brandt's attention. Carson frantically tried to staunch spurting arteries. Brandt could see frustration in his eyes and almost anger at his own human limitations. Blood pooled on the ground as men moaned through clenched teeth. The man on the poncho rolled toward Brandt. Corporal Altobelli, a machine gunner. The ragged stump of a right leg waved in the air. "My foot hurts. God, my foot hurts," Altobelli cried. The words froze Corporal Singleton, who held the foot, still in its boot, about to place it on the poncho, ensuring that it would get to the hospital with his friend.

Brandt's eyes narrowed, his nostrils flared, and he jammed down the push-to-talk button, fingertips turning white.

"Kingpin 6, I've got a medevac chopper standing by to pick up four of my men. They're lying here bleeding. A shitload of automatic weapons in that village are keeping me down behind a motherfuckin' rice paddy dike, and you're telling me that this is a friendly fuckin' village?"

"Sorry, November 6," the voice faltered. "That's affirmative. I, I can't help you. Out."

Brandt threw the handset as hard as he could. It stretched the cord to its limit, then snapped back, glancing off Jenkins' helmet as the RTO rolled to avoid the boomerang.

Brandt's breathing deepened and his muscles tensed.

Friendly village. Win their hearts and minds, but carry a rifle. Don't Search and Destroy anymore; do Reconnaissance-in-Force. Same shit, different day.

Brandt nodded slowly, then muttered to himself, "Now I understand. It's just a matter of semantics."

"What, sir?" Jenkins asked.

"Hand me that radio, Jenkins."

Brandt wedged himself into the corner of the dikes, peered just over the top, and located where the last artillery round hit.

"Kingpin 6, this is November 6. Over."

"I can't fire into that village. You know I can't."

"Listen carefully," Brandt said in a calm but forceful voice. "I don't want you to fire artillery shells into that village. What I want is for you to fire my mission as an airburst over the village. Do you roger that? Over."

"November 6, that's crazy. I want to help you, but I can't."

Brandt could sense the pain in his voice, the understanding.

"My men are bleeding. The bastards are shooting at the medevac. I need your help. Just an airburst. That's all."

After a long pause, "This is a crazy fucking war, November 6."

A deep breath.

"From your last adjustment, drop 50, Fire for Effect. Battery four. HE-Air. On the way."

Brandt picked up the PRC-6. "Get your heads down. Artillery on the way."

Brandt and Jenkins scrunched down behind the dike.

Fear and confusion contorted Jenkins' face. "What the fuck is going on, sir?"

"This isn't a war, Jenkins," Brandt said. "It's a fucking word game. And the assholes at the top make up the rules. Like that 'hearts and minds' bullshit. I didn't go to a school for diplomats. I went to a school for soldiers. If they wanted diplomacy, they should have sent diplomats."

Brandt paused. A thin smile creased his face.

"A word game. And I'm finally learning how to play."

Jenkins nodded as the confusion on his face disappeared. The fear remained. "Goddamn, sir. Shit's gonna hit the fan."

"I have to kill gooks to keep my own men alive. The assholes have forgotten those words. Jenkins, it's a good thing there are still some men who remember what's important. Men we can count on, like that battery commander."

Brandt looked up at a very distinctive sound, like a giant drill boring its way through the air. Artillery shells exploded 50 meters above the village followed by thousands of ripping noises as shrapnel shredded leaves and branches. More 105 mm howitzer rounds exploded in rapid succession. Steel hail raked the village, tearing through trees, thatched roofs, and walls. One long, rolling thunderclap filled Brandt's ears and shook his body. A cloud bank of smoke and dust formed a dark, mottled shroud over the area.

Sudden silence. A mixture of smells drifted toward Brandt. A sense of things charred.

Jenkins handed Brandt the PRC-6.

"Be a bitch if it rains tonight," Brandt said in a voice devoid of humor.

He keyed the radio. "First and 2nd Squads, base of fire. November 5, take 3rd squad out on the flank. Pound the shit out of 'em. Now."

★ ★ ★

Brandt, Jenkins, and Ferguson stood in the center of the so-called friendly village, coordinating the mop-up operation as the sun dipped behind the ridge.

Dead enemy soldiers lay on edge of the rice paddy, while the prisoners, under the watchful eyes of 3rd Squad, waited for a helicopter. Next stop for them, a base camp and questioning. A medevac helicopter landed and loaded the enemy wounded.

Yeah. Enemy soldiers firing at a chopper bearing a red cross. Same one now taking them to a hospital. And how do they treat prisoners?

"Surprisingly, no villagers were injured in the battle," Brandt said.

"Yeah," Ferguson said. "Probably hid in their root cellars when they saw the enemy soldiers move into action. Good thing it was an air burst. Only surface damage. That saved them."

"Guess they're well trained, too," Brandt said.

"Sir," Ferguson asked, "since we never got there, what happened with the cordon operation?"

"Delta Company managed to get a platoon there and they're in position now."

"Good. Did the gooks know our plans, somehow?"

"I don't think so. I figure the platoon in this village was the security element that you warned me about. Probably just got here and only had time to set up a hasty ambush when they saw us moving across the paddy. That's why we took so few casualties when they sprang the ambush. We were lucky." Brandt shook his head. "No, *we* screwed up *their* plans. Seven killed, nine wounded, and five captured." He paused and gazed around the village. "But if it weren't for that artillery commander, their platoon leader would be standing here reciting similar numbers to his platoon sergeant."

Ferguson nodded. "Got that right."

"Lieutenant." Jenkins interrupted, arm extended. "It's Big 6, sir. Wants to talk to whoever called in that artillery. He's pissed."

"Well, sir," Ferguson said in a fatherly voice, "this is where it starts. The battalion commander. Then who knows how high up it'll go."

Brandt stared at the ground, silent, hands on hips.

"What you gonna say, sir?"

Brandt drew in a deep breath, let it out slowly, and looked into Ferguson's eyes.

"What difference does it make? Shit rolls downhill, right?"

Ferguson gently placed his arm across Brandt's shoulders. "Fuck 'em, lieutenant. What they gonna do? Put you in the infantry? Send you to Nam?"

Brandt snatched the handset from Jenkins and held it up to the side of his head, fingers resting on the push-to-talk button. He gazed around the village at his men, the enemy soldiers, and then back at Jenkins and Ferguson. Brandt shrugged, and a smile spread across his face.

"Big 6, this is November 6. Over."

A MATTER OF SEMANTICS

★ ★ ★

Brandt stood at attention. He tried to swallow, but his mouth was dry. He tried to take a deep breath, but his chest constricted.

Alexander sat behind his desk, arms crossed, eyes narrowed and flashing. He breathed heavily through his nose.

"Brandt." The name escaped through clenched jaws. "What am I going to do with you?"

Brandt's stomach churned.

Alexander took a deep breath and leaned forward. "I just met with the Brigade Commander." He pounded his fists on the table. "The general wants to know why I can't control my subordinate commanders."

He held the forward lean, took several breaths, and spoke in an even tone. "Fortunately, no villagers were injured." He paused, then said in a sarcastic tone. "As a result of your brilliant tactical decision."

Alexander sat back.

"The way the general sees it, no harm, no foul. He says the Army and this war are getting enough bad press at home." He shook his head. "And his commander at II Corps doesn't need to be bothered with a royal fuckup by a second lieutenant."

Alexander seethed, face flushed and nostrils flared. He leaned forward again.

"Of course," his voice exploded, "my commander is aware of it." He pounded his fists again.

Alexander took more deep breaths. "And the general's tied my hands."

"So," he said again, "what am I going to do with you?" He raised his arms palms up. "I can't court-martial you." He raised his chin. "But I haven't written your Efficiency Report yet. Keep that in mind."

Brandt exhaled.

"No, Brandt, I'm not going to relieve you of command. No, you're not going to get a cushy job. You're not going to sleep in a bed, eat real food at a table, and take a shower every day." He paused. "No, Brandt, I'm keeping you out in the field. Infantry platoon leader humping the boonies in Vietnam. Sleep in the mud with snakes and scorpions. Eat ham and lima beans from a can. Wash your butt from your helmet every three days."

Brandt's shoulders relaxed and his chest expanded.

Sergeant Ferguson was right.

Alexander sat back, a self-satisfied smile on his face.

"Dismissed."

CHAPTER 13

★ ★ ★

Captain Parker wrapped up the Operations Order. "That's it, gentlemen. Rest well tonight. We're likely to get some action tomorrow." Parker gave some instructions to his RTO, and then rummaged in his rucksack. The three lieutenants tucked away their notebooks and chatted easily among themselves, a rare opportunity to converse with someone of their own rank. News from home, baseball standings, movies, music—the closest thing to relaxing in enemy territory—five minutes of it every month or so.

Reluctantly, they broke and turned toward their platoon sectors.

"Lieutenant Brandt," Parker called. "Hang on a minute."

Foster and Merriweather smiled and stifled a chuckle as they hustled away.

Brandt completed a 180 degree spin and took a few steps toward Parker.

"Yes, sir?"

"I have a surprise for you."

"My last surprise was a platoon sergeant. Hard to top that one, sir."

He handed Brandt a bulky tube. "Well, I think you'll like this one almost as much."

"Damn, it's heavy."

"Six pounds with the battery, but I think you'll find it well worth humping the weight."

"What is it?"

"It's called a Starlight Scope. Originally developed as a rifle sight for snipers so they could shoot at night. The scope gathers ambient light from the moon and stars, hence the name Starlight, and multiplies it a thousand times. But, of course, the Army has a long, bureaucratic acronym for it that none of us can remember."

"How did we get one?"

"Well, they're experimental. This is one of the first in Vietnam. The Supply Officer told me that snipers don't want them because they still have too many glitches. Like they won't hold a zero. Bright light nearby blinds it. Even the muzzle flash of the rifle it's mounted on shuts it down." Parker paused. "To say nothing of putting a six-pound scope on your rifle."

"Then why did we get it?"

"The Supply Officer said to try using it as a handheld device. It does a decent job of detecting enemy movement at night. Even as far as 200 meters or more."

Brandt's eyes widened. "Sounds great."

"Right. When I heard that, I thought you might be able to put it to good use." Parker reached into his shirt pocket and pulled a folded sheet of paper. "Here's a spec sheet on it. You'll need to study it."

Brandt's eyes sparkled and a wide grin spread across his face. "Hell, I'll memorize it tonight."

★ ★ ★

Brandt held his left hand high over his head. "Jenkins, tell the squad leaders to halt in place."

He faced west, pulled his map and compass, took readings, and nodded his head.

Ferguson joined Brandt. "This the valley we're supposed to recon?"

"This is it, sergeant. Runs east–west."

A MATTER OF SEMANTICS

"It's small. Less than two kilometers long, but about a kilometer wide here at the mouth." Ferguson pointed. "Look how it narrows sharply at the far end. Shaped like a funnel."

"Yeah. And this trail we found slices through the middle, then climbs steeply into the mountains. Map shows another trail coming in from the north. Should be an intersection about half way up the valley."

Ferguson rubbed his chin. "Intel says the NVA has been infiltrating troops in this area, right?"

"Right," Brandt said. "Groups of four or five, some up to a dozen. Squad size. And the company's mission is to find active trails and intercept enemy patrols."

Ferguson looked left and right. "These valley walls are steep. Covered with thick vegetation. Only way in or out of the valley is on the trails."

"Right." Brandt scanned the valley floor. "It's dry and dusty. Nothing but clumps of short scrub grass—no concealment, let alone cover." He pondered a moment. "I think Bravo will want to set up a blocking position here at the mouth of the valley, not out there at the intersection."

Ferguson nodded. "Makes sense, sir. Good concealment here. Best place to catch anybody coming out of the mountains. With three platoons, we could handle anything coming down those trails."

Brandt pointed to his right, half way up the valley. "There's a notch in the valley wall. Probably where the other trail enters. Let's go check out the intersection and that notch to verify it. We can take a break there in the concealment of the notch and rest the troops. We'll come back and join the company for the night."

After a quick march up the valley, the platoon found the intersection and followed the north–south trail into the notch, an area about 40 meters wide and 60 meters long. Another funnel, another steep trail coming down.

Jenkins approached Brandt. "Bravo 6, sir."

"Bravo 6, this is November 6. Over."

Brandt checked his map. "I am at, from Yankees, down one, right one-half."

"That's good. I am at, from Dodgers, up three, left one, with Lima and Mike. We are laagered up here. I want you to set up a blocking position where you are on that north–south trail tonight and cover that intersection with an OP. Let me know coordinates when you're set up for the night. Six out."

Ferguson strode toward him. "What's up, sir?"

"We're not rejoining the company. Bravo wants us to set up a blocking position here tonight covering this trail." Brandt pointed. "Look at how steep that is. Same with these slopes on either side of us. All we need to do is set up inside this notch."

Ferguson grunted, his expression deadpan.

Brandt did an about face. "But there's one more thing. An OP out there." Brandt pointed. "On the intersection."

Ferguson gazed at the intersection. The deadpan expression turned into a frown. "Nasty mission, sir."

Brandt nodded. "Right. We have to sit on this trail to protect his right flank and also block the other trail?"

Brandt shook his head. "The intersection is 600 meters out from here. I don't like putting an OP out so far. Especially one so vulnerable. If anyone comes down that east–west trail, they'd be sitting ducks."

"I agree, but Bravo said—"

Brandt cut him off. "Jenkins." Brandt held out his hand for the radio handset.

"Bravo 6, November 6. Over."

"Bravo 6."

"Six, that OP on the trail intersection. It's a long way out. I'd like to have it in closer so I can support them if necessary. We can put some trip flares and Claymores on the intersection."

"When I give you an order, I don't expect a discussion." Brandt yanked the handset away from his ear. "I want bodies on that intersection. If NVA troops come through here tonight, like Intelligence expects, I want to know as soon as possible. Set it up. Six out."

Brandt returned the handset, placed his hands on his hips, and stared at the ground.

"Well, sir, who do we—?"

"Sergeant," Brandt said, uncharacteristically cutting off his platoon sergeant again. "Get a perimeter set up. Put two machine guns covering this trail and one aimed at that intersection. Our perimeter will fill the gap between the high ground on our left and right, creating the block for Bravo's right flank."

"Airborne, sir." Ferguson walked away, but looked back over his shoulder, deep furrows in his brow.

Brandt took a deep breath and let it out slowly. Then he walked to a clump of bushes, shrugged off his rucksack, plopped down, and leaned against it. He jumped up, swatted the air around him, grabbed his rucksack and charged out of the swarm of mosquitos.

Damn those things.

Brandt moved to another spot, checked the undergrowth, settled down and watched the squad leaders position their men. He drew his canteen, took a long drink, and replaced it.

Ferguson asked, "Who?"

He looked into the faces of his men.

Right. Who do I send out there?

He let out a sigh. "Son of a bitch."

Brandt scrambled to his feet and walked west in the shade of trees against the steep slope bordering the open field. As he passed the westernmost position of his platoon, Corporal Singleton stopped digging. "Sir, is Bravo getting short?"

Brandt paused before answering.

Word travels fast on the grapevine. He's asking if Parker is using us to protect himself.

"Corporal, that question is way above my pay grade. How about yours?"

Singleton looked down and away. "Sorry, sir."

Brandt hustled away, stopped about 50 meters west, backed into the foliage, and squatted at the base of the steep slope.

"What have I been told to do?" he said to himself. "Block the trail coming in from the north to protect the company's right flank. Put an OP on the trail coming in from the west to give early warning for the company's front."

The little voice in his head responded. "Put a three man OP out 600 meters in the middle of flat, bare ground?"

Shit. He kicked a rock, sending it flying into the thick vegetation. Birds scattered.

"That did a lot of good," the voice chided. "Solve the problem."

He took a deep breath and knelt on one knee facing the valley.

"O.K.," he continued the conversation with himself, "what have I been taught about Observation Posts? Place them within small-arms range of the unit. Not here. The position should offer adequate cover and concealment. Not here. There should be concealed routes to and from the OP. Not here." Brandt sighed. "What's a three man OP going to do if the enemy comes down that trail? There's no way they can get back safely. The enemy could come down both trails to meet up. There's no way we can support the men in the OP." He shook his head. "What's my duty? Do what my commander tells me to do and put my men in danger, or accomplish the mission he gave me?"

Brandt surveyed the 180 degree view in front of him.

"The only way through this valley is on those two trails. And that trail coming in from the west is only 250 meters away from where I am now. They can't maneuver, but we can. We're not locked into any one formation. But how can I use this advantage?"

Formations. Football. An image of his football coach formed in his mind. "You always have options, Brandt. You can audible at the line if you don't like what you see."

Brandt nodded as the coach faded. Loose connections coalesced into a single image. *Shift formations.* Brandt sat, laid his rifle across his legs, and plucked his notebook and pen from his shirt pocket. He sketched the outlines of the valley and drew the trails. Then he marked positions for the OP and his squads. *Shift.* Permutations and possibilities cascaded. He hastily jotted more notes.

"We can do this." Brandt jumped up and walked briskly back to the platoon. He saw Singleton sitting on the edge of his foxhole, eating a can of spaghetti and meatballs. Brandt veered toward him, and Singleton scrambled to his feet, an apprehensive look on his face. Brandt leaned in and whispered, "Bravo's got 67-and-a-wake-up."

A smile lit up Singleton's face. "Thank you, sir." He shook his head, then sat down and finished his dinner.

Brandt spun away without responding and hurried to his rucksack.

Ferguson approached. "Sir, we got some decisions to make."

"Right. I got some ideas I want to run by you first."

Brandt opened his notebook and used his pen to point to terrain features, trails, and squad positions and then explained his solution to the problem.

"Complicated. Tricky to do at night." Ferguson shook his head. "I like it, but from what I heard on the radio, I don't think Bravo is going to go for it."

"Let me take care of that. Any suggestions?"

"Well, I think we should mark the positions we shift into now, before it gets dark. Less chance of confusion later."

"Good idea. Now let's talk to the squad leaders."

The three sergeants and Jenkins converged on the command post. Brandt motioned, and they sat. Stiffly erect. No one spoke.

"What's our mission?" Brandt started. "As I see it, we need to protect the company's right flank and set up an ambush on two trails about 600 meters apart." He looked at each of them. "So that's what we're going to do."

"To protect Bravo's ass? How the hell are we going to do that?" Ski blurted. "Uh, sorry, sir."

"I'm getting to that."

"Sir, about that OP we're supposed to send out," Hart interjected.

Brandt held up his hand, palm facing Hart. "I share your concern, sergeant."

Brandt hesitated and then said, "You guys ever heard of the Rockne Shift?" Puzzled looks came from the younger ones. He nodded to Ferguson.

"Sure," Ferguson said. "Notre Dame football coach. The Four Horsemen. They were the first ones to have the backfield shift positions to confuse the defense."

"Right. And that's what we're going to do," Brandt said. "Set up, let the defense see us, and then shift."

"Sir?" A chorus came from befuddled faces. Ski continued, "But what the hell does that have to do with anything?"

"Look." Brandt traced the two trails on the map with a grease pencil, then drew a line from their current location west along the bottom of the steep slope. "This valley's a funnel that narrows sharply. See how close this line is to the trail at the head of the valley? We're going to set up where we are now, then shift to new positions after it gets dark. Take advantage of the terrain. Sergeant Hart, 1st Squad will cover this trail we're on now, but about 50 meters out into the valley. Here." Brandt drew a rectangle on the map. "The OP will set up on the intersection and place a Claymore with a trip wire on the trail 50 meters to the west. When the sun dips below the peak of the mountains, the OP will pull back to a position 250 meters in front of your squad. Here." Brandt drew a circle on the map.

A MATTER OF SEMANTICS

"Because," Martinez interjected, "that is the most difficult time for anyone to see?"

Brandt smiled. "Right. It's the best concealment we have here."

"Only concealment," Ski grumbled.

Brandt ignored Ski's comment and pointed to Hart. "At that distance, your squad can cover the OP with small arms. The OP can still cover the intersection with small arms." He paused.

"Yeah," Hart said. "I see. That's slick, sir."

"Good. Now, when the OP moves back from the intersection, 2nd Squad and 3rd Squad will shift west." Brandt drew another rectangle 25 meters west of 1st Squad. "Second will be here, Ski. Set trip flares in this notch. If anyone comes down that trail, 1st and 2nd squads will have them in a crossfire."

Ski pumped his fist. "You got it, sir."

Martinez leaned forward and jabbed the map. "And 3rd Squad will be here, 25 meters to the west of 2nd Squad." He looked up expectantly.

"Airborne, sergeant." Brandt drew a third rectangle around Martinez' finger. "From that position, it's only 250 meters out to the east–west trail. We can get very effective small-arms fire on it. If they come at us, we'll have them in a crossfire between 2nd and 3rd Squads."

Brandt sat back. They all nodded enthusiastically.

"I will be with 3rd Squad because I think the action will be coming from the west. Any questions?"

Martinez asked, "Why do you think they'll come on the trail from the west?"

"It's the most direct path off the Ho Chi Minh Trail. Sergeant Ferguson and I feel it's the most likely route they'd follow."

Brandt gestured to Ferguson.

"I will be with 1st Squad. I'll help set up the OP, oversee the Claymore placement, and coordinate their shift."

"Any more questions?"

They shook their heads.

"O.K. I will give the command to shift."

He leaned toward Jenkins and reached for the radio handset. "Bravo 6, November 6. Over."

"This is Bravo 6. Report."

"The OP is on its way out to the designated position. They will be at, from John, up three, left one. From my last position, we have the north blocked and the west covered."

"Excellent. Six out."

Brandt returned the handset and looked into faces filled with disbelief.

Ferguson stood before anyone could comment. "O.K., gentlemen, let's get to it. We got a lot of work to do, and it's getting late."

★ ★ ★

Brandt looked up at the sky. Stars and a quarter moon peeked between passing clouds casting shadows, restricting visibility to objects close by. A good night for traveling if you didn't want to be seen.

Can't wait to see if this new toy makes a difference. Starlight Scope, they call it. Well, we'll see.

He breathed a silent chuckle.

No pun intended.

Martinez tapped Brandt on the shoulder. "My eyes are going buggy looking through this thing," he said, handing the Starlight Scope to Brandt. "But I think I might have seen something. Just a fuzzy green blob. Right where the trail comes down into the valley. Can't be sure."

"That's about 300 meters away. Far limit of the detection range. Let's give it a few minutes and check again. Another hundred meters closer and we should be able to recognize what it is. Could be a deer. If anything."

Time plodded as he waited. Sounds of insects drifted over from the vegetation behind them. Brandt looked at his watch. 0314. He raised the scope to his eye. "You were right. I see two, now three, heading into the valley on the trail." He handed the scope to Martinez.

"I got 'em. Little green men walking." He lowered the scope. "This thing is amazing. How's it work?"

"It gathers light from the stars and magnifies it."

Martinez raised the scope again. "Like magic. Now I see," he paused, counting, "twelve. One out in front on point. And they're moving fast." He paused and watched. "Yeah. In a hurry. Not being careful."

"Probably FNGs," Brandt said. "Don't know any better."

"Or their commander's pushing them." Martinez snorted. "Naw, can't imagine that."

Brandt reached for the scope. "Just hand me the scope, sergeant." He scanned the trail behind them and up the slope. "Don't see any more behind them. It's just a squad, like Intel said. Walking right into the kill zone." He nodded.

Just as I planned it.

Brandt picked up the PRC-6 radio. "November, this is November 6. We got visitors headed straight for the Claymore. They're almost there. When it blows, open fire. Acknowledge. Over."

"Roger. Wilco," came the reply from all three squads.

"November 5, did you monitor that?"

"Roger that. November 1 and the OP are in place and ready."

Brandt looked into the scope again. "They're close to the trip wire. Get ready."

He put down the scope and picked up his CAR-15.

Brilliant light illuminated the center of the valley followed by a sharp explosion. Darkness and silence settled for an instant. The rifles of November shattered the silence; a line of fiery muzzle flashes streaked along their side of the valley. Red tracers from the machine guns raked back and forth across the kill zone. Explosions from the grenade launchers flashed like giant fireflies.

Brandt picked up the PRC-6 radio. "Cease fire. That should do it. Let's get out there and clean it up."

As the men rose, green lines of tracers clawed at November's right flank. Bullets ripped into bushes and trees behind them.

"We're taking fire from the right," Martinez shouted.

"What the fuck?" Brandt grabbed the Starlight Scope. "Shit. There's another element coming into the valley from the trail. Looks like about 20 men."

He picked up the PRC-6 radio again. "November, this is 6. More enemy coming down the trail. Looks like about 20. Focus your grenade launchers and machine guns on our right flank."

Before he finished the sentence, another volley of fire erupted from November.

Jenkins handed him the PRC-25 handset. "Bravo 6."

"November 6. Over."

"What the hell is going on out there?"

"A squad of enemy came down the trail. Didn't seem like any more. They tripped our Claymore and we fired. Then another 20 came down the trail. They're trying to maneuver on our right flank. Firing seems to be equal now. Over."

"I sent Lima out to reinforce you. Any friendly casualties?"

"Negative. They're firing too high. Must be new recruits."

"O.K. Hang tight. Lima should be there any minute. Six out."

Brandt exchanged radios with Jenkins. "November, this is 6. Lima is on the way to reinforce us. They'll be on our left flank. Make sure you don't fire into them. November 5, did you monitor that?"

"Affirmative. I see them now. Will coordinate the linkup."

Brandt rose from the ground and looked around. *Equal firing on both sides. Enemy unable to maneuver.*

Jenkins tapped him on the shoulder and handed him the handset for the PRC-25. "Lima 6."

"This is November 6."

"Lima 6 here. We're on line at the trail intersection. Lima 5 and November 5 connected. I can see your line of muzzle flashes. Clearly marks your positions. We will be firing up the long axis of the valley in front of you. Into their flank and front."

"Airborne, Lima 6. Give 'em hell."

A bright line of muzzle flashes crossed the valley at right angles to November. Enemy fire rose sharply in response but sputtered quickly and then died out. Brandt rose up and glanced at Lima's line of muzzle flashes and down November's, a perfect L-shape drawn by fire. The far end of the valley was now dark, devoid of green tracers and yellow muzzle flashes—only darkness cut by red tracers.

Brandt picked up the PRC-6. He hesitated, put the radio down, and scanned the area with the Starlight Scope. Across the valley floor, up the steep trail, nothing moved. He put the scope down and picked up the radio again. He took a deep breath. "Cease fire. Cease fire."

Rifle fire diminished sporadically, then stopped. Silence settled, stars faded, and the sky looked gray-blue in the predawn half-light. The now-familiar violent tranquility following a firefight engulfed the valley. No one moved. Brandt could feel the eyes of his men on him. He listened, scanned the valley, took a deep breath, and rose slowly. He surveyed the scene, stood tall, chest out, pulse pounding.

I survived again.

"O.K.," he bellowed. "Let's check the kill zone. Be careful. A wounded man can still pull a trigger."

CHAPTER 14

★ ★ ★

Brandt swished through the waist-high grass of the valley floor and sensed dampness seep into his skin. He glanced down at his fatigue pants. Once green and now almost black, they stuck to the front of his legs. He looked up at the cloudless blue sky, wiped sweat from his forehead, and frowned.

Carson accelerated his pace and veered toward Brandt. "Sir."

"Yeah, Doc. What is it?"

"We got to stop when we get out of this wet grass and check for leeches."

"Why? Leeches live in streams and ponds."

"There's another kind. Land leeches. Small ones that live in places that are always damp or wet, like this grass."

Brandt looked up at the sky again. "How the hell does it stay so wet?"

"Feel how soft the ground is here? In the rainy season, areas like this turn into a marsh. Still is like that back there near the river bank. So down around our ankles, it's a humid wonderland for all sorts of vermin."

Brandt shook his head. "O.K. How about that spot?" Brandt pointed. "Up ahead where the ground rises, just before the jungle starts."

"Looks good, sir."

A hundred meters later, the platoon set up a hasty perimeter. Carson, Ferguson, and the three squad leaders converged on Brandt.

"O.K.," Brandt said, "Doc tells me that we need to check for leeches. Land leeches. That's a new one for me."

Ferguson chuckled. "Like I said before, Nam always has a new surprise for you, lieutenant." He addressed the squad leaders. "You know the drill. Make sure the troops do a thorough job of checking, especially the three new replacements." He turned to Brandt. "Anything else, sir?"

"How about sending the new guys to me?" Carson interjected. "I'd like to brief them on the importance of the procedure myself."

Ferguson looked at Brandt.

"Fine with me. Let's get to it."

The three new soldiers hustled to the CP. Brandt studied them. *Ricci, Landers, and Hawk. All probably 18 or 19 years old, ranging from five ten to six feet tall. All about 190 pounds.* They stood uneasily, apprehensive looks on their faces.

"Stand at ease." Brandt nodded in Carson's direction. "Doc will demonstrate how to check for leeches. Usually, you only have to do that after going through water, but there's another kind that lives in places that are always wet." He gestured with his thumb over his shoulder. "Like that grass we just walked through." He looked at Carson. "Doc."

"O.K., gentlemen, everyone has to take their clothes off and check each other for the leeches."

"You're kidding," Landers said. "We should be able to see them on our clothes. Pants are tucked in our boots. We're wearing belts. Got all that equipment on."

"No, I'm not kidding. Unlike the big water leeches, land leeches are small. About an inch long. These things can find a way to get inside your clothing."

Carson started unbuttoning his shirt. "Go ahead. I'll check you, then you will check me."

Ricci and Hawk got right to it. Landers had his fingers on his top button but hesitated.

Brandt glared at him. "Soldier, this isn't a junior high gym class locker room." Brandt dropped his shirt on the ground. "This is serious business."

In minutes, 36 men in varying stages of undress paired up. Some were discreetly half naked; some hopped precariously on one foot, the other tangled in a pant leg; and some proudly displayed physiques like Michelangelo's *David*. A few hesitantly removed clothing and glanced furtively as if a throng of women might suddenly appear, sauntering down this remote, deserted mountain valley.

Brandt chuckled. "Looks like a nude beach with a bunch of monkeys grooming each other."

"Yeah, but it's not funny, sir," Carson said. "You don't want one of those things crawling up your penis or your anus."

"What?" Landers screamed. His eyes grew wide and his jaw dropped.

"I'm serious, soldier. Seen it before." Carson pointed to a black blob on Landers' calf.

Landers jumped then reached down to brush it off.

Carson grabbed his arm. "Don't touch it."

Landers froze.

"If you try to pull it off, you will tear your skin. Nasty wound, easily infected."

Revulsion charged Landers' voice and contorted his face. "Then how do I get this thing off me?"

"Two ways. Hold a cigarette lighter under it or squirt some insect repellent on it. Either way will cause it to release its grip and fall off."

Carson pulled a bottle of insect repellent from the camouflage band around his helmet, knelt and positioned the bottle over the swelling black blob.

"Watch this, soldiers."

Ricci and Hawk leaned in close.

Revulsion rose to panic in Landers' voice. "Hurry."

Carson looked at each of them, the bottle poised above the leech. "You need to be careful not to get the bug juice on the wound. That stings like hell." He squeezed out a drop of liquid and the inch-long leech writhed and shriveled. "Hah. Take that you blood sucker."

The leech dropped to the ground.

Carson looked up. "See how that works?"

Landers' jaw dropped and eyes widened again. The round, red sore oozed blood. He looked away. "Oh, God."

"Relax, Landers. You're not going to die. Leeches secrete an anti-coagulant that keeps your blood flowing, but it will stop. I'm going to put some antiseptic and a bandage on it." Carson sat back on his haunches and smiled. "Just like your momma used to do, soldier. Make sure you keep it clean to prevent infection."

"Clean?" Brandt snorted. "What the hell stays clean anywhere in this country, Doc?"

Carson laughed. "I know, sir. We just have to do our best."

After the leech lesson, Brandt and Ferguson discussed the route ahead. Brandt traced a path on the map with his finger. "It should be a straight shot over level ground to the base of this ridge. The slope looks more like a wall on the map. What do you think?"

"It won't be fun busting through this thick undergrowth in front of us, but then it should open up. We should be able to make good time. The climb will be tough, but that's nothing new. We should give the troops a rest on top before we start searching. We might find more than just signs of Charlie."

"Good idea. We should eat some lunch before we start the climb. Probably won't have time later. Anything else?"

Ferguson shook his head. "No."

"Let's brief the squad leaders."

Minutes later, the leadership team assembled. Brandt turned the map so the squad leaders could read it.

"We are here." Brandt tapped his grease pencil on the map. "We've got to get up there." He pointed up, away from the map, over the trees. "On top of that ridge. To get there, we'll have to go through this jungle in front of us. The land is flat for about four kilometers, but then we climb. And it's steep. We'll eat lunch before we start the climb. Once on top, we'll take a break, then follow the ridge and look for signs of a hospital. There's supposed to be one in this area."

"What about this jungle?" Ski asked. "We might walk right into one here."

Brandt shook his head. "I doubt it. It's too exposed, even if you can't see it from here. The wide, flat ground between the river and the jungle is room enough for a battalion to land choppers and attack straight at it."

Olszewski nodded thoughtfully. "Makes sense."

Brandt looked at Ferguson. "What do you think, sergeant?"

"I agree, sir. They like to put them in places that are harder to get to. Like narrow valleys that force us into small-unit advances and give them ambush sites. Crossfires. I expect we'll see some likely places coming off that ridge."

Ski persisted. "O.K., but what if we find one? We supposed to take on a whole base camp? A hospital is bound to be well guarded."

"No. We're just looking for anything that confirms the intel and narrows it down to a general location. If we can do that, Big 6 might send in a small recon team to observe movement. Maybe send in some ambushes to confirm, then launch a battalion-sized operation against it."

Ski nodded. "So we find something. Then what?"

"We hightail it to our extraction point and choppers take us back to base camp. Showers and real food for a change."

"Yeah." Ski rolled his eyes. "I heard that one before."

"O.K., 2nd Squad is on point today. I will be with them. I want to be near the point going through this jungle. Any questions?"

They shook their heads.

"Sergeant Ferguson, anything to add?"

"No, sir."

"Let's get moving."

As 2nd Squad breached the wall of vegetation guarding the jungle, Brandt could hear frequent shouts of "Wait a minute," followed by expletives of frustration. He smiled, pardoned the lapse in sound discipline, and blended into the file.

Grass and broad-leafed plants covered the ground, and skinny-trunked trees supported interlaced vines. All crowded the jungle fringe and competed for the precious valley sunlight. Brandt's irregular strides, serpentine route, and bobbing and weaving like a boxer all failed to keep him from the clutches of genus *Smilax*. The thorny Wait-a-Minute vine grabbed at his arms, legs, rifle, and equipment, causing himself to also break sound discipline.

Like walking through a spider web that won't break. Hard to believe this damn vine is in the lily family.

Brandt couldn't see the ground in such dense foliage and kept tripping on exposed roots.

Hate not being able to see where I put my feet. At least the roots aren't slithering.

Brandt looked up, shaded his eyes against sunlight, and checked their direction. He could only see peaks of mountains to the left and right and a glimpse of the ridge straight ahead. The jungle rose above terrain features as if he were walking into deep water. Brandt pulled his compass from his shirt pocket and checked the azimuth to the ridge, but he couldn't see far enough to pick out a straight path and replaced the compass as he looked ahead.

What did the Ranger School instructors say about dense vegetation? Balance left around a tree or bush and right around the next one to maintain compass heading.

Shafts of sunlight streamed through trees and glared off bright green leaves; deep shadows hung between them. As Brandt threaded his way through, it occurred to him that Ski just might be right. They could pop out of this thicket and bump into an NVA patrol headed for the valley. But he couldn't do anything about that. He needed to focus, to keep a sense of direction.

Another 50 meters, and Brandt no longer fought undergrowth. He could see where he was placing his feet. His stumbling gait flowed into purposeful strides. The dense jungle had opened up to reveal a tropical forest. The trees grew larger and were spaced farther apart. Bushes were scattered in between; their small leaves on sparse branches gathered the soft, filtered sunlight sifting in through the canopy of leaves and vines overhead. Brandt did a one-eighty as he walked. He was taken by an incredible variety of plant species and hundreds of shades of green, from pale pastels to almost black.

Brandt could no longer see the top of the ridge, but he could see about a hundred meters ahead. He pulled the compass, sighted along the azimuth, and focused on a tree with humped roots and multiple twisted trunks. He let out a deep breath. *Direction and distance much easier now. Better control of the platoon. Easier to spot Victor Charlie and maneuver.*

Two hundred meters past the tree, a small, shallow stream only a few feet wide splashed between moss-covered rocks. The light grew noticeably dimmer, the plants fewer and more widely spaced, and huge leaves attempted to gather the available light, the branches sprouting them supported by thicker trunks. Brandt looked up and visualized a second canopy over the forest. Taller trees successfully fought for sunlight above the first canopy. But that gave them fewer distinctive trees to use as guideposts. He checked the compass heading more often.

Brandt settled into a smooth rhythm, conserved energy, and cruised deeper into the rainforest. Eventually, the light grew even dimmer. A soft carpet of decayed leaves covered the ground, emanating musty smells. The air felt dank and humid. Hardly any plants grew here, the widely scattered tree trunks were huge, maybe 15 feet around, and there were no branches or leaves below the first canopy.

Fewer places for Charlie to hide.

He did another one-eighty and then spun around again.

But harder to spot him.

The Brandt looked up again. *Triple canopy.* It was eerie. There was no sense of sky above, no mountains visible, no landmarks in sight.

Damn. Wouldn't do any good to call in artillery or air support here. It would never reach the ground.

"Jenkins, tell the squads to halt in place. Let's eat lunch now. And tell the squad leaders and Sgt. Ferguson I want to talk to them."

The forest felt spacious, like a huge gymnasium. He checked his watch. 11:17. But it looked like dusk. He took out his Kodak camera, but the red light in the viewfinder blinked steadily—not enough light to take a picture.

Hart, Martinez, and Ferguson joined Brandt and Jenkins. Each found a spot on the ground and formed a semi-circle. Brandt waited for Olszewski to come in from point.

Ski strode into the group shaking his head. "This place is weird," he announced. "I don't like it." He shook his head as he sat down. "Spooky. Like there might be ghosts flying around."

Hart leaned toward Ski. "Boo."

Everyone laughed. Ski flipped him off.

"Yeah, well, I seen some weird shit in here, sir. A plant that looked like a funnel. Had black scum in the bottom of it and half a small lizard. The thing drooled when I looked down into it. Creeped me out. Then I saw a hollow tree. I mean the trunk looked like wooden chicken wire. Tell me that's normal."

Brandt smiled and nodded. "This is a triple-canopy rainforest."

"Not a jungle?" Martinez asked. "I hear people calling it a triple-canopy jungle."

"That's incorrect. Jungle refers to any place with dense, tangled vegetation. Like we busted our way through on the edge of the valley. We all say jungle because it's easier to call everything here a jungle."

Martinez nodded. "O.K."

Brandt continued. "A tropical rainforest can have one, two, or three canopies. You saw the differences on the way in here. As the light got dimmer, the vegetation changed. Right here, it's like there are three roofs over our heads. That's why it's so dark. Hardly any sunlight gets through."

"But what about all that weird stuff I saw?" Ski asked.

"The funnel is called a pitcher plant. Insects fly down into it to get nectar and get stuck in the fluid, which actually digests the insects. The lizard probably crawled down into the funnel to eat the insects and got stuck. The plant digests little animals too."

"Gross. But what about the tree?"

"Well, it's not a tree. It's a vine. It grows rapidly up a tree to the top so it can get to sunlight and completely surrounds the trunk and branches. It tightens and suffocates the tree. Down here, the tree decays fast and disappears. Because it has the structure of chicken wire, the vine is strong enough to support itself. It's called a strangler fig."

"O.K., but I saw something worse. A plant that looked like a mouth. Wide open, with fangs for teeth."

"That's a Venus flytrap. Eats bugs that fly into it. The jaws close, the fangs form a cage, and it secretes juice that digests the bug."

Hart jumped in, a smile on his face. "It eats meat?"

"Yeah," Brandt said slowly, wary of the look on Hart's face.

"Maybe Ski can feed it. He got stuck with Ham and Motherfuckers last resupply."

Brandt looked down at the ground, shaking his head. "How do you guys think of shit like that?"

Ferguson cleared his throat. "Actually," he said, "I seen a guy do that once. My last tour in Nam."

Hart, Martinez, Ski, and Jenkins stared at him, mouths open. Brandt snickered. They looked like Venus flytraps.

But Ferguson had that dead serious look of old on his face. "As a matter of fact, it was First Sergeant Klein." He nodded his head, looking at each of them, drawing it out. "We were together in the 101st then, somewhere in Kon Tum Province. A place just like this. He took out his P-38 and opened a can of Ham and Lima Beans." Ferguson pantomimed working the Army version of a field can opener. "We noticed one of those flytrap plants." He held up his hands in an exaggerated circle. "This big. Shaking and drooling. Well, First Sergeant Klein, being the kind and gentle soul you all know he is, spooned some into those wide-open jaws." Ferguson leaned forward, extending his arm. "Damn thing clamped down on it so fast, it bit his finger." Ferguson jerked his hand back and shook it as if stung.

Brandt put his hand up to his face and stifled a laugh, while the others were held in rapt attention.

Ferguson continued. "Once that thing got a taste of the shit they feed us, it gagged and spit it out. All over Sergeant Klein."

Brandt could no longer contain the laugh.

"That's impossible." Martinez sat back and shook his head. "No way."

The spell broken, the others laughed.

"No. It's true. It's true." Ferguson shook his head but chuckled through a smile that spread from ear to ear.

"Feel better, Ski?" Brandt asked.

"Well, I'm wondering what kind of nasty snakes are crawling around here. I don't like those things."

"You won't see any snakes crawling around on the ground. Not enough food down here."

"No shit? Finally some good news."

Brandt raised his arm and pointed overhead. "They're up there. In the canopy. Lots of food for them like tree frogs, birds, and lizards. Big spiders, too."

Ski looked up. "Aw shit. That's even worse. They could drop down on us."

Hart put a hand on Ski's shoulder. "Don't worry. They won't want to eat you. You got a natural repellant about you."

Before Ski could respond, Martinez leaned forward. "Sir, you never been in one of these places before. How do you know so much about it?"

"Well, my senior year in college I had a pretty good idea that I would be sent here, right?"

They all chuckled. Someone had found out he'd gone to a military college, and word had got around.

"So, I spent a lot of time in the library researching Nam, jungles, snakes. Stuff like that. Figured it would come in handy. But enough of the biology lesson. I figure we're close to the base of the ridge and we'll be climbing out soon. Like the sound of that, Ski?"

"Sounds good to me."

"Well, we need to be careful as we climb out." Brandt paused for emphasis.

Brandt looked at Ferguson. "Sergeant, you want to tell them?"

Ferguson smiled. "Gentlemen, you remember all the nasty things the lieutenant told you about crawling around in those canopies overhead?"

They all nodded.

"Well, we're going to climb through them as we go up the ridge."

★ ★ ★

After lunch, Brandt took his first gradual uphill steps. He walked with Ski in the lead element of the platoon, again in single file, anticipating rainforest canopies. They reached the first ceiling, only 15 feet above the forest floor, quickly, and they popped through a thin layer of broad leaves, branches, and vines. Tree frogs hopped away; spiders and insects scurried.

A longer, steeper uphill climb brought them to the second canopy, much denser and deeper than the first. The point man hacked a tunnel through small leaves, branches, and tangled vines. After they passed through, Brandt tapped Ski on the arm and pointed down to the surface of the canopy.

"Now the roof looks like a floor. Like you could walk across it. Not that I'd want to." Brandt pointed to his right. "Look." A thick-bodied, bright green snake with thin, widely spaced yellow bands attempted to move away from them.

Ski jumped back.

"Don't worry. He can't bite you now. In fact, he's having a difficult time trying to get away from us. Look closer."

Ski leaned forward but just a little bit. The thick body flopped from side to side and the tail whipped up and down as the snake struggled to retreat, anchored by the large rodent half-swallowed in its unhinged, distended jaws.

"Damn." Ski shook his head. "Never seen anything like that before. Is it poisonous?"

"Yeah. It's a Wagler's Pit Viper."

"Let's get out of here." Ski climbed with renewed motivation.

Brandt followed him up a longer, steeper slope. He trudged up three steps and slid back one, breathing labored and heart rate increased. The dim light gradually brightened, and they emerged into sunlight.

Brandt stopped and took deep breaths. His eyes widened. The emergent layer, the top of the rainforest. Broad-leafed trees and evergreens over 200 feet tall broke through the canopies, spread their limbs under blue sky and ruled the rainforest. Birds flew around him, even below him. A vista of the valley spread into the distance.

Amazing. Like flying with the birds. This is what it must have been like when Jack climbed the beanstalk.

Brandt continued the climb and left the triple-canopy rainforest far below, the fascinating biology experience driven from his thoughts by arduous exertion. Brandt leaned into the steep slope, a wall of short, parched grass, and his world contracted into the ground before him. The sun beat down, and sweat drenched his fatigues. He gasped for air between each step. He trudged three steps up, then slid two steps back. Three steps up; two steps back. Three steps up; two steps back. Again and again.

Brandt paused and took several deep breaths.

I feel like a lizard clinging to a wall. Exposed to predators; no cover, no concealment. No control over my platoon; impossible to maneuver.

He looked up.

Not much further. Get your butt moving, Ranger.

He resumed the plodding pace, dug the inside edges of his boots into the dirt, fought gravity, and resisted the downward slide, driven upward by single-minded determination.

He paused again. His legs quivered with fatigue, the weight of the rucksack pulling him away from the slope. As he gathered the energy to take another step, a large hand appeared in front of his face. He looked up. Ski smiled. Brandt took the hand and felt himself hoisted over the crest.

Ski's smile spread wider. "Welcome back from the underworld, sir."

Brandt gulped enough air to say, "Thanks."

During the rest break, Brandt conferred with Ferguson. "This ridge is like the edge of a serrated knife. Not wide enough to maneuver. I guess we walk on the trail."

"Yes, sir. I already told the squad leaders to be extra careful. We're in the middle of nowhere, but look at this trail. Two feet wide. No grass growing on it."

Jenkins joined them. "Ski reported another trail ahead. Comes up the left side of this ridge. His point man found some punji stakes around the trail junction."

Ferguson lifted his helmet and wiped sweat. "Well, lieutenant. That confirms it. Charlie uses this trail and he doesn't want anybody snooping around up here."

"Which is exactly why we're here, sergeant. Let's get moving. I'll be in the center of the file now. You bring up the rear, as usual."

After about 80 meters, Brandt inspected the trail intersection. Dry, dying grass crowded each side, and long thin blades hung over the edge of the trails, perfect camouflage for the tan, sharpened bamboo stakes.

Brandt turned to Jenkins. "Difficult to see. Point man's got a sharp eye."

"Good thing for us, sir. They look nasty."

Brandt reported the discovery and his current location to Captain Parker. He resumed the pace, and the ridge gradually widened.

An easy walk. And quiet. No city noise. No highway traffic. Like a hike through a National Park. Except for the punji stakes.

Jenkins approached. "Ski reports that another trail comes in from the right, up from the valley. They found some bloody bandages in the weeds off to the side of the trail."

"Well, Charlie screwed up. Didn't clean up very well. Call Bravo and report that."

Brandt took the platoon radio. "November 5, did you monitor that report from the point?"

"Affirmative," Ferguson responded. "Let's stay sharp. Sounds like they've been here recently."

The ridge curved to the right, and Brandt saw a distant mountain directly ahead. He pulled his compass and sighted on it.

O.K. The trail should be heading down soon. Decision time coming up.

Brandt continued the pace with deliberately placed steps, scanned his surroundings while trying not to drift off the trail. Just the opposite of standard procedure. Another kilometer and the ridge descended gradually; forward momentum increased, and Brandt leaned back slightly.

"Sir." Jenkins hung the radio handset on a web-gear D-ring. "Point reports that the ridge flattens out, widens, and splits into two fingers; three trails heading down. Lots of trees. Ski's waiting there."

"O.K. Call the squad leaders and tell them we'll set up a perimeter there and decide what to do."

★ ★ ★

Brandt and Ferguson stood with Olszewski in the center of a wide, flat clearing. Skinny-trunked trees about 15 feet tall formed an airy umbrella overhead, a welcome relief from the sun. As 1st and 3rd squads searched the area, Ski pointed to the trail on the right.

"That one looks like the shortest way back into the main valley we came out of. It drops down quick, but it's not steep. Kind of arcs down, like a pitcher throwing a sinker ball."

A half-turn and he pointed to the trail in the middle. "That one has a gradual slope. Looks like it runs a long way before reaching the valley. Between them is solid jungle. No way you could walk into it."

He pointed to the far left side of the perimeter. "That trail heads down the side of this ridge, into a saddle, and over to a hill, away from the main valley. Didn't go down far. It's steep. Afraid I might slide all the way down on my ass."

Brandt gave Ski a thumbs-up. "Good briefing. We'll wait until the search is done, then decide which way to go." He paused. "By the way, who's on point today?"

"Allison." Ski pointed. A soldier sat under a tree a few yards away, swigging water from his canteen. "I told him to take a break. He's been busting his butt all day."

A MATTER OF SEMANTICS

Brandt walked over to him, and Allison clambered to his feet, his flushed face subsiding to normal color.

"Great job on point today, Allison. The grass hid those punji stakes. Very difficult to see them. You probably saved somebody from a nasty leg wound."

Allison's slumped shoulders straightened, a smile spread across his face. "Thank you, sir."

"It's a tough job. Keep up the good work."

Brandt noticed Ferguson writing in his notebook.

"Lieutenant." Martinez called for them to join him. "We found a pile of sticks about six feet long." He led them to a clump of bushes and pushed aside grass with the muzzle of his M-16.

Brandt looked down at the stout tree limbs trimmed of foliage and cut to equal lengths. He looked at Ferguson. "What do you make of these?"

"Well, I seen these before," Ferguson said. "Charlie uses them to make stretchers."

"So a hospital is near?"

"Sure seems like it, but which way? It could be in any one of these small valleys around the ridge and the fingers coming off this spot."

Brandt took the radio handset from Jenkins, called Captain Parker, and reported their location and additional discovery.

"Sounds like you confirmed the likelihood of a hospital in that area."

"Affirmative. But exactly where is the question. This spot is like the hub of a wheel. The fingers and trails coming into it are like spokes on a wheel. Several small valleys between."

"That's not your job. Let me know when you head to the extraction point. Good work, November 6."

Brandt studied his map, walked to the head of each trail, and pondered his choices. A scowl formed on his face. He put the map away and walked down the trail to the right. He paused about 30 meters down, searched, and listened. He repeated the procedure on the middle trail.

Gentle slopes and lots of vegetation, just like Ski said.

Then he walked to the left trail, peered over the edge, and stepped down gingerly, but only about five meters. He perched precariously and worked to maintain his balance. The almost vertical drop smoothed into a saddle, then back up to a flat, round hilltop, lower in elevation. Brandt could see, through sparse trees and vegetation, clear views all around. The scowl returned to his face.

"Don't like this place," Brandt muttered. He shook his head. "But why? A quiet, peaceful-looking valley. Just like all the rest."

The little voice in his head said "Looks can be deceiving. How do you feel?"

Brandt gazed up and down the valley on both sides of the saddle, around the hilltop, and then focused on the trail through the saddle.

Again, he muttered, "It's peaceful, but it's an unsettled peace. Not pastoral. Not picturesque. Somehow, an ominous scene."

Brandt returned to his command post. They all had concerned, expectant looks. "We're going down the trail to the right. It goes directly down into the main valley we climbed out of. It's the quickest route to our extraction point."

He extended his hand and Jenkins gave him the handset.

"Bravo 6, November 6. Over."

"Bravo 6. Over."

"Proceeding from my current location to planned extraction point. Be there in about one hour."

"I copy one hour to extraction point. Will notify the lift ships. Six out."

Brandt looked back over his shoulder at the steep trail and the saddle. "Let's get out of here."

About 200 meters down the trail, Brandt heard shots behind him, the distinctive sound of an AK-47. He pulled the rucksack quick release cord and hit the ground facing uphill. He bounced up immediately and scanned the trail, but the slope and thick vegetation truncated his view. Jenkins appeared beside him.

"Hart says a gook on the trail fired at them and then ran. No one got hit. They're chasing him."

Brandt picked up his rucksack. "O.K. Let's follow. Tell the other squads."

About 50 meters up the trail, Jenkins called to Brandt, "Sir, Hart reported that the guy just disappeared."

"Sniper harassment. Tell the squad leaders we're heading back down."

As soon as they headed down again, Brandt heard the AK-47. This time Brandt yelled at Jenkins, "We're going after him. Tell the squad leaders."

A hundred meters up the trail, Hart reported no casualties and the sniper had disappeared again.

A sniper that can't shoot straight? Firing from the middle of a trail? Doesn't make sense.

"Forget him. We need to get to the extraction point. Jenkins, tell the squad leaders. We're going down."

Immediately after they started down, Brandt heard shots again.

"Damn it. We're going to get that son of a bitch this time."

Brandt charged up the trail and found Hart at the trail intersection, hands on hips, jaw clenched, eyes narrowed. Ferguson joined them.

"The little fucker disappeared again." Hart pointed to the steep trail on the left. "Down that trail."

"O.K.," Brandt said. "Tell me what you saw."

"We hear a shot behind us and hit the ground. One guy is standing on the trail, turns and runs like hell. We don't have time to take a well-aimed shot, so we chase but can't find him. As soon as we head back down, he shoots again. Same thing over and over. He can't shoot for shit, because he hasn't hit anybody yet."

Brandt shook his head. "This doesn't make sense. Why would they pick such a poor shot as a sniper?"

"Right," Ferguson said. "Know what I think, lieutenant?"

Brandt threw his hands up. "Hell, yes. I want to know what you think."

Ferguson smiled. "Well, I don't think he's trying to hit anybody. I think he's trying to get us to chase him. Which we are."

"Shit. I think you're right."

"That's what it feels like to me," Hart agreed.

"Last you saw of him, he went down that trail?" Brandt pointed.

"Right."

"Let's take a good look at that saddle down there."

Brandt, Ferguson, and Hart crawled to the edge of the ridge under some bushes, just to the side of the steep trail. Jenkins followed.

Brandt focused his binoculars on the saddle, spoke softly, and described the scene. "The short, dry grass up here turns into bushes on both sides of the trail where the trail levels off and widens into the saddle. Looks wide and long enough to set up an ambush there. Then the trail rises to the hilltop. Lots of widely spaced trees and dry grass on the hilltop, just like here."

Brandt handed the binoculars to Ferguson. "Take a look."

Ferguson studied the terrain for several minutes. "Damn," he said. "Those bushes in the saddle are big, but lots of space between the branches. Small, football shaped leaves. I think I see some reflections down there. Like sunlight off metal. The sun's hitting it just right." He passed the binoculars back to Brandt. "Check the left side of the saddle."

"You're right. They've set up an ambush. Good call, sergeant. Jenkins, get Martinez and Ski up here."

"Take another look," Ferguson said. "At the trail going up to the hilltop. About halfway up. I saw a small bush broken, pointing downhill. Like maybe somebody slipped on his ass going down and grabbed it to stop himself."

Brandt found the spot. "I think you're right. That means they came from that direction. If there's a hospital on the other side of that hill, the ambush is probably a standing protective position. Early warning for the hospital."

They crawled back to the center of the perimeter, and Brandt briefed Martinez and Ski.

"So, they probably spotted me when I did my recon of the trails." Brandt looked at Hart. "Then sent that," Brandt paused and looked at Hart, "little shit to lure us down into the ambush."

Hart chuckled. "Right."

"But thanks to Sergeant Ferguson, we're not falling for it."

"So, what are we going to do?" Ski asked.

"Well, it's obvious we can't maneuver to get behind them. They know how to use terrain."

"Can we call in artillery?" Ski suggested.

"No." Brandt shook his head. "We're out of artillery range, but we might get some air support. There's supposed to be a Forward Air Controller in the area."

"If we get that," Ferguson said, "We need to be ready to cover their exit. They might head up to the hilltop when they see aircraft coming."

"Right." Brandt looked at Hart. "Your squad's overlooking the saddle. Here's your chance to get even with that little shit."

"I'm ready for it. I'll put my best shots lined up on that trail."

Brandt spread his map on the ground and called the Forward Air Controller somewhere overhead in a Piper Cub. "Bird Dog, I have enemy troops on the ground. Hidden in bushes, set up for an ambush. Steep, narrow valleys here. It's a tight shot in a saddle." He gave the enemy grid coordinates in the clear.

"You're a lucky man, November 6. I got just what you need only minutes away. A light fire team's been prowling the area like a hungry tiger." After a brief silence, Bird Dog said, "Two Huey gunships are headed in your direction."

"Roger that, Bird Dog. Thanks."

"Hawk 36 will be coming up on your frequency shortly. Good luck, November 6. Bird Dog out."

"Damn," Ski said. "That's the first time we've gotten air support that quick."

"Yeah," Brandt said. "I guess Big 6 wants that hospital."

Ferguson snorted. "I guess Big 6 feels bad about sending us beyond artillery support." Brandt put his map away and looked at each man. "Let's get ready to kick some ass."

Brandt again crawled to the edge, Ferguson and Hart on one side, Jenkins on the other. "Sir, Bravo 6."

"I heard your request for air support. What is your situation? Over."

"Sniper harassment. He tried to lead us into an ambush, but we spotted them. I am at my previous location. A little delay in getting to the extraction point. Over."

"Roger that. Keep me informed. Six out."

This time Brandt kept the handset, eyes focused on the sky. Two dark spots appeared in the distance and he heard, "November 6, this is Hawk 36. Hawk 32 and I have your target in sight. We've got miniguns and rockets hot and ready. Pop smoke your location."

Ferguson had a purple smoke grenade ready and placed it at the top of the steep trail.

The dark spots in the sky grew larger, resolved into helicopter silhouettes, and dove into the valley.

The pilot said "I identify grape smoke."

"That's affirmative," Brandt responded. "Target is directly down the trail from the smoke. In the bushes in the saddle."

"Got them in my sights. Here we come."

Rotor blades pounded the air, and engine roar reverberated.

Hart raised his arm and pointed. "Look," he shouted. Two enemy soldiers ran up the far side of the trail.

Two M-16 rifles fired. The two enemy soldiers dropped, hit face first and slid down and off the trail.

A strange sound rose above rotor blades. Like a loud, continuing fart. The minigun's six rotating barrels spewed 7.62 mm bullets at 4,000 rounds per minute. Small clouds of dust mushroomed on the slope leading up to the saddle then moved over the trail. Dirt kicked up into the air from every square foot of the saddle.

Immediately after the fart ended, another sound rose above the rotor blades. A loud whooshing followed multiple explosions. A barrage of rockets mowed down grass and bushes as if a giant scythe had cut a swath across the saddle.

The lead helicopter pulled up into a steep climb and turned sharply. The second helicopter flew in and raked the saddle, miniguns and rockets blazing, a repeat performance of aerial gunnery.

No one cheered. No one cracked a joke. Silence settled over the saddle. Rocket craters punctured bare ground, and scattered remnants of bushes and piles of branches partially hid broken bodies.

The radio transmission broke the spell. "That do the job for you, November 6?"

"Nice shooting, Hawk 36. You got 'em. Nothing's moving down there."

"Hawk 36 RTB to reload. Out."

Brandt watched until the helicopters flew out of sight on a Return To Base for more ammunition.

"That, gentlemen," Brandt said, "is some damn fine close-air support. What would we do without them?"

The chorus replied, "Airborne, sir."

They pulled back from the scene of devastation. Ferguson said to Brandt, "We shouldn't hang around here very long. Those runners we dropped on the trail were headed over that hilltop. Probably to a base camp on the other side. Charlie had to hear those gunships doing their work. Bound to send troops over to check out what happened. Especially after those guys don't report in."

"Right," Brandt agreed. "If there's a hospital around here, they must have a lot of troops guarding it."

Brandt took the handset from Jenkins and reported to Captain Parker.

"We dropped two enemy soldiers with small arms, and the gunships cleared the saddle with miniguns and rockets. Estimated eight enemy KIA. On our way to planned extraction route."

"Estimated?" Brandt held the radio receiver away from his ear. "I don't want estimates on body count. Get down there and confirm that number."

Everyone within several feet could hear Captain Parker.

"That's a dangerous spot, 6. There must be a lot of enemy troops in the area. We could get caught down there."

"November 6, when I give you an order, I don't want a discussion. I want an accurate body count to turn in. Get it now, and get it fast. Six out."

The three squad leaders joined Brandt and Ferguson. Their eyes bored into Brandt. Ferguson remained silent, his face expressionless, eyes expectant. Some of the men nearby craned their necks to look.

Brandt took a deep breath. "Everyone get back to your positions. I'll let you know what the plan is."

Brandt crawled back to the edge overlooking the ambush site, checked his watch, pulled his binoculars, and scanned the saddle.

"Two that ran, six bodies on the ground," he enumerated. "But three hanging over the edge. Could be more further down the slope blown off by rockets. Some could be hidden by the remaining bushes."

Brandt shifted position and peered again into the bushes. "Hard to tell."

He pulled back from the edge, replaced the binoculars, and rubbed his chin.

No more than 12 men could fit in that saddle for an ambush. Eight? Twelve? What's the difference?

Brandt shook his head and muttered. "Charlie's going to check out what happened, and we'd get caught down there. So how do I report this?"

The little voice said, "What are your Standing Orders, Ranger."

"Well, Number 4 says that you can lie all you please when you tell other folks about the Rangers, but don't never lie to another Ranger or an officer. But Number 5 says don't never take a chance you don't have to."

Don't lie. Don't take unnecessary chances.

An image formed in Brandt's mind. He stood on the sideline after a blown third-down play; the fullback limped off the field, and the punter trotted onto the field. The voice of his football coach drifted in.

"Brandt, the coach calls the plays from the sideline, but when you walk up to the line of scrimmage and see the defense, you have to make the call. The men in front of you depend on your decision."

Brandt crawled back from the edge and sat near Jenkins. He checked his watch again, then spread his map on the ground and studied it. He took a sip of water from his canteen.

Duty. Honor. Loyalty.

Brandt stared at the ground, rubbed the back of his neck, and looked up.

The men in front of me.

"Jenkins, we need to get to the extraction point and get down there fast. Get Ski and Ferguson."

Jenkins rose to one knee and shouldered the radio.

Brandt raised a hand. "And leave the radio. You've been humping that thing all day. Take a break."

"Don't take the radio?" Jenkins hesitated. "Uh, well, O.K., sir." He shrugged off the PRC-25 and jogged away.

Brandt picked up the handset, brought it half way up to his ear and paused.

Send my men down there for the difference between eight and 12?

He raised his chin, pulled his shoulders back.

No way.

He depressed the push-to-talk button.

"Bravo 6, November 6. Over."

"Bravo 6. Over."

"I report 12 confirmed enemy KIA. Proceeding on planned route to extraction point. ETA, one hour. Over."

"I copy 12 confirmed enemy KIA. Nice job, November 6. I will notify the choppers. Let me know when you get to the extraction point. Six out."

Brandt lowered the handset but stopped at his shoulder. He breathed heavily, nostrils flaring. "Shit." The expletive came out as a hiss.

He threw the handset at a tree. The coiled cord stretched to its limit before the handset hit the trunk and snapped back, glanced off the radio and up toward his face. He twisted in time to avoid it. As it bounced and settled on the ground, Brandt sensed a presence and looked up. Ferguson, Ski, and Jenkins stared at him, frozen in mid-stride. He waved them over.

"I just reported to Bravo. Ski, you're still on point. We're going to have to move fast, but be careful, too."

"No problem, sir."

"Sergeant Ferguson, make sure the rear guard keeps up with the pace so we don't get strung out. But you'll also have to use those eyes you have in the back of your head. No telling what might come after us this time."

"You got it, lieutenant."

"Any questions?"

They shook their heads.

Brandt folded his map, stood, and slid it into his pocket.

"O.K. Let's get the fuck out of this place."

Ski and Jenkins hustled to line up on the trail. Ferguson hesitated in mid-turn, about to say something. His eyes searched Brandt's. A long moment passed. Then Ferguson raised his hand to his helmet brim, tipped it to Brandt, and turned and jogged away.

Brandt blended into the file, charged down the trail, and picked up the pace, faster than Quick March, almost a Double Time. He took one last glance over his shoulder, the clearing eclipsed by the crest.

A day's work completed. An hour to extraction and a long chopper ride.

As he descended, walls of vegetation closing in, Brandt pondered his debriefing—across a table from Big 6, the S-3, and Captain Parker.

Yeah, elaborate on the intelligence we developed, detail about terrain, and the likelihood of a hospital location. And then look them in the eye to confirm 12 enemy soldiers KIA.

CHAPTER 15

★ ★ ★

Brandt stood in the back corner of the battalion Tactical Operations Center against a wall of green plastic sandbags. All battalion officers present, standing room only for lieutenants. In the dank bunker interior, the wall felt cool, a rare sensation in Vietnam. Major Owens, the S-3, had just finished an operations order and opened the briefing for questions.

Brandt leaned to his left and whispered to Bob McKnight. "What the hell is going on? I can't remember an operation this size. All four rifle companies in a coordinated helicopter attack? There isn't an enemy force in that area large enough to justify a battalion-size Combat Assault. Doesn't make sense, Bob."

McKnight smiled from ear to ear. "Not hard to figure out, Bill. Alexander is getting short here. For a lieutenant colonel, battalion command is a make-or-break assignment."

Brandt shrugged. "So?"

"Think about it. Alexander's been here almost six months. He'll be rotating to a staff job at Corps level, maybe even Saigon. Up there, he'll be the one sent out for coffee. Career officers in command positions need to get their tickets punched if they have any hope of making general. And so far, this has been a nothing tour for him. No big battles with him flying overhead maneuvering rifle companies. No great victories. No medals."

Brandt nodded. "So this is a safe way to rack up some brownie points. He gets recognition, but he doesn't have to put his ass on the line."

A MATTER OF SEMANTICS

"Now you're catching on," McKnight said. "After this is over, he and Parker can put each other in for medals. Bronze Star for a captain, Silver Star for a lieutenant colonel. Maybe even a decoration from the Vietnamese."

Brandt groaned.

McKnight flashed that devilish smile of his and leaned closer to Brandt. "I mean, what do you think the Brigade Commander's going to write on Lieutenant Colonel Dalton Alexander's Efficiency Report? What's the only thing that got him the general's attention so far? A near war crime on a friendly village. Thanks to you, Brandt."

Brandt raised his right hand to chest level, elbowed McKnight in the ribs, and flipped him the bird.

After a brief silence, Owens said, "If there are no more questions, that concludes my briefing." He gestured to Alexander. "Colonel." Owens stepped aside.

Lieutenant Colonel Alexander marched to the map display. "Gentlemen." Alexander cleared his throat. "This is a great opportunity to bring credit upon yourselves, the Second Battalion, 503rd Airborne Infantry, and the United States Army. What you do here will become history. I challenge you to live up to the tradition of the paratroopers gone before you. Brave men like the soldiers of the First Battalion, 504th Airborne Infantry, whose actions in Italy during World War II inspired a German commander to write in his diary, 'I am surrounded by devils in baggy pants.'" He paused and scanned the room. "Strike a blow that will change the course of the war."

Alexander lowered his head as if in prayer. A moment later he looked up, raised his right fist high. "Sky Soldiers, give 'em hell. Good hunting, men."

Officers stood and shuffled toward the doorway bottleneck and chattered excitedly. While they waited for room to move, Brandt said to McKnight, "At least nobody will get wasted in this operation. I can live with that."

Brandt inched forward, followed the press.

"Lieutenant Brandt." Alexander's tone was magnanimous. "May I have a word with you?"

May I?

Brandt squeezed between the man in front of him and McKnight. Brandt jumped. McKnight had goosed him. He flashed McKnight a dirty look as he walked toward Alexander.

Brandt stood at attention. "Yes, sir?"

Alexander put his arm around Brandt's shoulders and led him aside.

What the—?

Brandt glanced over his shoulder. McKnight shrugged, gave the victory sign, and darted out.

"Lieutenant, I've directed Captain Parker to give you a very important role in this operation." He leaned in close and spoke conspiratorially. "TV networks are interested in filming this attack. I will be coming in on the lead chopper with the rest of Bravo Company. I want you to be on the ground to secure the LZ."

Uh oh.

He pulled back, eyes narrowed, but said, "Yes, sir."

Alexander nodded. "Good." He moved to the map board. "Intelligence informs me that this village," he jabbed a pudgy finger into a red circle on the map, "is a VC headquarters and likely reinforced with North Vietnamese Army regulars. I want you to have your platoon lay down a base of fire as we disembark the helicopters." He paused and scrutinized Brandt. "Any questions?"

Brandt pulled back a half-step. "Sir, I went through that village last week."

Alexander cut him off. "Precisely why I want you to secure a possible hot LZ, lieutenant."

"But sir, that village. There's nothing there. We searched the root cellars. Kids climbed trees to pick coconuts for us. My medic treated sick people. The *mamasan* even told us not to follow a certain trail out of the village."

Alexander's face glowed crimson. His eyes narrowed. He jabbed a fat, crooked finger in Brandt's face. "Goddammit, lieutenant. I don't remember you having any compunctions about firing artillery into friendly villages. Call in a fucking airburst if it makes you feel any better. That area is at the end of a major spur off the Ho Chi Minh Trail. Enemy patrols are moving through there all the time. You've ambushed a few yourself. Intel says a VC headquarters is out there somewhere. That's why this village is in a Free Fire Zone. You can shoot anything that moves. This operation is the beginning of a big push toward that hospital *you* located."

Alexander paused in his tirade and took a few deep breaths.

In a more controlled voice, he continued. "Not you, nor any fucking *mamasan*, is going to screw this up for me. When those choppers land, I want your machine guns blazing. Do you understand that, lieutenant?"

Alexander's nostrils flared. He leaned into Brandt. "Brandt," he said in a low, deliberate voice. "You've stepped in deep shit more than once. You've got a chance to redeem yourself now. I haven't written your Efficiency Report yet."

Brandt stepped back again.

Just keep your mouth shut and get out of here.

Brandt snapped to attention and saluted.

Alexander smiled and returned the salute. "I'm counting on you, lieutenant. Dismissed."

Brandt bolted out of the TOC, squinted against the sunlight, searched left and right, spotted a low sandbag wall alongside the mess tent, and ran toward it. He sat hunched over, arms on his knees, and stared at the red, parched dirt.

What's happening here? What am I being ordered to do? What are my choices?

Thoughts and feelings swirled, but answers remained elusive. He looked up and around the scattered tents, at the sky and the distant mountains of the Central Highlands. Still no answers.

Brandt looked down again. He remembered something Sergeant Williams had said to him. "Lieutenant, this is the Army. You got no choice."

"Yeah. The Army answer," he muttered. "That's why the 600 rode into the valley of death."

He shook his head.

This isn't helping. What am I looking at here? A direct order in combat. A village I know is clear of the enemy. Is it a lawful order? Who decides that? Me? Officers on a court-martial board?

He closed his eyes and rubbed his forehead.

Call in a fucking air burst. Yeah, I did that. And I could have been court-martialed for it. But can I tell my men to do this and place them in jeopardy?

He let out a deep sigh.

Alexander said this is a chance to redeem myself. If I do this, I'll get a good Efficiency Report. He'll probably put me in for a medal. Things a career officer needs.

He looked up at the sound of voices. Soldiers walking to the mess hall for the midday meal. Brandt hopped off the wall and started walking, away from people and out of the battalion area, aimlessly, pondering, eyes following the ruts in the dirt road.

"Good afternoon, Bill."

Brandt started.

Lt. Col. Everett smiled. "Lost in thought?"

"Not just in thought, sir. Do you have a minute?"

"Sure." Everett gestured toward his office door.

Brandt sat in the folding chair, eyes downcast. Everett moved his chair from behind his desk to the left of it, sat with his right arm resting on the desk, and crossed his legs.

"So, lost in more than just thought?"

Brandt looked up and nodded.

"Well, what do you do when you're temporarily disoriented in the field?"

"Use a map and compass to find the right direction to go."

Everett shrugged and spread his arms wide, palms up.

"I don't seem to have a map for this terrain, sir."

Everett raised his eyebrows.

"Sir, can I ask you some hypothetical questions?"

"Sure."

"Say an officer is given an order and then he has to give an order. But he's not sure it's the right thing to do. He knows the mission comes first. It's his duty. A commander expects loyalty. But does loyalty also go down the chain of command?"

Everett maintained a steady gaze and waited silently.

"What if the order places his men in jeopardy? Can they expect loyalty from him?"

"Bill, you are describing some very difficult terrain, and you're right, there isn't a map for it. Your hypothetical officer is trying to decide if the order is lawful or unlawful."

"I know about Nuremberg, of course. Leaders of a defeated country just following orders didn't work. But a junior officer in combat? Never had any classes about that. How does he decide what to do? Actually, who decides? Him? His commander? A court-martial board?"

"You may not have a map, but you do have a compass, a moral compass. You are wrestling with some deep concepts. As a good soldier, you've focused on duty and loyalty, but they are only part of a hierarchy.

At the top rests ethics, your set of moral principles that helps you decide between good and bad."

"Yeah, but we grow up learning that killing is wrong. Our country, our church tell us that. Here, they tell us it's O.K. That's like holding a compass next to my rifle. The compass doesn't work. The needle keeps bouncing back and forth."

"What did you do when you got caught in an ambush?"

"Fought my way out."

"And how did you feel afterward?"

"I felt good. I survived."

"And you had to kill to do it. Self-defense, survival, underlies all you've been taught. There's no conflict." Everett smiled. "So don't hold your compass next to your rifle."

Brandt chuckled. "O.K., sir. What's the rest of the hierarchy?"

"Below ethics is loyalty. Most people think it means allegiance to a country or a superior, but it can also refer to a group or a cause. So yes, loyalty can, and should, go both up and down. Duty arises from your position in the chain of command, an obligation to your superiors to carry out tasks and missions. And even though it is the first thing that comes to your mind, it is number three."

"But Robert E. Lee said that duty is the sublimest word in our language."

"True, but back to your hypothetical question. Your officer is trying to decide what his duty is in a particular situation. He might do well to consider that Abraham Lincoln said we should dare to do our duty as we understand it."

Brandt cocked his head. "Never heard that one, sir. It kind of muddies the water."

"Actually, it means that the water is deeper than you think."

Brandt let out a deep sigh.

"I know you live by an honor code, Bill. However, honesty is fourth on the list. Your hypothetical officer needs to answer his questions within the structure of this hierarchy."

Brandt nodded thoughtfully. "But I still don't have a map."

"You didn't always have a map in Ranger School, did you?"

"No. Sometimes we had to use a compass with dead reckoning on terrain features."

"Well, there are some salient terrain features here. You're looking at a saddle. On one side is a mountain of military tradition of obeying orders without question and placing duty above all else. On the other side is a mountain of legal history confirming that a soldier has an obligation not to obey an unlawful order. Between the peaks is the low, connecting ridge, the seat of the saddle."

"So, I climb a mountain or take the easy path through the seat of the saddle?"

"In the field, do you usually take your platoon through the seat of a saddle?"

"No, sir. It's a likely place for an ambush from the high ground on both sides, or it could be filled with booby traps."

"Same thing here."

"So it all rests on the lowest ranking officer?"

"Bill, war is planned and executed by good and bad men on both sides. But every plan unfolds into reality when opposing forces meet. It's like looking into a kaleidoscope. You see the intricate design of the plan, the way it's supposed to happen. But with the first move to execute the plan, when you take your first step outside the perimeter, when you give your men the order to march into battle, you turn the kaleidoscope cylinder. What happens? All the pieces shift position. This is a platoon leader's war. You are the man turning the cylinder of a commander's kaleidoscope. You make the call on the ground based on what the enemy is doing. Combat operations are messy affairs. Noise. Confusion. Errant artillery rounds." Everett paused. "Sometimes radios don't work when you need them the most. You've experienced it."

"Yeah. I sure have."

"And that's why the Army emphasizes duty and mission."

"O.K., sir. That helps a lot."

"Bill, when you ask yourself these questions, you have to consider short-term versus long-term consequences. I've followed you enough here to know that you're a good soldier. Among the best. You've got a career ahead of you."

"Thank you, sir."

"You know, I've asked myself those same hypothetical questions, and I can still live with my answers." Everett paused. "But maybe that's why I'm not a general."

"Well, I think I've taken enough of your time, sir. Thank you."

"My door is always open to you."

Brandt stood and headed to the door.

"By the way, Bill."

Brandt stopped, hand on the door handle.

"On a lighter note, how's your family? Heard from them lately?"

"I got a letter a couple of days ago. Everyone is well, but my father's a little concerned about my youngest brother. Seems he's showing signs of some leadership ability."

Everett raised his eyebrows. "Why concern?"

"Well, he and some of his friends found some snakes in the woods near their house. They elected him president of their snake club."

Everett laughed. "Sounds like Ranger material to me."

"Yes, sir. And how about your family?"

"Everyone is fine," Everett said, smiling.

"Glad to hear it," Brandt said as he stepped toward the door.

"Bill." Everett's voice held Brandt again.

Brandt paused, half-turned, hand on the door. Everett's smile dissolved into a pensive look, as if making a decision.

"I just got a letter, too."

Brandt returned to the chair.

"My son got into a scrape with the law for not pulling over to get out of the way of a police car. Claimed he didn't hear the siren. He felt strongly about it because he was driving a Mustang convertible, top down. He talked to my brother, an attorney, about it and they took it to court. My brother had the patrol car inspected. Turned out the siren wasn't functioning. The judge said that if he didn't hear a siren, he didn't disobey the law."

"Glad to hear it, sir."

An inscrutable look veiled Everett's face. "Something you might think about, Bill."

★ ★ ★

Brandt followed his men up the tailgate of the Chinook and walked down the center of the huge chopper counting heads. He returned to the tail, stood by the only open seat, and glanced up and down the two rows of soldiers on either side of the helicopter.

They've done everything I've asked of them, and more. Because they trust me.

When we land, they'll charge out of this chopper into what? A pastoral valley and an easy hike through the hills? Or a landing zone filled with booby traps? A hot LZ with small arms and automatic weapons blazing? We never know. But is today different? They'll go because I gave the order. Like so many times before.

Brandt felt a tap on his left thigh and looked down.

Ski yanked on his pant leg. "Sit down, sir. Look at the crew chief. The bus driver wants to go."

The crew chief raised his arm high and moved his hand in a circular motion, and the twin rotor blades rumbled to life. Brandt squatted and plopped into the cotton-strap webbing that passed for seats in Army aircraft. There was no graceful way to do that.

"Thanks," he said, glancing at Ski.

A big smile spread across Ski's face. "Just doing my job, sir."

How many times have I heard that? And is it his job to repeat my order to attack that village today?

Brandt leaned back in his seat, resting his head against the webbing, and closed his eyes. An image coalesced in his mind of a young officer standing at attention, right hand raised, reciting the Oath of Office, "…and that I will well and faithfully discharge the duties…"

The helicopter rose, banked, and surged forward on a northwesterly course, rocking Brandt to his right. His eyes flew open. The noise from the engine dampened the sounds of conversation, and vibrations rippled through the fuselage and lulled men into somnolence. Some leaned toward the man in the next seat and spoke. Some responded with laughter, and some with a punch to the shoulder. Others stared straight ahead. Most appeared to drift into sleep.

An hour's flight. The dead time filled with palpable tension, and each man dealt with it in his own way.

But they don't bear the weight of decision making. Alexander had said, "I'm counting on you." Yeah, and that's what these men think when they look at me. Everett said that loyalty can go down as well as up, but survival underlies everything. A chance to redeem myself.

Brandt closed his eyes and rocked his head from side to side. The strains of a melody drifted into his mind, but the lyrics escaped him.

Civil War. Something about a terrible swift sword.

Brandt leaned forward and looked around the chopper. Ferguson sat in his usual position near the front of the chopper—last to come out—flipping pages in his notebook, pencil in hand.

What more could he be working on? Probably stuff I haven't even thought of, and he'll have the answers ready for me.

Brandt glanced at the tailgate a few feet away, closed his eyes, pictured his map, and reviewed the plan.

A ridge about 400 meters high separates the LZ from the target. Come in low, unseen from the target. Disembark and head west through scrub vegetation, then forest. Climb the ridge, survey the target, make final plans for the assault, and move down into position. Just a walk in the park. If we don't walk into an ambush. Or a sniper. Or punji stakes.

The melody intruded again.

Damn. What is it? Something about sifting hearts of men. Associated with Lincoln.

Brandt shifted position and stretched his legs. He checked his watch.

Almost there.

The engines rumbled, and he leaned back, closed his eyes, and let thoughts drift with the monotonous thrum. An image of a book formed, pages flipping in a breeze—The Uniform Code of Military Justice. The breeze died and the pages settled. "Punitive Articles. Number 92. Failure to obey order...which it is his duty to obey."

Brandt felt a pressure on his left shoulder. The chopper angled downward. Brandt opened his eyes. The crew chief signaled to prepare for landing.

Level flight.

Soldiers sat erect, rifles firmly grasped, poised and ready. Brandt's hunting falcons. Ferguson gave a thumbs up. Brandt stood, and the tailgate dropped.

"Go," Brandt shouted.

Three men led the charge, and Brandt and Ski sprinted after them. Brandt blinked into the sudden brightness, then squinted against the maelstrom of dust and grit kicked up by the rotor's wash. He sprinted in an arc to the west and pulled up to a jog.

Not a good idea to outrun the point man.

He slowed to a walk, spun 180 degrees, and walked backwards. His falcons flew in perfect formation, 7.62 mm talons extended as they hit the ground.

Brandt did another one-eighty, jogged to the tree line, and knelt beside a thicket. No shots fired at them, no explosions. He took a deep breath and waited. Silence. He studied the top of the ridge. No reflections. No movement. He scanned back across the LZ, left, then right, the Chinook already a dark spot in the southern sky.

Jenkins appeared beside him, arm extended with the PRC-6 radio.

"November, this is November 6. Form up in a file and move out."

He heard each squad leader reply, "Roger. Wilco."

After an easy, uneventful climb, Brandt knelt, map spread on the ground and Ferguson, the squad leaders, and Jenkins arrayed in front of him. They huddled just below the crest of the ridge and overlooked the objective.

Brandt looked at Olszewski, anticipating his usual remark to get things started, but Ski remained silent.

"The village," Brandt began, "is a rectangle on the north side of the dry rice paddy. The choppers with the attacking force will be coming in from the south. We're on the east side of the village. I want 2nd Squad on the left, here." He marked a line on the map with a grease pencil. "First Squad here, in the middle and 3rd Squad on the right." He completed the diagram of an arc cradling the east side of the village. "I will be on the far left with 2nd Squad instead of in the center as usual. That position gives me the best view of the long axis of the rice paddy where the assault choppers will be coming in. I'll know when to start the attack."

They nodded slowly.

"And me, sir?" Ferguson asked.

"I want you on the far right with 3rd Squad. From that position, you and Martinez need to keep tight control on the direction of fire. Make sure that no one fires into the rice paddy into our attacking troops."

"Right, sir." Ferguson pointed to the map. "I'll be here with the machine gun."

Martinez hesitated, then said, "I'll be here with the M-79."

Brandt looked up.

Why the flat tone of voice?

"That's good." Brandt continued, "Sergeant Hart and Sergeant Martinez, coordinate the placement of your machine guns and grenade launchers. We need them working together."

Again, hesitation. "Yes, sir."

Brandt searched their faces. He saw no enthusiasm, only concern.

"This deployment will give us fire down the long axis of the village and a crossfire on the village from the left and right. I want your men to put stakes in the ground to guide their lines of fire. Just like we set Final Protective Lines of Fire at night. Like I said before, we don't want to be shooting into our own troops."

"Right, sir."

Another flat response. He looked at each man in turn.

They know what's going on.

He looked to Ferguson.

"Sergeant Ferguson, anything to add?"

"Well, sir, I'd like to probe the village with 3rd Squad. See if we can get them to give away any positions they might have set up."

What the hell?

Brandt looked into his eyes and held the gaze.

Damn. Ferguson must be a good poker player.

Brandt opened his mouth to speak. Ferguson cut him off.

"It would help us direct our fire more effectively during the attack."

Brandt looked away first. "O.K., sergeant."

Brandt stood. "Let's move down into position now."

The squad leaders headed back to their squads, followed by Ferguson. Brandt noted the absence of the usual, "Airborne, sir!"

He watched them disperse, his hands on his hips, standing alone in silence. He looked down on the village, but his focus blurred, and that melody drifted into his mind again and an image of Abraham Lincoln followed. "Do your duty as you understand it."

★ ★ ★

Sergeant First Class Ferguson sat down beside Brandt on the edge of the rice paddy in the shade of a broad-leafed tree. He took off his helmet, placed it on the ground beside him, and wiped sweat from his forehead. "The village looks clear, sir. No response to our probes."

Brandt looked away.

"People walking around like normal, sir. They haven't seen us."

Brandt stared across the parched stubble of the paddy.

A shadow of concern darkened Ferguson's face. "We still gonna open up on this village, sir?"

Without shifting his gaze, Brandt answered, "On my command, sergeant. Tell the squad leaders, *only* on *my* command."

Jenkins knelt next to Brandt and offered the radio handset. "Big 6, sir. He says he's five minutes out."

Brandt accepted the handset, took a deep breath, and put it to his ear. "Big 6, this is November 6. Over."

"November 6, we are inbound your position."

A MATTER OF SEMANTICS

Brandt jammed his thumb on the push-to-talk button, severed communications, and lowered the handset into his lap, thumb clamped, knuckles white.

"Sir, nobody can talk on the net." His voice shaky, Jenkins glanced back and forth between Brandt and Ferguson.

"Sir."

Brandt's jaw locked, muscle twitching.

"Sir?"

Ferguson shook his head and a smile brightened his face. "Hmm," he murmured, "can't disobey an order you didn't hear." He waved a hand dismissively at Jenkins, replaced his helmet, and clambered up to a standing position. "I best go talk to the squad leaders, lieutenant. Make them aware of your wishes." He leaned down, put a hand on Brandt's shoulder, and squeezed it.

Brandt continued to stare across the rice paddy as Ferguson jogged away.

The faint beating of helicopter rotors grew into a deafening roar. The rotor blades pounded the air above the paddy, kicking up stubble and grit. Brandt had never seen so many helicopters in one flight. Men in fatigues jumped out of the lead birds and ran to the edges of the paddy like seasoned soldiers. Some, Brandt noticed, aimed TV cameras instead of rifles and charged forward behind the soldiers.

No cover fire erupted from Brandt's platoon, and no enemy fire from came from the village. There were no explosions. It was an unopposed landing. The men lowered their cameras, exchanged glances, and ambled to the shade. One man, hands free of a camera or rifle, stomped toward November's position.

Brandt could see the red face between pumping arms fifty meters away. He pushed the radio handset toward Jenkins as he stood. He took a deep breath, let it out slowly, and walked out to meet the charging water buffalo.

Alexander sputtered, spit, and stuttered. "You're relieved of command, Brandt. Get on the chopper."

CHAPTER 16

★ ★ ★

Brandt stood at attention. Alexander sat behind his desk, face crimson, mouth drawn so tight he struggled to force out words. He flexed his fingers, took a deep breath, let it out slowly, and placed his palms down flat.

"I'm not going to court-martial you, lieutenant," Alexander finally blurted. "That would only make me look bad." His lips curled and teeth bared, "Worse than you already have." He leaned forward, pounded the desk with his fist and shouted, "More than once."

He sat back and gulped air, and a vein in his temple pulsed. "And I'm not going to send you back out into the field either." He continued in a low, controlled voice. "No. You love it out there." He paused and lifted his chin. "I'm going to keep you here in base camp." He leaned forward. "Under my thumb."

He continued in a normal tone. "I'm appointing you Assistant S-1." A self-satisfied smile creased his face. "I'm going to assign you every shitty little personnel job that rolls downhill from Brigade Headquarters."

Alexander pulled open his desk drawer, removed a large routing envelope, and handed it to Brandt. "Here's the first one."

Brandt took the envelope and drew out a thick stack of papers.

"There's a presidential campaign going on back home," Alexander stated matter-of-factly. "You are now the Battalion Voting Officer, responsible for ensuring that every soldier in this battalion has the opportunity to vote. The instructions, procedures, and timeline are in your hand."

Brandt glanced at the papers. "Yes, sir."

"Have I made your new position and responsibilities clear?"

"Yes, sir."

"Consider yourself the Battalion Point Man for Paperwork."

"Yes, sir."

He shouted, "Have I made myself clear?"

"Yes, sir."

"Dismissed."

★ ★ ★

Brandt settled into a folding chair in the Battalion Personnel Office. On the green folding field table in front of him rose neatly arranged piles of paper up to eye level.

Right. Up to my eyeballs in paperwork.

"Lieutenant."

Brandt turned toward the sound of the voice. Sergeant Wilson, the Personnel Sergeant, smiled. "We got the absentee ballots from headquarters this morning. I counted them out and put them in stacks for each company. They're ready to go."

"Thank you, sergeant."

"Counting was the easy part, sir. The company executive officers can distribute most of them, but some of the units are scattered in the boonies. Some are in contact almost every day. It's going to be tight getting them all back in time."

Brandt nodded. "Then I better get on it. I'll take these ballots to the company execs, now."

He rose, gathered up a stack in his arms, and backed out the screen door.

"Hey, lieutenant."

Brandt paused and looked questioningly at the sergeant.

"Who you gonna vote for, sir?"

Brandt smiled. "Anybody who'll get us out of this fucking place."

"Airborne, sir."

★ ★ ★

Brandt carried his tray through the serving line and scanned the almost deserted officer's mess hall.

Captain Cousins, the Battalion Headquarters and Headquarters Company Commander, sat alone, tray pushed aside, coffee mug in hand.

"Mind if I join you, sir?"

Cousins gestured to the chair across the table. "Please."

Brandt placed his tray on the table and eagerly went to work on the food—mashed potatoes and gravy, mystery meat—but not from a can—and green beans. A real meal.

Cousins sipped his coffee. "Better be careful, Bill," he said. "I've seen young officers come in from the field for a staff job and put on 20 pounds real fast."

Brandt stopped chewing and started to respond. His mother's voice echoed in his ears. "Don't talk with your mouth full, William. Take smaller bites."

A knowing smile spread across Cousins' face.

Brandt chewed through the uncomfortable moment, swallowed, and opened his mouth to respond.

Cousins held up his hand. "I know. We've all been through it."

"I'll keep that in mind, sir."

Brandt took smaller bites of the mystery meat, and Cousins stirred coffee.

"You seem to be settling into the S-1 job well."

"Thanks, sir. But all the regulations, documentation, reports—never imagined so much paperwork in a war zone." Brandt shook his head. "It's been a long week. I'm having to learn a lot fast."

"Bill, I was the S-1 before I became Headquarters Company Commander, so if you have any questions, don't hesitate to ask."

The door to the mess hall creaked open and slammed shut behind Lieutenant Colonel Alexander.

Oh, shit.

Alexander poured himself a mug of coffee, then sat down next to Cousins and across from Brandt.

"Gentlemen."

"Evening, sir," they responded in chorus.

Alexander fingered the handle of his coffee mug, rotating it clockwise, then counterclockwise. "Lieutenant, how's the absentee-ballot job going?"

"Well, sir, Alpha, Bravo, Charlie, and Headquarters Companies are 100 percent. Delta is securing a firebase near the Cambodian border. One platoon is out patrolling the valleys around the mountain, and those men haven't been able to mark their ballots." Brandt shook his head. "We've only got a few days left until the deadline."

Alexander nodded. "Yes, I'm aware of that." He pursed his lips. "Be a shame if those boys didn't get a chance to vote. Out there defending democracy and all."

"I know. I've been thinking about that and it bothers me."

Alexander shook his head. "Shame nothing can be done about it."

"Well, maybe there is, sir."

"Oh?" A thin smile spread across his face.

Brandt took a deep breath. "They're due to get a resupply day after tomorrow. I could go out on the first chopper, distribute and collect the ballots, and come back on the last chopper."

Brandt held his breath as Alexander seemed to be mulling it over. "If that's alright with you, sir," Brandt added.

Brandt noticed Cousins looking back and forth between them like he was watching a tennis match.

Alexander studied his coffee mug and pursed his lips.

"O.K., lieutenant. Coordinate with Delta and get it done."

"Yes, sir."

Alexander stood up. "Have a good evening, gentlemen."

As the door creaked and slammed again, Cousins looked down at Alexander's full mug of coffee. A concerned look spread over his face.

Brandt finished his meal, carried the tray back to the kitchen, returned to the table, and took a final sip of coffee. "I'd better get going. Got a recommendation for a Bronze Star to finish before I turn in." He rose and pushed in his chair.

"Bill," Cousins waited for eye contact. "If you want to talk about anything, my door is always open to you. After all, I am your company commander."

"I appreciate that, sir."

As Brandt headed out the door, Cousins called after him, "Be careful out there on that resupply."

★ ★ ★

The next morning, Brandt carried a stack of reports up to Brigade Headquarters, passed the Inspector General's office on the way back, and saw Lieutenant Colonel Everett behind his desk. Brandt peeked in the door. "Sir, do you have a minute?"

Everett looked up. "Bill, come in," he said and gestured to the chair in front of his desk.

Brandt sat down.

How the hell do I start?

After a long moment, Everett said, "So, the Battalion Point Man for Paperwork."

"You know already, sir?"

"It is my job."

Everett chuckled.

"And I know more than you think."

"But so quickly? Well, anyway," Brandt hesitated again.

"How do you feel about your decision not to fire on that village?"

"I feel good."

"What do you mean?"

"I made the right decision."

"Why?"

"I think firing on that village would have been a war crime, and it would have placed my men in jeopardy for following my order to do so."

Everett sat back and nodded slowly. "But?"

"I know I did the right thing. But now," Brandt shrugged, "I'm not sure where I stand."

"Bill, you didn't get a court-martial. You got reassigned. Every career officer has at least one incident like that on his record. Hell, I've got more. As long as you feel good about what you did, you came out on top on this one."

"Do you think so, sir?"

"Sure. Just do this new job the best you can."

"Well, it just seems like shuffling a lot of papers."

"It is a lot of paperwork, but you're not just moving paper from an In Box to an Out Box. Just think about what you are doing. You are making sure these soldiers get their promotions on time. That's important to them. You write up and process recommendations for awards and medals. That makes their families proud. And when it comes to casualty reports, you ensure the right parents get notified."

"And process Article 15s and Courts-Martial."

"Right. Not a fun part of the job. But maintaining discipline in the Army, especially in a war zone, is of paramount importance."

Brandt nodded. "I see what you mean. I didn't think of it that way."

Everett looked over Brandt's shoulder. "Bill, I have a soldier outside waiting for an appointment."

"Oh, sorry, sir. Didn't mean to take up so much of your time."

"No problem. I'm glad you came to see me. Stay in touch, O.K.?"

Brandt stood. "O.K. Thank you, sir. This helped a lot."

"And Bill," Everett called after him. "Watch your back out there."

"I'm always watching my back out in the field."

"Bill, it's a jungle in here, too."

★ ★ ★

Brandt stood just outside the reach of the rotor blades and watched the crew chief finish loading hot food containers, the first thing in on a resupply. He sensed a presence behind him, like eyes boring into his back, and he looked over his shoulder. Alexander stood on the edge of the helipad, hands clasped behind his back, rocking to and fro on his feet, with that thin smile on his face.

Brandt focused on the chopper again. He checked his web-gear— canteen, ammo pouch, and knife. He checked the tape sealing the plastic bag holding the ballots. It wouldn't do to have them get wet after all this.

The crew chief shoved containers around, created a spot large enough for one passenger, and waved. Brandt checked the safety on the M-16 drawn from Supply and sprinted to the chopper. He placed one hand on the cargo area floor, spun 180 degrees, and plopped his butt squarely in the area cleared for him, legs dangling over the edge. The crew chief tapped him on the shoulder and gave a thumbs up. Brandt returned the gesture. The crew chief spoke into his headset and the chopper lifted off. The ground fell away, and the Central Highlands of Vietnam filled Brandt's field of view. Framed between Brandt's feet, verdant terrain zipped by—streams cascading down mountainsides, smooth dark ribbons cut by white water, falls plunging into pools.

They look just like the streams I fished back home. Wonder if there's any trout in them? Yeah, I wonder. Never did let my men fish. Always insisted on conserving grenades, maintaining sound discipline. Was I too strict? A real asshole?

The helicopter banked sharply. Sky filled the frame between his boots. The chopper leveled, angled downward, and dropped. Trees filled the field of view, and the chopper settled on level ground. Brandt pushed off, landed firmly, and sprinted into the center of the perimeter. He slowed to a walk and threaded his way between soldiers running to the chopper.

The platoon leader, platoon sergeant, and squad leaders sat clustered around a map on the ground. The familiar sight triggered a twinge of nostalgia.

The freckled face of Lieutenant McKnight looked up. "Bill, good to see you. Damn nice of you to do this. The men have been alerted and the squad leaders are ready."

"Great."

Brandt handed stacks of ballots to each of the squad leaders, and they hustled away. He handed a small stack to McKnight for the platoon command post. The platoon sergeant rose. "I'll get the chow line set up first, then I'll come back and mark my ballot."

McKnight nodded, and the sergeant took off at a jog. He opened his ballot and studied it.

"You're lucky, Bob. All you need to do is a make an "X."

McKnight flipped him off. "This is supposed to be a secret ballot. Don't look."

A MATTER OF SEMANTICS

A moment later, McKnight faced Brandt and handed him the folded ballot. Brandt slipped it in the plastic bag.

"So, Bill," McKnight said through a wide smile, "how's it feel to be a Rear Echelon Mother Fucker now?"

"Fuck you, too. At least I get to eat real food."

"Yeah," McKnight poked a finger into Brandt's belly. "I can see that."

"Besides, I'm incarcerated in base camp. That doesn't make me a REMF."

The platoon sergeant strode up to them and handed Brandt three stacks of ballots. "I'll mark mine now," he said. He turned, marked the ballot and handed Brandt the folded paper.

"Sir, the men wanted me to tell you, they never seen a REMF—" He stopped in mid-sentence, looked down, and then looked up again. "Never seen anybody from the rear area come out and do something like this for them. They sure do appreciate it."

"They're worth it, sergeant."

Another chopper landed. "Looks like my ride is here. You men be careful out here."

As Brandt jogged toward the chopper, he looked over his shoulder. "Hey Bob, who'd you vote for?"

"Anybody who will get us out of this fucking place."

★ ★ ★

After a smooth helicopter ride back to LZ English, Brandt bounded up the steps to the S-1 Office, settled behind his desk, lifted the box of ballots, and began to inventory the contents.

"Sir," Sergeant Wilson said, "I checked and they're all there. I figured you were bringing in the last of the ballots. They're ready to go."

"Thank you, sergeant. I guess the voting is complete."

Captain Johnson, the Personnel Officer, rose, walked to Brandt, and shook his hand. "You did a great job, Bill."

"Thank you, sir. I'll take the ballots up to headquarters now."

★ ★ ★

A few days later, Brandt returned from his rounds to each company headquarters, opened the S-1 Office door, and noticed Sergeant Wilson scurry out the back door. Alexander stood in front of the S-1's desk. Captain Johnson sat at attention in his chair.

Oh, not good.

Brandt slunk into a corner.

Alexander leaned over Johnson's desk and raised his voice. "Captain, I just got back from a battalion commanders' meeting at headquarters. The Brigade S-1 complained that all four battalions are way beyond timelines for Article 15s. Then the Brigade Commander jumped all over us. Wants to know why we can't run our units efficiently."

Alexander paused for a breath, leaned back, and Johnson jumped in. "But, sir, we have three companies out in the field all the time. We have to wait until they come back in for perimeter duty to get paperwork signed."

Alexander exploded. "Damn it, captain, you think I'm going to give that excuse to the Brigade Commander? In front of the other battalion commanders? The general knows that. He doesn't give a shit." He leaned on Johnson's desk, spittle at the corners of his mouth. "He reamed our asses, and I don't like the feeling."

Johnson spread his arms wide, mouth open, but no words came out, a helpless look on his face.

"Uh, sir," Brandt interjected.

Alexander spun around. "Oh, Brandt. You have something to add to our conversation, do you, lieutenant?"

"Well," Brandt hesitated, "I could take the 15s out on resupply choppers to get them signed."

The old thin smile creased Alexander's face. "Still trying to get back into the field, Brandt?"

"No, sir, but—"

Alexander cut off Brandt. "Well, captain, can you spare," Alexander looked over his shoulder at Brandt and continued in a sarcastic tone, "this *valuable* officer from your very busy office?"

A look of relief washed over Johnson. "I think it's an excellent idea, sir."

Alexander placed his hands on his hips. "O.K., let's try it. But however you do it, I want that pile of 15s out of my battalion area and back up at Brigade as soon as possible."

The door slammed shut, and Johnson let out a deep sigh. "Thanks for saving my butt, Bill."

"It just makes sense, sir."

"Well, get it done as soon as you can, Bill."

"Yes, sir. I need to make the mail run up to headquarters now. I'll coordinate with the company execs when I get back."

"Sir," Sergeant Wilson piped up as he re-entered the back door, "I'll sort the Article 15s by company. There aren't very many. They'll be on your desk when you get back."

"Thank you, sergeant."

★ ★ ★

The next day, Brandt rose from his table in the mess hall and gulped one more sip of morning coffee before picking up his tray. Captain Cousins was just placing his own tray down and took a seat.

"Left half of your potatoes, I see."

"Good morning, sir. Yeah, when I picked up the last of the ballots from Lieutenant McKnight's platoon, he poked me in the belly and said I looked like a REMF. I'm taking your advice to heart."

Cousins chuckled, then turned serious. "And my advice about being careful out there?"

"Always, sir. I'm going out to Charlie Company now. Got to get an Article 15 signed."

Cousins raised his coffee mug in a toast. "And be aware of what's going on around you in here."

★ ★ ★

Brandt charged toward the chopper, climbed into the cargo area, and wedged himself between ammunition boxes on one side and grenades on the other. As the helicopter lifted off, he saw Alexander on the helipad, hands clasped behind his back, rocking on his feet. Brandt shook his head.

I wonder if he's got that shit-eating smile on his face.

The crew chief tapped Brandt's shoulder and shouted over the engine noise. "It's a short flight, sir. Only 20 minutes. You're coming back on our next run, right?"

"That's right."

"So 40 minutes plus for our round trip. That be enough time for you?"

"Should be plenty. I just need to get some papers signed."

The crew chief gave him a thumbs-up and spoke into his headset as he moved away.

Brandt adjusted position between boxes to achieve a semblance of comfort—at least the Army version of comfort. The helicopter cruised smoothly, and his body and mind resonated with the rhythmic thrum. Time and miles flew by. Literally.

A sharp bank and the descent jarred him into alertness. He saw sandy ground, sparse vegetation, palm trees, and miles of white sand and blue ocean.

That's right. Charlie Company is operating along the coast north of Bong Son. Beautiful place, but how can you enjoy it? Can't catch any rays on the beach. Can't swim.

Brandt shook his head, frowned, and envisioned a soldier standing in front of him.

Damn, what's this going to be like? A man is out there fighting a war and I'm going to ask him to sign a paper agreeing to a reduction in pay for three months. How's he going to react? What have I gotten myself into?

The helicopter settled, and Brandt worked his way through the bustle of resupply activity.

"Morning, soldier." Brandt addressed a private heading toward the chopper. "Where's the company CP?"

The young man pointed.

"Thanks."

Brandt jogged in that direction. A stocky man stood solidly on pillars of muscle, hands gesticulating, while three younger men stood before him taking notes—the company commander and three platoon leaders. Brandt slowed to a walk and stopped a few feet away.

The captain turned and closed the distance between them. "Lieutenant Brandt, so nice of you to join our beach party. We're having a ball out here. Sun, sand, and surf. What more could you ask for? My platoon leaders," he made a sweeping gesture toward them, "are just now organizing the festivities."

Brandt knew Captain McCarthy by sight. Brandt had not interacted with him much but had heard about the captain's sense of humor and that his men loved him. But Brandt had also heard that he could use that sense of humor like a bayonet if he'd been displeased.

"Good morning, sir."

"Did you bring that volleyball net I requested?"

Brandt chuckled. "No, sir. The crew chief said to tell you it'll be on the next run."

McCarthy registered surprise at the rejoinder, then feigned an exaggerated look of disappointment.

"Just an Article 15 to be signed, sir."

McCarthy called over his shoulder to his RTO, "Get Worthington up here."

"I got the paperwork ready. All he has to do is sign it." Brandt glanced down, lips drawn into a thin line.

"What is it, lieutenant?"

"Well, how's he going to feel about this? I mean, well, I feel a little uncomfortable in this situation. Out here in enemy territory. Ask the man to agree to a reduction in pay for three months. And he's got a rifle on his shoulder."

McCarthy chuckled. "Yeah, it's not your usual disciplinary setting, I'll grant you that. But he understands. He's a crackerjack of a soldier, just made an immature mistake. Last time we were in base camp for perimeter duty, he got drunk and mouthed off to his squad leader. A little pushing and shoving. He apologized, and things are good between them."

Worthington stepped hesitantly toward Brandt, the boyish face contrite, apprehensive.

"Private Worthington," Brandt began, "your company commander has decided to give you an Article 15, Non-Judicial Punishment. Do you understand the charges and the punishment?"

"Yes, sir. Captain McCarthy explained it all to me."

"Do you understand that you have the right under the Uniform Code of Military Justice to refuse Non-Judicial Punishment and request a court-martial?"

"Yes, sir."

"And do you waive that right?"

"Yes, sir."

Brandt handed him the clipboard and pen.

"Sign here." Brandt pointed to a line at the bottom of the paper.

Worthington signed his name, handed back the clipboard and pen, and stood at attention.

"Thank you, sir."

McCarthy said, "You're dismissed."

Worthington walked away slowly, head down, shoulders slumped.

Brandt looked at McCarthy questioningly. "Thank you?"

"Like I said, lieutenant, he's a good kid. He knows it won't go on his permanent record. He'll learn from it." McCarthy paused. "And so will you. Never be afraid to mete out discipline."

"Yes, sir. Not the fun part of my job, but I know it's necessary."

Both men looked toward the sound of an approaching helicopter.

"I need to catch my ride, sir."

"O.K. I appreciate your coming out here to take care of this. I hate stuff like that hanging over a man's head." McCarthy smiled and nodded. "He can move on, now."

"Airborne, sir."

Brandt headed for the chopper.

"Hey, Brandt," McCarthy called.

Brandt stopped and looked over his shoulder. He saw a big smile on the ruddy face.

"Do you think that volleyball net will be on the chopper?"

"I doubt it, sir. You know the Army. Probably got it on backorder."

Captain McCarthy lifted his helmet, laughed out loud, and ran his fingers through red curly hair.

"Are you sure you can't stay for our beach barbecue this evening?"

"I think Big 6 has other plans for my evening, sir."

Brandt started again.

"Brandt." McCarthy spoke in a serious tone, a serious look. "You ever want to get back in the field, you give me a call."

★ ★ ★

Brandt handed the Article 15 form to Sergeant Wilson. "That wasn't much fun, but we got it done."

Wilson smiled. "I'll trade you, sir. You'll like these. Captain Johnson is meeting with the Battalion Commander, and I thought you'd like to handle this. I sent word down to Bravo Company, and the sergeant should be here soon."

Brandt scanned the papers and smiled. "Yes, indeed."

Sergeant Martinez stepped smartly through the door of the S-1 Office, marched to Brandt's desk, and stood at attention. Brandt sat back and appraised him.

Just like the first day I met him. How does he manage to look so sharp even in wrinkled jungle fatigues?

"Relax, sergeant. This isn't an inspection."

Martinez snapped to Parade Rest. "And we're not out in the field now. Good to see you, sir."

Brandt handed him a piece of paper. "And here's your ticket for a Freedom Bird. You fly home from Cam Ranh Bay in one week."

A smile fought its way through the serious military bearing as Martinez took the DEROS orders.

"Thank you, sir."

Brandt slid a piece of paper to the edge of his desk and placed a pen on it. "And I have a paper for you to sign, if you so choose. I understand you intend to reenlist."

"Yes, sir."

Martinez leaned forward and signed the paper.

"Have you thought about where you'd like to be assigned?"

"No, sir. I've just concentrated on getting back here safely." He shrugged. "But I don't think I'll have much say about it. You know, E-5, Infantry."

Brandt slid another piece of paper toward him. "This is a request for reassignment. All filled out. All you need to do is sign it."

Martinez picked it up and scanned the form. His eyes grew large; his jaw dropped.

"Ranger School?"

"Otherwise known as the Bad-ass School."

"But do you think it's possible? I'm just an E-5."

Brandt handed him another piece of paper. "Here's a letter of recommendation to accompany it."

★ ★ ★

A few days later, Alexander stomped into the S-1 Office. Johnson, Brandt, and Wilson rose to their feet.

Alexander nodded curtly at Johnson and said, "At ease. Return to your work."

He faced Brandt. Wilson shrugged and sat down. Alexander raised a file folder to chest level and presented it to Brandt. It had red tape border and a red, all-capital title in the center, "CONGRESSIONAL INQUIRY."

"Your new project, lieutenant. Ever seen one of these?"

"No sir."

"This is a direct question from the junior senator from Kansas. He would like to know why one of his constituents, a mother of a soldier in the 2nd Battalion, received a letter from her son two weeks after she was notified that he was killed in action."

Brandt gulped. "I'll do my best on it, sir."

"Brandt, I will personally review your report before it is sent to Brigade Headquarters."

"Yes, sir."

Alexander stepped toward the door, paused, and said, "And I'm sure the 2nd Battalion's procedures were flawless in this case." He held Brandt in his gaze for a moment and then exited.

Brandt dropped the file on his desk. "Oh, shit."

Johnson said, "Bill, I'll help you with this one. Especially with the wording of the report. Somebody, somewhere along the line, is going to be in big trouble."

Brandt sat down. "I'll appreciate any help and guidance sir." He shook his head. "Like where to start."

"Well," Johnson suggested, "this will take a few days. Follow the chain of events from start to finish. Talk to the company commander and executive officer, then the people at B Medical, and end at the Graves Registration Office. They process all bodies going through LZ English."

★ ★ ★

The next day, Brandt sat at his desk reviewing casualty reports for the past month. He frowned.

Lots of different handwriting. No consistency in the way they're filled out. No apparent breaks in protocol, but difficult to verify accounting. Well, they're often filled out in the heat of battle, sometimes at night.

Brandt sat back and rubbed his chin.

Wonder if there's any follow-up once the medevacs arrive at B Med?

The door creaked open, and Sergeant Hart hopped through the doorway. "Geez! Where is everybody? You chase 'em away, sir?"

Brandt put down his pen and moved a pad of paper aside.

"No. Sergeant Wilson is up at headquarters, and Captain Johnson is in a battalion staff meeting. I'm not important enough to go to those." Brandt gestured toward a chair. "Have a seat."

Hart sat down and glanced around. "Nice office. First lieutenant's bar on your collar. You're moving up in the world, sir."

"Going from second to first lieutenant is like sitting in a chair and then standing. You're still on the bottom floor." He shrugged. "Anyway, how's perimeter duty?"

"Only good things about perimeter duty are real food in a mess hall and taking a shower for the first time in a month." He shook his head. "Those bunkers are nasty. Dark and muddy inside. And November's sector is downhill from the 8 inch howitzer battery. When they shoot at night, we bounce up off the ground. I sleep better out in the field."

Brandt chuckled. "Yeah, I remember that."

"Anyway, First Sergeant Klein told me to report to you. What's up, sir?"

"Well, how would you like to sleep in a real bunk nowhere near a perimeter and eat in a mess hall every meal?"

Hart cocked his head to the side. "Uh, what's the catch, sir?"

"Did I mention showers every day?"

"Now it sounds too good to be true. Something's fishy here."

Brandt chuckled. "There's an opening for an instructor in Jungle School. You have enough experience, and I think you'd make an excellent instructor."

Hart remained silent for a moment. "So I'd be moving to An Khe?"

"That's right."

Another moment.

"O.K., sir. I'll take it."

"Great. We'll cut the transfer orders today, and you'll fly to An Khe tomorrow."

★ ★ ★

Midafternoon. In the deserted mess hall, Brandt and Johnson each drew a cup of coffee and sat at a table. Brandt plopped the Congressional Inquiry folder on the table.

"So," Johnson began, "you concluded your investigation yesterday. And the breakdown in the system was at Graves Registration?"

"Yes, sir. I spent today writing up the report." He tapped the folder. "It's ready for you to proof."

"Tell me about it."

"Well, when I got there," Brandt shook his head. "there was no officer. No NCO. Just a Spec 4."

Johnson raised his chin. "I wonder how often that happens?"

"Yeah. Anyway, the *Specialist Fourth Class,*" Brandt emphasized the rank, "had an attitude. I didn't care for the tone of voice, the way he answered questions." Brandt paused. "Like he thought his rank made him special. He forgot he's just one rank above private."

"Uh-huh. And you impressed upon him that this was no laughing matter?"

"Yes, sir. And when I told him I was going to take a look around for myself, he got this wise-ass smile on his face. Like he just knew I'd be freaked out by dead bodies."

"And what did you find?"

"I unzipped a few body bags. In the third one, the body was in full uniform, so I searched and found a letter in a shirt pocket."

Johnson whistled.

Brandt continued. "I called the specialist over and told him to search the body. Well, when he found the letter, that wise-ass smile disappeared real fast."

"I'll bet it did. Bill, you did an excellent job on this. After I proofread it, I'll take the report to Colonel Alexander myself."

Brandt let out a deep breath. "I would appreciate that, sir."

Johnson sat back and sipped some coffee. "Did you learn anything else?"

"Well, sir, when the units take casualties, they report to their headquarters here in base camp. Personnel here fill out the forms and deliver them to us and we send them up the line to Brigade. The wounded soldiers are picked up by the medevac chopper, taken to B Med, and treated. If they're not returned to their unit, they're sent to Cam Ranh Bay and Japan." Brandt paused. "And the deceased to Graves Registration."

"O.K.," Johnson said. "Is there a problem?"

"I didn't find any recent discrepancies, but I think there's a potential for errors."

Johnson nodded. "I see. And what would you recommend?"

"I think it would be prudent for me to meet the medevacs at B Med so I can verify the reporting."

"No one's done that before, but it sounds like a good idea. If you want to take it on, I'll support you."

★ ★ ★

During the next week, Brandt settled into a routine of reports, meetings, coordinating with each company headquarters, and jeep trips to Brigade Headquarters.

One afternoon, Brandt sat back and looked at Sergeant Wilson. "Another Report of Survey completed." He tossed the papers aside with a flourish. "What's next? Let me guess, company strength reports."

"Nope. You guessed wrong, sir." Wilson held up a few pieces of paper. "These orders are ready. Kinda nice for you to get something enjoyable for a change."

Brandt took the papers and scanned them. "You got that right, sergeant."

"He's on his way up here."

As if on cue, Jenkins walked through the door. "Good afternoon, sir."

"Specialist Jenkins." Brandt gestured to a chair next to his desk. "Have a seat."

Sergeant Wilson whistled. "Well, some people get special treatment."

"Sergeant, this young man did the equivalent of two tours of duty just trying to keep up with me out in the field."

"Yeah," Jenkins said. "And Captain Parker didn't have to staple my ass to yours to do it."

"Sergeant, if it weren't for the Specialist, I'd still be drinking iodine-flavored water and burning my lips with a metal canteen."

Wilson laughed. "Oh, that's all part of the training for a lieutenant, sir."

Brandt smiled. "So, Specialist, they brought you in early. You don't DEROS for a few weeks."

"Yes, sir. The company clerk is overwhelmed with paperwork and the First Sergeant heard that I could spell real well. Can't imagine who might have told him that."

"First Sergeants know everything. How do you like rear area life?"

Jenkins raised his arms, palms up. "Sleep in a bed, wear clean clothes, eat real food. What's not to like?"

Brandt looked down, then up again. "On to business. I understand you turned down a promotion to sergeant because you are not going to re-enlist."

"How did you know, sir?"

Brandt sat back, paused a moment. "It's my job to know."

"What *is* your job, sir?"

"Basically, my job is to carry stacks of paper to and from Brigade Headquarters and to listen to the advice Sergeant Wilson gives me."

Wilson snorted.

Jenkins said, "Well, I hear some of that paperwork is heavier than your old rucksack."

Brandt's eyes widened. "How did you know that?"

Jenkins smiled. "I'm your RTO. I hear everything."

Brandt laughed and shook his head. "O.K. So what are you going to do when you get home? Buy a fast car? Date beautiful women? Drink beer with your old high school buddies? Enjoy the Real World?"

Jenkins shook his head. "Actually, sir, I'm going to go to college."

"That's great. I'm glad to hear it. How did you come to that decision?"

"I want to learn all that weird stuff you used to say. The stuff you thought I didn't hear. *Quo vadis*. Dante's Inferno."

A sheepish smile spread across Brandt's face. "O.K., you need a letter of recommendation, you let me know."

Brandt looked to Sergeant Wilson, who nodded in return.

"And now Specialist," Brandt said as he stood. "Stand at attention."

Jenkins shrugged and rose.

Wilson picked up a dark blue case with gold lettering, carried it to Brandt, and opened the case. Brandt removed a hexagonal bronze medal suspended from a green-and-white ribbon and pinned it on Jenkins' shirt.

Jenkins' jaw dropped.

Wilson walked back to his desk, snatched a sheet of paper, handed it to Brandt, and stood at attention.

Brandt cleared his throat and read, "Attention to orders. The Secretary of the Army has awarded the Army Commendation Medal to Specialist Wallace Jenkins for sustained meritorious service in ground operations against hostile forces in the Republic of Vietnam."

★ ★ ★

Brandt sat at his desk, alone in the S-1 Office. Johnson and Wilson had left for dinner a while ago. He finished writing a Bronze Star recommendation, set it aside, and pulled a letter from his shirt pocket. After reading it, he tore a blank page from a notepad and began writing.

"Dear Jim,"

"You asked what a rear-area job is like in a war zone. Well, it's like working for a big company back home. Lots of offices, warehouses, cafeterias; the need for transportation, supplies, planning, payroll—everything needed for running a large organization efficiently. And for the most part, regular hours for work, meals, and sleep. Except that all this can be suddenly interrupted by a mortar or ground attack or responding to casualties brought in from the field. In any one of the 24 hours in a day."

"My job in S-1, the Personnel Department, is dealing with paperwork. Lots of it. It's amazing how much paperwork it takes to keep an army functioning in the field. But it's not boring. Having to learn a lot real fast challenges me. And most of it is important."

He paused and looked at Jim's letter.

"Yes, I am relatively safer in base camp, and I know that makes my parents feel better. I eat fresh food on a plate with silverware, sitting at a table, and sleep on a mattress in a bunk with a roof over my head."

Brandt sat back, gazed up at the ceiling, and resumed writing.

"However, during lulls in activity, my thoughts drift back to my platoon. To the aggressive anticipation of enemy contact. Planning and executing a successful ambush. The adrenalin rush from standing up in the deep silence after a firefight and knowing I beat death again. It's like withdrawal from an addiction. I miss it. And that is a disturbing realization."

Brandt re-read the last paragraph, lips drawn tight and brow wrinkled. He took a deep breath.

"Geez. I sure didn't think this letter would end like that. Thanks for listening, Jim."

"Be well,"

"Bill"

★ ★ ★

Captain Johnson strode into the office after a trip to Brigade Headquarters and placed a file on Brandt's desk. "Bill, this is a high-priority case. The Red Cross contacted headquarters. The mother of an Alpha Company soldier is seriously ill. They've made arrangements to fly him home. We need to get him to An Khe as soon as possible."

"Wow. Red Cross does that?"

"Only in dire situations, Bill. I'd suggest you start with Major Owens at Operations. See if he can get the soldier brought in on a chopper today. Then notify the company exec and first sergeant."

"I'll get right on it, sir."

Brandt rose and headed for the door.

"And Bill," Johnson added, "when you talk to the soldier, I'd suggest having the Battalion Chaplin here with you."

★ ★ ★

Brandt sat in an empty mess hall. Another late dinner. The door creaked open, and Brandt looked up. Captain Cousins walked in.

"Eating late again, Bill?"

"Yes, sir. And you?"

"I ate at a reasonable hour for a change. I just needed a cup of coffee. Mind if I join you?"

"Please." Brandt gestured toward a chair.

Cousins stirred his coffee and took a sip. "Hey, it's still fresh."

"I guess the mess sergeant thought I look like I needed it."

Cousins laughed. "I hear you worked with the Red Cross today."

"Yes, sir. That surprised me. I didn't know the Red Cross and the Army worked together like that."

"It's a good thing for you to remember. Especially when you get in command positions. The Red Cross can be a big help."

The door creaked again, slowly this time. Sergeant Wilson poked his head into the doorway. "Lieutenant, Charlie Company is in contact, and they've requested a medevac."

Brandt stood. "I'd better get over to B Med. I want to verify names as they bring in the wounded. It's getting dark. Chance for lots of confusion out there."

Cousins raised an eyebrow. "Nobody's done that before."

"Well, remember that Congressional Inquiry I investigated? Mother received a letter from her son two weeks after she was notified of his death."

Cousins nodded slowly. "Yes, I remember. But the problem was at Graves Registration, right?"

"Yes, but I'll be damned if I notify the wrong mother that her son was wounded or killed in action."

"Sounds like a good idea, Bill."

Brandt stood, left his half-finished meal, and hustled to the door.

"Hey, Bill," Cousins called after him, "should I have the mess sergeant save this for you?"

Brandt looked back over his shoulder. "No. I'm still taking your advice on that, sir."

★ ★ ★

Brandt marched through the tents and bunkers of the battalion area, bounded up the S-1 Office steps, and sprang through the door. "Good morning."

"Good morning, Bill." Captain Johnson sat back in his chair.

"Morning, sir." Sergeant Wilson placed his elbows on his desk, his chin on his folded hands.

Brandt looked back and forth between them and said after a pregnant pause, "Are there any more Article 15s to serve?"

"No," Johnson answered. "You got us caught up and Colonel Alexander is happy. And that makes me happy."

But not a happy tone of voice. No smile.

Johnson extended his arm and offered a routing envelope to Brandt. "Colonel Alexander left another project for you. Looks like this one is complicated."

"Great. Just what I need. I was starting to get bored."

"You don't need this one, sir." Sergeant Wilson shook his head emphatically.

Brandt looked to Johnson.

"Bill, there's going to be a currency change. Too many Military Payment Certificates are getting into Vietnamese hands and flooding the black market. You understand about international balance of payments, gold flowing out of the U.S., right?"

"Yes, sir. The Army pays us in MPC because a country holding dollars can demand payment in gold and a country hosting U.S. troops doesn't want its own economy undermined by a black market. But I didn't know it was such a big problem here in Nam."

"Apparently it is. I got a briefing at headquarters this morning. The original series was issued in 1965. The large troop buildup in the three years since then brought with it a tremendous increase in the amount of American money here and a corresponding increase in black market activity. Last year, there were over 60 courts-martial for currency and commodity violations on the black market. So far this year, October 1968, there have been over 200 commodity violations and over 200 currency violations. The government is very concerned, and the Army is going to issue a new series of Military Payment Certificates. The old series of MPCs will be invalid. The new series will be a different color as well."

"Damn." Brandt opened the routing envelope and spread the papers across his desk. "Looks like this is going to happen fast. I guess I can understand why, but how is it going to work?"

"Bill, you are going to collect every MPC from every soldier in the battalion and replace them with ones from the new series. Right down to the last dollar. This will have to be done all in one day. The day of the change is a secret held very closely for obvious reasons. On the specified day, you will get a bag of new MPCs from HQ, bring them back to our area, collect the old money, and count out the new money. All of our troops will be restricted to base. No one will be allowed in or out."

He paused, then nodded toward Brandt.

"You will be responsible for having the total amount of the exchange for the battalion come out even. That's cash for over 500 men. Work with the company execs on a schedule. They may have to bring MPCs in from the field for you to exchange. I'll have to confirm that. Only authorized personnel can handle the money. The procedures for the exchange are very strict."

Brandt sat back. "Wow. We're going to stop the war for a day to change money."

"That's right. After C-Day, which is what they are calling it, Conversion Day, no old certificates will be accepted for conversion. Again, for obvious reasons."

"Yeah. A lot of people dealing in the black market are going to be royally pissed off."

"To say the least."

Brandt whistled. "Sergeant Wilson, you were right about this one."

"Airborne, sir," Wilson said in flat tone.

"Don't worry about anything else during this time, Bill. We'll handle the routine tasks and whatever rolls down the hill." Johnson continued, "And I'll help you as much as I can on this one."

"O.K., sir. I'll appreciate any help."

Wilson added, "Anything, sir. You got it."

Brandt gathered the papers and shoved them back in the routing envelope. "I guess I'd better alert the company execs now." He rose and headed for the door.

"And you might check in with S-3 at the Tactical Operations Center. They're going to be figuring out how to get troops in and out for the change. It's going to be tricky. We're not the First Cav. We don't have that many helicopters available, and it's going to be on very short notice."

"Good idea, sir. I'll get over there right away."

★ ★ ★

Brandt trudged back into the S-1 Office, plopped into his chair, and exhaled loudly.

Captain Johnson smiled. "Put on some miles this morning, Bill?"

"You got that right, sir. I tracked down everyone in the battalion area who has a need to know about the currency change. They're all briefed."

"How'd it go with S-3?"

"Well, like you said, they have a nightmare on their hands, but I talked to Major Owens and it looks like it's going to work out."

"Yeah, he's an excellent Operations Officer."

"There is one problem, sir.

"Oh?" Johnson leaned forward. "And that is?"

"The Recon Platoon is on a long-range mission. In the middle of nowhere. Big 6 doesn't want to pull them out now, and we don't know the date for C-Day. That means they're going to lose whatever money they have."

"Damn. That's a shame. There's nothing they can do?"

"Not according to Big 6." Brandt paused, shook his head, and pursed his lips.

"O.K., Bill." Johnson leaned back in his chair. "However?"

"Well, sir. The Recon Platoon is due to get a resupply tomorrow. I could go out there, pick up their MPCs, and hold them until C-Day."

"Whoa, lieutenant!" Wilson exclaimed. "That's a long way out there. And it's Recon Platoon, about 20 men. That's not like landing in the middle of a 150 man infantry company."

"Yeah, I know. But the chopper pilots and the crew chief are going out there and it's only one run. All I'm going to do is pick up the MPCs and get back on the chopper."

Johnson leaned forward again. "Bill, I appreciate your concern for the men and your dedication to getting our job done. You've transformed our operation here." He paused and shook his head. "But I think that is above and beyond."

Brandt sighed. "Sir, I just can't help thinking how I'd feel if I lost a month's pay just because the Army wants its money to be a new color."

Johnson's eyes fell to his desk for a long moment and then fixed on Brandt. "Bill, it's your call. If you feel O.K. with it, make it happen."

CHAPTER 17

★ ★ ★

I can feel those eyes boring into my back. I'll bet he's got that shit-eating smile on his face again. Don't look back.

The crew chief signaled. Brandt dashed for the chopper, scrambled into a gap between boxes, and settled down, butt on the floor, back against the rear bulkhead.

Don't look. Fuck that asshole.

Brandt crossed his arms on his knees, gazed at the floor between his feet, and focused on the rhythmic beat of the rotor blades, the vibration of the helicopter drifting through his body.

★ ★ ★

As if coming out of a trance, Brandt started.

"Sorry, sir," the crew chief apologized, his hand recoiling from Brandt's shoulder. "Pilot says you've been to this mountain before. He'd like you to come up front."

Brandt gave him a thumbs-up, weaved his way forward, and knelt next to the pilot.

"We're getting close," the pilot said. "Since you're familiar with this area, I'd like you to help me confirm the LZ. Lots of these mountaintops look the same."

Brandt smiled. "Yeah. You ought to try looking at them from the bottom."

"What?" the pilot said through a broad smile. "You Airborne Rangers can see through triple canopies?"

Brandt shook his head. "Only when we're wearing our floppy bush-hats. These helmets they make us wear are made of Kryptonite."

The pilot laughed. "That's why God made helicopters."

Brandt leaned forward, squinted into the glare of the sun, raised his arm, and pointed. "That's the mountain, the bare ground to the south," he shouted over the noise of the Huey's engine. "Green smoke," he continued. "The landing zone's secure."

"Secure, my ass," the pilot yelled back over his shoulder. He flipped his sun visor down, but the decal pasted on the olive-drab helmet revealed more than his face. Crossed spears dripping blood cradled the words, "Death from Above." "That just means they're not sure Charlie's around."

"Don't worry," Brandt shouted back. "Sergeant Anderson's the acting platoon leader right now. He knows what he's doing."

"Don't take too long," the pilot said. "We're sitting ducks down there."

"All I'm going to do is pick up some MPCs and get out. I don't like having a bull's-eye painted on my ass any more than you."

"Right. After we kick out the resupply boxes, I'll lift off and circle back around to pick you up."

"Yeah. See how much I trust you?"

A smile fought its way through the bushy mustache beneath the opaque visor. The cryptic head rotated to the front, the pilot leaned to the left as if aiming the spears, and the helicopter responded with a wide descending turn and circled the mountaintop.

He's making an aerial reconnaissance while setting up his approach. Good move.

A MATTER OF SEMANTICS

Brandt saw the LZ straight ahead and moved back into the cargo area through stacks of boxes, ammunition, and rations for the Recon Platoon. No hot food on this resupply, just those light bags of freeze-dried food. The helicopter dropped rapidly. Brandt sat on the edge of the cargo door opening and glanced to his right. The door gunner leaned out of the chopper, strained against the safety harness and adjusted a belt of ammo across his lap with one hand. His other hand grasped the pistol grip of the M-60 machine gun, index finger resting on the trigger guard.

Brandt focused his attention down to the probable landing site. The ground rushed up to meet him. His actions became automatic. Brandt checked the safety on his M-16 rifle and pulled back the charging handle. A twitch of the thumb released it. Lethal brass leaped into the chamber. Almost simultaneously, a reborn warrior jumped into the dust-filled whirlwind. Swirling grit stung his face and arms. Braced for the familiar jolt from the 70 pounds of equipment he no longer carried in a rucksack, Brandt stumbled, then regained his balance.

He crouched low and ran until he dipped below the crest, careful not to silhouette himself on the skyline of the hill, the conditioned responses that had kept him alive as a rifle platoon leader still sharp. Brandt knelt on one knee and peered into the thick undergrowth ahead. No human forms visible. Then, two bushes in the tree line rose, grew legs, and approached him, branches sprouting from steel helmets. Three more men rose from the tall grass to his right and rushed to the boxes tumbling out of the helicopter.

The tall, slender figure in front of him moved with a smooth, sure step, exuding a toughness that ensures survival by bending in a gale rather than breaking. He bore the insignia of three chevrons and a rocker as if it were carved into bark.

His companion, short and stocky, faltered behind. Inked across the camouflage cover of his helmet were the words, "God Is My Jumpmaster," a token attempt at individual expression.

Brandt smiled and muttered, "No peace symbols in this platoon."

Staff Sergeant Anderson and one of his riflemen stopped in front of him.

The sergeant held out a stack of MPCs wrapped in a piece of notepaper. "Here it is, sir. I already collected it and wrote down the totals for each man."

"Good work, sergeant. I appreciate it."

"Thank *you*, sir." Anderson protested. "I appreciate the hell out of you coming out here like this. I don't know who else would've done it."

Brandt looked over the list of names and figures.

"That's the whole platoon, lieutenant," he continued. "Except for Perkins, here. I told him what's happening, but he don't seem to understand, and I thought maybe you could explain it to him, sir."

Perkins seemed a little frightened and unsure of himself, but he stood solidly on both feet, his jaw set.

"Perkins," Brandt said, "Do you know why the army pays you in MPCs instead of real dollars?"

Leaves fluttered as the paratrooper shook his head.

"Well, the U.S. dollar is backed by gold. When a foreign country holds dollars, it can demand payment in the amount of gold the dollars represent. When that happens, gold flows out of our country. To stop that, our government issues Military Payment Certificates to soldiers in Vietnam."

The blank stare on Perkins' face stopped Brandt. He tried a different tack.

"MPCs have found their way into the black market, and dealers are using them like dollars. The sorry scumbags are making a fortune off supplies that should be going out here to the GI risking his ass every day. That's why the Department of Defense is making a currency change. MPCs will be a new color from now on. The new series will go into effect all over Nam on the same day. The old series will be invalid."

A confused expression clouded Perkins' face. Brandt took a deep breath and brought it down to a personal level.

"You know that you're supposed to exchange MPCs for Piasters, Vietnamese currency, when you go downtown. But that's a pain in the ass, right? Well, a lot of other GI's think so, too. That's how MPCs get into the hands of the black marketers, greasing their supply lines, which undermines the Vietnamese economy."

The look of confusion gave way to one of frustration. Perkins couldn't grasp the concepts. And he still didn't want to part with his money. Brandt sighed and looked away.

I can't get him to understand. Maybe Sergeant Anderson can influence the kid now.

Brandt addressed Anderson. "Talk to him again sergeant. See if you can figure out what the problem is because I can't." Then Brandt turned his back on the two men and took a couple of steps, granting them a facade of privacy.

"I don't know, sarge," Perkins blurted out. "How do I know I can trust this lieutenant?"

"Well, *Private* Perkins," Anderson answered in a controlled voice filled with disbelief, "I give him my money. I trust him."

Brandt shook his head as he listened, then allowed his mind to wander while his eyes followed the rise and fall of the mountains rolling toward the horizon. He treasured these rare moments, free to appreciate the beauty of this country, the essence of Vietnam, its unspoiled wilderness, old-growth forests, abundant wildlife, and crystal streams splashing over rocks and dancing down mountainsides.

Reminds me of camping in national parks at home. That time seems so long ago.

Movement jarred Brandt out of his reverie. The corner of his eye registered a presence in the tree line. He brought the M-16 up to a ready position and flipped off the safety. Brandt's eyes pierced the shadows in the nearby brush. An instant later, his shoulders relaxed. He lowered the rifle, reset the safety, and smiled. A deer emerged and then darted across the clearing.

Huh. Why would he sprint across open ground like that with humans around. He must have heard us. Wonder what scared him. Probably just the chopper.

The spell broken, Brandt acknowledged the bleak desolation of the abandoned firebase. The first time he landed on this mountaintop, his platoon came in first to secure it, while others followed with 105 mm howitzers, radios, tents, and a kitchen. Within hours, soldiers cleared vegetation, built fortifications, and laid in supplies. They transformed a mountaintop into a small, isolated village ready to provide artillery support for infantry operations.

The mountain had been pristine, a once-idyllic spot that could have been Eden before men pressed it into service. No longer desired, it now lay exposed, ravaged, and razed.

Brandt's eyes fled this footprint of man and returned to the verdant carpet that enveloped the surrounding hills between Kon Tum and Dak To.

Raised voices behind him drew his attention back to the problem at hand.

"I don't know, sarge. I just don't like it," Perkins insisted.

Sergeant Anderson took a deep breath, raised his arms palms up, and said, "Look at it this way, Perkins. The lieutenant risked his ass coming out here. Don't that mean anything to you?"

Artillery shells pounded a hill to the east, the explosions muted into dull thuds by the thick jungle canopies of the Central Highlands. Brandt turned and saw the look of exasperation disappear as the sergeant's eyes darted toward the ominous sound. Brandt scanned the area, too.

Alpha Company's over there. Probably just firing artillery registration points for tonight. Probably.

Satisfied that they were in no immediate danger, Anderson returned his attention to Perkins. "Look, the man brought three days' worth of food with him. Just for us, private."

Brandt shifted his attention to the waiting helicopter. It looked like a jittery bird anxious to get back to its nest. The pilot waved to him.

Brandt glanced at his watch. "Shit. I don't know if he's telling me to hurry or flipping me off."

The voices behind Brandt rose again, and the truth finally exploded from Perkins.

"Well, how do I know he ain't going to collect all our money and run off with it?"

"Jesus—fucking—H—Christ, Perkins!" Anderson answered with equal emotion, "You're talking about what's less than two days' pay for him. The lieutenant, here, makes more in jump pay than you make regular in a week."

Brandt shook his head.

Time to put an end to this bullshit before that pilot heads back without me.

He retraced his steps, and stopped directly in front of Perkins.

"Look, private, I'll explain it one more time. You've got money that's a funny color, but you can buy stuff here because Nam is like a big Monopoly game. But now the banker is pissed off because somebody is giving too much money to the gooks. They can buy the same shit as you. You like that? Hell no, and neither does the banker. So he's going to fuck over Charlie by giving you new-color money. The old color won't be any good, and all Charlie will be able to do with it is wipe his ass. Isn't that a slick idea? Fuck Charlie without firing a shot. Think about it."

He glared at Anderson. "Sergeant, I'm going to leave you two alone for one minute. When I come back, I don't want to hear shit. I want one of you to hand me the money or just walk away and let me get my ass on that chopper before it takes off and I become your platoon leader."

Brandt spun around, walked about twenty yards, automatically squatted to lower his silhouette, and laid his rifle across his knees. He let out a slow, deep breath and gazed over the valley. A beautiful mountain on the horizon drew his attention, but the smell of napalm clawed at his nostrils and dragged his thoughts back to the charred ground in front of him.

His shoulders sagged. He helped build this firebase, lived in it, and defended it. Now, it was completely destroyed with not a trace left, just like the Romans left Carthage. *But we did this to our own camp. Tore it down, bombed the hell out of it, and finally dropped napalm on it as a finishing touch. All so the enemy couldn't use it.*

"My God, what we do to the Earth and each other," Brandt whispered. "War. Why do we keep doing it?" He hung his head. "Why can't we find another way?"

Brandt sighed and rose, ready to settle this matter of a few dollars.

He walked slowly, studying the two men in front of him. Perkins squared his shoulders and thrust his jaw forward. He looked like a badger digging in for a fight. His eyes spewed distrust. Anderson just looked disgusted.

Brandt stopped a few feet away from them and waited.

Platoon Sergeant Anderson handed Brandt a thin stack of MPCs. "Add this to my total, lieutenant. Perkins, here, loaned me his money. I'll pay him back after the change."

Brandt blinked as he took the MPCs from Sergeant Anderson and put them with the rest of the platoon's money in his right breast pocket.

Now I understand. Perkins is just a nineteen-year-old kid trying to survive in a hostile, topsy-turvy world filled with fear. When the first enemy bullet aimed at him cracked over his head, that single bullet unleashed feelings the kid never thought possible. All the rules of conduct learned at home, in school, and in Sunday school shattered. The only thing left for him to trust was his surrogate father figure, his platoon sergeant.

Anderson gave Brandt a knowing glance and said, "Thanks, lieutenant. See you back at base camp."

The three men turned. Perkins and Anderson jogged to the tree line, and Brandt took a long stride toward the helicopter. Midway through the second stride, Brandt froze. He heard a loud whoosh, saw a bright flash, and a sharp explosion blasted the ground near the helicopter.

Rocket Propelled Grenade. Got to be a sniper nearby, too.

A MATTER OF SEMANTICS

The chopper rose, carved a tight turn, and sped away. A volley of AK-47 fire chased the chopper. Brandt spun around, sprinted to the tree line, dove into high grass, and low-crawled through brush until he reached Sergeant Anderson.

One of Recon's squad leaders crawled up to them. "We spotted an NVA patrol on the trail coming up the mountain. Looks like seven or eight men. They're about 50 meters west of us."

The other squad leader joined them.

Anderson turned to Brandt, a questioning look on his face.

"It's your platoon to lead, sergeant."

"O.K. The platoon is on line overlooking that trail." He pointed and shook his head. "Didn't expect company so soon." Anderson said to the squad leader, "What did you see?"

The squad leader said, "They just got to the crest. Don't know we're here. Surprised the hell out of them to see the chopper. They took a quick shot at it. Probably why they missed."

Anderson nodded. "O.K. First Squad, you move forward until you see them, then lay down a base of fire. I'll take Second Squad on our right flank and swing like a gate. We'll trap them against the bare ground on top."

Anderson turned to Brandt. "Lieutenant, you got ammo?"

"Got a round in the chamber, full magazine, and four spares."

Anderson smiled. "Alright. We got us an extra fighting man." He pointed forward and swung his arm in an arc. "Lieutenant, we're on a wide, flat finger trailing off this mountain, but it has a sharp slope. It would be easy for us to drift downhill. You move with my First Squad and make sure we stay anchored along the tree line. I don't want them sneaking around us on our flank."

"You got it, sergeant."

Anderson turned to his squad leaders. "Tell your men to maintain an even line moving forward, five meters apart. Try to stay in sight of the man on your left and right. That might get difficult, so maintain the pace." He paused. "Anybody got any questions?" Anderson looked at each man. "No? Then let's go."

The men rose as one and fanned out. Brandt bounced on his toes, eyes aglow, heart pounding. He took a few deep breaths, back erect, shoulders back. Like standing in the door of a plane, ready to jump.

Let's go.

He strode forward, positioned himself just inside the tree line, held his rifle chest high, flipped the selector switch from safe to single shot, and placed his finger on the trigger guard. He glanced to his right. He could see men down the line to the fourth man. They all moved forward as one, and Brandt matched their pace. He settled into a rhythm, scanning into the forest ahead, then left to check the open ground beyond the tree line and then right to stay on line. After 25 meters, the vegetation grew denser, and he could only see one man on his right. Another 10 meters and he could no longer see the man on his right. And he could not hear the man moving through brush.

Those guys are good.

He maintained the pace set by First Squad. Another five meters, and Brandt gingerly worked his way through vines interlaced with branches. He took one more step forward and entered a clearing about five meters across. He stopped and listened. Sounds drifted across the clearing of twigs snapping and branches swishing.

Another spooked deer?

Brandt waited. The interlaced vines in the thicket ahead shook, branches pulled, and leaves fluttered. He raised his rifle to his shoulder, placed his finger on the trigger, and took a deep breath and let it halfway out.

An enemy soldier burst through brush, jaw clenched and eyes narrowed. Vines cut across his flushed face, and he jerked his AK-47 skyward.

Frustrated. Used the rifle to break through vines. An FNG mistake.

The vines snapped, and the soldier froze. His jaw dropped and eyes opened wide. He hesitated, then started to bring the rifle to his shoulder.

Brandt squeezed his trigger. The enemy soldier crumpled, dropped his rifle, and fell backwards. Brandt stepped forward, rifle pointed at the center of body mass. The man's chest heaved, then sunk with a gurgling sound, and pink foam bubbled from his mouth. Brandt stood over him, eyes drawn to his boyish face.

A volley of M-16 rifle firing on his right broke the silence.

First Squad's base of fire.

He heard AK-47s roar in return. The cracking of the enemy rifles inched toward the tree line, closer and closer. Brandt stepped over the body and crouched to lower his silhouette. A sudden punch to his head knocked him to the ground. His head bounced. He felt consciousness fade as his steel helmet rolled away.

Brandt opened his eyes and grasped for awareness. Balls of light flashed on and off. He struggled to get up but crumpled in pain. He'd always been able to get up before, even if a 275 pound defensive end put him down. Now, a bullet weighing a couple of ounces riveted him to the ground. Renewed efforts made everything go blurry, and Brandt fought frantically to focus his attention.

When he regained control, he heard a rifle firing and looked up. Private Perkins knelt over him, rifle aimed at the tree line. Disciplined three-round bursts exploded above him. He heard more rifles firing in the distance—Second Squad swinging the gate and slamming it shut.

He felt a hand on his forehead, felt fingers opening his eyes. A face appeared above him, very close. He blinked and recognized Jones, the Recon Platoon's medic.

Perkins lowered his rifle. "Couldn't find blood anywhere, Doc, but he was out cold."

"Thanks, Perkins."

Brandt's jaw moved but no words came out of his mouth. Jones palpated his chest, stomach, arms, and legs.

"You're a lucky fucking man, lieutenant," Jones said. "You got the best damn medic in the Army."

Men shouted over helicopter noise.

The helicopter is back.

Brandt grasped for comprehension, but meaning drifted away. Jones' face began to blur. Brandt struggled to keep his eyes open.

"You stay with me, now. You're going to be all right."

Going to be all right. How many soldiers has he said that to? Probably every one he's worked on.

Jones and Perkins slid Brandt onto a poncho. Four men grabbed a corner each, cradled Brandt in the center, and jogged to the helicopter. Jones ran alongside him squeezing his hand. "Damn it. You stay with me, now."

Brandt tried to see who carried him, but vague shapes blurred into darkness.

CHAPTER 18

★ ★ ★

Brandt awoke. He saw a canvas ceiling, smelled antiseptic smells, and heard strange voices.

Where the hell am I?

He raised his head and shoulders, but his eyes squeezed shut, his teeth clenched, and spots flashed in his vision. Then he collapsed.

"Bill, take it easy."

Captain Johnson's voice.

"You're in B Med, Bill. You caught a bullet with your helmet. Knocked you out, but you're O.K."

"Well, lieutenant, you're trying to sit up today?"

A gentle, melodious voice drifted from behind him. An angelic face appeared over him.

"Welcome back. Let me help you."

Welcome back?

A soft but strong hand slid behind his shoulders.

"Move slowly."

Brandt rolled his shoulders forward.

"How's that? Any pain?"

"No."

"Just move slowly for a while."

She offered him a small paper cup and a glass of water.

"Some pain medication. It will help."

Brandt took the offering and swallowed.

"Do you know where you are?"

"Heaven?"

The angelic voice turned austere. "Lieutenant, get serious."

"Mobile Army Surgical Hospital Bravo, LZ English."

"What's your name?"

"Are you asking me for a date?"

"Lieutenant." Stern voice again.

"Brandt, William F., lieutenant, OF 112342. That's all I'm required to give by the Geneva Accords."

"O.K., lieutenant," she said in an exasperated voice. "That's the first time in three days you've been able to answer those questions." She smiled. "I think you'll be released today." The angel spun on her heel and marched away.

Brandt looked at Johnson. "Three days?"

Johnson nodded. "Do you remember how you got here?"

Brandt frowned, thought for a moment, and said, "Last thing I remember, I got on a resupply helicopter up on the helipad."

"Anything else?"

Brandt started to shake his head but winced.

"Bill, you got on the helicopter to collect MPCs from Recon because they couldn't get back before the change. Do you remember the currency change?"

"Vaguely. Something about changing MPCs."

"Right. The Army wanted to issue a new series because so much had gotten into the black market." He paused until Brandt nodded tentatively. "Anyway, you went out on the resupply chopper. Sergeant Anderson told me what happened. After you got the MPCs, you ran to the chopper, but an RPG exploded wide of the chopper. You turned, sprinted to the tree line and joined Recon. An NVA patrol happened to climb the mountain just at that moment. Sergeant Anderson maneuvered the platoon and ambushed the patrol. He said you anchored their left flank on the tree line. They tried to sneak by Recon on the left, but you stopped it cold. Killed their point man."

Johnson paused, waiting for recollection to occur.

"Yeah. It's coming back. Like looking through fog."

"Good. That trapped them against the bare ground on the peak. Then all hell broke loose. Shooting in all directions. But your training to lower your silhouette saved you. A bullet hit your helmet instead of your chest."

Brandt sensed another presence and looked to the side, slowly. A tall, lanky captain stood beside his bed, hair a little shaggy by Army standards, Medical Corps insignia on his collar. *A doctor.*

"That's right," the doctor interjected. "They put the helmet on the medevac with you." He shook his head. "Damnedest thing. The bullet pierced the helmet, traveled around your head between the metal helmet and the plastic liner and came out the same hole." He paused. "As a result, you have traumatic brain injury."

"What?"

"You ever had your bell rung playing football?"

"Yes, sir."

"Well, put this on the far end of a logarithmic scale. You have one hell of a concussion. Not a lot of fun, but it beats having that hole in your head."

"But three days?"

"Not unusual. You've been in and out of a coma during that time. Amnesia, memory loss, is a common symptom. You may have a sense of lost time. You'll experience headaches for a while. All this will subside in time, and you'll be back to normal. Just take it easy."

"O.K. When can I get back to my unit?"

"Other than the headache, how do you feel?"

"Pretty good, I guess."

"Can you stand up?"

Brandt started to hop out of the bed, stopped, and gingerly slid off.

"Walk around to the other side and back."

Brandt performed the task.

"Got your balance back. Feel any nausea?"

"No, sir."

"Well, I agree with my nurse," the doctor said. "You are definitely ready to go back to your unit."

Brandt followed Johnson through the infirmary door to a waiting jeep and climbed into the back alongside him. The captain leaned forward and tapped the driver on the shoulder. "Drive slowly. Smooth a ride as possible."

The driver turned, a wide grin on his face. "Oh, so we're pampering lieutenants now?"

Brandt looked up at the familiar voice, and his jaw dropped. "Corporal Singleton! What are you doing here?"

Singleton raised his arm and pointed to stripes on his sleeve. "Sergeant Singleton now, sir. I'm the Battalion Commander's driver."

Brandt leaned forward, winced, and shook Singleton's hand. "Good for you. You earned it." He turned to Johnson, slowly. "Wow. That happened fast."

The jeep pulled away. Johnson settled back and said, "Bill, a lot has happened while you've been in B Med. Do you remember why you went out on the resupply chopper for Recon?"

Brandt looked down and pressed his lips together. "Something important I needed to finish?"

"MPCs?"

"Recon's resupply. Yeah, they couldn't get back in time. I went out to collect their MPCs for the change."

"Correct."

After a pause, recognition dawned on Brandt. "That's right. You told me about getting on the resupply chopper to get their MPCs." A long moment. "Holy shit. I've got to get ready for C-Day."

Johnson smiled. "The change took place two days ago." He paused to let that sink in. "On 28 October, 1968."

"How did it go?"

"Everything went smoothly. You did a great job of setting it up. We just needed to execute your plan."

"And Recon's money?"

"You got the money in just under the wire. We got a call from B Med. Said they found a pile of money on one of our troops. Not the usual case they get, so they figured they'd better let us know. I picked up the money that afternoon. Recon came in from the field yesterday and I gave them the new series."

"Well, I'm glad it all worked out."

"By the way, Bill," Johnson added, "a Private Perkins in Recon said something puzzling. He said to tell you he's sorry and to say thanks."

"Perkins? Sorry?" Another long moment passed. "Oh, yeah. It's a long story."

The jeep slowed and swerved but hit a dip that ran across the width of the road.

"Damn, that hurt."

"Sorry, sir. I couldn't avoid it."

Johnson patted Singleton on the shoulder. "I know you tried to soften it."

Johnson looked at Brandt and waited. "Better, now?"

"Yeah."

Johnson cleared his throat. "And now for the big news."

"Big news? The MPC change wasn't big?"

Johnson took a deep breath. "This morning, the Brigade Commander relieved Lieutenant Colonel Alexander of his duties. He's already left the battalion area."

"No shit?" Brandt took a deep breath and let it out slowly. "Couldn't happen to a better guy."

"Bill, for some time now, the Brigade Commander has been dissatisfied with Alexander's," Johnson affected a sarcastic tone of voice, "*leadership.*" Johnson shook his head. "It's been difficult for all of us on his staff. He's continually placed his troops in jeopardy trying to make a name for himself. He's a poor tactician. Doesn't know how to fight a battalion effectively. You couldn't see it as a platoon leader in the field, but the staff and company commanders were very frustrated. We walked a fine line between supporting him and looking out for the troops. Except for Parker. He and Alexander scratched each other's backs. The Brigade Commander transferred Parker to a Corps Headquarters staff position."

"Damn."

"Alexander used vindictiveness," Johnson continued, "as if it were a leadership tool. You weren't the only one who felt it, although you caught the brunt of his rancor. Every time he dumped what he thought was a shit job on you, you turned it into a positive and excelled. Each time you succeeded, it increased his chagrin and made things worse."

"Yeah, I sure felt it."

"And that fiasco of a," Johnson used the sarcastic tone again, "*combat assault* on the village." Johnson shook his head. "That gave the general sufficient reason to act. He just needed time to line up replacements."

The jeep crested a rise, pulled into the battalion area, and eased to a stop alongside the S-1 Office. Brandt and Johnson climbed out.

"Hello, Bill. How are you feeling?"

Brandt looked up at another familiar voice. "Colonel Everett." Brandt took a step back, mouth open. He regained his composure and said, "I feel great, sir."

"I told you to watch your back, Bill. I should have told you to watch what you walk into. How's your head?"

"Just a little headache now and then, sir."

Everett tilted his head to the side, crossed his arms on his chest. "Uh-huh."

Johnson stepped forward and gestured to Everett. "Bill, meet your new Battalion Commander."

Brandt gasped.

"Would you gentlemen join me in the Tactical Operations Center? I've called a meeting of all battalion officers." Everett strode past them and led the way.

Brandt gazed around the bunker. Uncertainty filled the atmosphere, suppressing the usual pre-meeting chatter. The presence of the Brigade Commander and the absence of Alexander raised tensions.

The Brigade Commander stepped up to the podium. He held no notes and wore a somber expression. Everett stood behind him, poker faced.

"Gentlemen." The general paused and surveyed the room, unnecessarily waiting for attention. "I have relieved Lieutenant Colonel Alexander as commander of this battalion." He paused. Audible gasps filled the room, followed by deep silence. He turned to Everett and nodded. Everett stepped forward. "Lieutenant Colonel Everett is your new battalion commander." Again he paused. "I will now turn the meeting over to him." The general stepped away and strode out of the bunker.

"Officers of the 2nd Battalion, it is an honor to be appointed your battalion commander," Everett began. "In the coming days, I will get to know each one of you better, and you will get to know me. And to help you start getting to know me, I will tell you now that this battalion will start fighting this war the way infantry units are supposed to fight. The mission of the Infantry is to close with and destroy the enemy, and that is just what we will do. The duty of an officer is to lead, and that is what I expect of you." Everett paused and looked each officer in the eye. "In return, that is what you will get from me. I do not believe a battalion commander is a crew chief on a helicopter. I will be on the ground with you, and I challenge each company commander and platoon leader to keep up with me." He paused again and scanned the room. "Dismissed."

Brandt shuffled along, following the throng toward the door, last in the pack.

"Lieutenant Brandt," Everett called. Johnson stood next to him.

"Would you join us?"

Brandt turned and stood before them.

"Bill, as the doctor prescribed, you will be on light duty for a while. Captain Johnson will assign appropriate duties and supervise your activities."

"I don't need light duty, sir. I feel great. Can't I just do my job the way I have been. Get out into the field to get things done?"

"Bill." Everett waited for eye contact. "The Battalion Surgeon will tell you when you're ready to go back into the field."

"Yes, sir."

★ ★ ★

Brandt hopped to the first step of the S-1 Office, winced, grabbed the door handle, and waited for the pain to pass. He took a deep breath, opened the screen door, walked in, and tipped his hat to Staff Sergeant Wilson.

"Welcome back, sir."

He faced Captain Johnson. "Good morning, sir. What's up for today? Something light, I presume?"

Johnson smiled at Brandt's sarcasm. "Morning, lieutenant. And yes, a light stack of papers for you to handle. A couple of Reports of Survey and an Article 15 that needs a signature." He paused. "And one more piece of paper on the bottom."

He offered Brandt the documents. Brandt took them, sat at his desk, and flipped through the pages. "What's this, sir?"

"Your three-year commitment in the Regular Army is coming to a close soon. It's time for you to re-up. All you need to do is sign the form."

"Time does fly when you're having fun, doesn't it?" Brandt folded the paper and tucked it into his chest pocket. "Thank you, sir."

Brandt stood. "I'd better get started on this light duty."

Johnson sat back and studied Brandt. After a moment, he said, "All of those forms are for Alpha Company. They're back in base camp on perimeter duty now. The Reports of Survey deal with lost equipment. Two weeks ago, Alpha crossed a river. Charlie opened fire and caught the rear platoon in the river. In the scramble to get on the bank, a few troopers lost some equipment. The Article 15 needs to be signed and taken up to Brigade Headquarters. You can probably clear everything today."

"O.K. I'll head down to Alpha and start with the executive officer."

★ ★ ★

After dinner, Brandt sat on the edge of his bunk, yawned, and checked his watch.

Enough time to write a letter home.

He rummaged through his rucksack for a note pad, but his fingers crinkled paper and he drew it from the bottom. Folded as if for mailing. He smoothed it on his knee, unfolded it, and read the date. Brandt groaned.

Damn, never mailed it. Wrote it on that mountaintop firebase.

An image formed in Brandt's mind of pulling out in darkness that night, being flown to LZ English, then a sprint to waiting helicopters and being launched into a coordinated night assault with two other companies. In the distance, two AC-47 planes fitted with .50 caliber machine guns, Puff the Magic Dragon, circling the target, solid red lines of tracers extending to the ground and rotating like lighthouse beacons, and Singleton saying, "Damn. We're going there?"

Brandt shook his head and began reading, subvocalizing.

"Dear Jim,"

"You asked what it's like walking into an ambush. It's hard to explain. Deafening explosions left, right, front, and back. Rifles and machine guns firing. Crack, crack, crack, all around you. That's the sound a bullet makes, Jim. Not the report you hear when you fire the shot. Loud, angry, sharp. The bullet breaks the sound barrier over your head and slams you to the ground."

"You instinctively hug the ground and jettison the 70 pound rucksack. Someone is trying to kill you. You might die. And if you just lie there trying to hide, you *will* die. It's ground prepared for that by the enemy. You have to do what's not natural. You have to get up, determine where they are, return fire, and get the hell out of that kill zone. That's your only chance."

"You might be able to relate this to bird hunting. Remember when we'd go upland bird hunting in the fall? We'd be walking through fields of tall grass and bush enjoying just being out in the quiet, natural beauty of the countryside. Suddenly we'd jump a covey of quail. An explosion. So many wings flapping. Birds flying helter-skelter. All directions at once. That confusion of trying to pick out a bird to shoot. Close your eyes and picture that. Now imagine all those birds shooting AK-47s at you."

"That's the key to understanding an ambush. Sudden violence. Confusion. Fear."

Brandt sat back and closed his eyes, took a deep breath, and lips drawn tight, he continued writing.

"Jim, writing it down like that gives me a new perspective. Never thought about it that way when I executed a successful ambush. Now I know how the enemy feels."

"But that's my job. And I'm good at it."

"Well, you asked. I hope that gives you a glimpse into the true nature of war."

"Be well,"

"Bill"

Brandt sat back, gazed up at the ceiling, and looked at the letter again.

That's my job. Yeah, I'm good at it.

A deep sigh.

Brandt refolded the letter, reached for the rucksack, paused, and tucked the letter into his shirt pocket instead.

★ ★ ★

The next few days, Brandt proofread Noncommissioned Officer Efficiency Reports; balanced casualty reports, company strength reports, and replacement needs; wrote recommendations for awards and decorations and delivered them to Brigade Headquarters; and brought back more forms, promotion orders, and reports.

And so it went, day after day after day.

★ ★ ★

Brandt pushed a form to the side of his desk, tossed his pen on top of it, sat back, and stared at the canvas ceiling of the S-1 Office. He sighed as images of his father, grandfather, and great grandfather marched into his thoughts. He recollected his own participation in the New Market Day Ceremony back at VMI, cadets arrayed before the memorial inscribed with names of the fallen. As each name was called, a cadet from the same company responded. In turn, Brandt answered, "Died on the Field of Honor, sir."

Scenes of his successful ambushes flashed by: standing over lifeless, broken bodies; the medevac helicopter returning three times to carry away his men; calling in artillery on a village; directing a helicopter gunship to fire on an ambush.

All necessary to accomplish a mission, to save my own men. But Fields of Honor?

Brandt shook his head, picked up the pen, and twirled it in his fingers.

Sergeant Wilson put his pen down, placed an elbow on his desk, rested his chin on his hand, and gazed at Brandt. He shuffled a stack of papers, selected a few with rank insignia clipped to them, and presented them to Brandt.

Brandt sighed. "It's endless, isn't it?"

"Yes, sir. But you look like you could use a bright spot in the day." He offered Brandt the papers. "The captain won't be back for a while. Here's one of the better parts of your job. You'll like these."

Brandt flipped through the pages, smiled, and said, "Alright! Their orders finally came through."

"They're meeting with the Sergeant Major now. Everything is set. They should be coming in any minute."

Brandt sat at his desk, neatly arranged the papers, and stuffed the rank insignia in his shirt pockets. "This sure is better than dealing with those Article 15s."

The door creaked open, and Ferguson and Olszewski entered and stood at attention in front of Brandt.

"Good afternoon, sir," Olszewski said cheerfully.

Ferguson, in a serious tone said, "Sir, I just come from the Sergeant Major's office. He directed me to have Sergeant Olszewski report to you."

Brandt sat back, eyes narrowed. "I can see why. Sergeant Olszewski, you are out of uniform. And I know what I'm going to do about it."

Ski frowned. "What do you mean, sir?"

Brandt stood, stepped around his desk, pulled a pen knife out of his pocket, and cut off Ski's E-5 stripes.

Ski's head whipped back as if smacked. "Sir, I don't understand. What did I do to get busted?"

Brandt maintained a stern face. "Who said anything about busted?" He plucked a pair of E-6 stripes and safety pins from his left shirt pocket and pinned them to Ski's sleeves. "You are now Staff Sergeant Olszewski."

Realization dawned, and relief flushed Ski's cheeks.

Brandt extended his hand. "Congratulations." He picked up a piece paper, and handed it to Ski. "Your promotion orders."

Olszewski pulled his shoulders back and raised his chin. "Thank you, sir."

Ferguson raised his arm, hand balled into a fist, and punched Olszewski in the arm.

"Ow." Olszewski rubbed his arm.

Ferguson chuckled. "I just wanted to make sure those stripes stick."

Brandt turned again and picked up another piece of paper. "And here are your transfer orders."

"Transfer? Where? What if I don't want to leave November?"

"You don't have to leave. You are now Platoon Sergeant, November Platoon, Bravo Company."

Ski's jaw dropped. He glanced back and forth between Brandt and Ferguson.

Ferguson shrugged. "I guess the young bull pushed the old bull out of the herd."

Olszewski tilted his head to the side. "What's going on, sir."

Brandt reached into his right shirt pocket, pulled out a pair of E-8 stripes, handed them to Ferguson, and shook his hand. "Congratulations, First Sergeant Ferguson."

Brandt addressed Olszewski. "As First Sergeant Ferguson said, he just came from the Sergeant Major's office. He's being transferred to Delta Company. Their First Sergeant is ready to DEROS."

Olszewski shook Ferguson's hand. "Congratulations." He turned to Brandt. "I don't know about this, sir. I got some big shoes to fill."

Ferguson made an exaggerated motion of looking to the floor. "You got big feet, Ski. Just step into those shoes. You're ready."

Brandt cleared his throat. "I hate to break this up, but both of you gentlemen have new duties to attend to, and I have to make my daily run up to Brigade Headquarters."

★ ★ ★

On the twelfth day of Brandt's light duty, the jeep driver pulled into the battalion area after the daily trip to Brigade Headquarters and parked alongside the S-1 tent. Brandt hopped out, then braced for pain.

Alright! No pain. Finally.

Instead of entering the office, Brandt sat on the sandbag wall surrounding the office and pulled the re-enlistment form out of his chest pocket, the unmailed letter to Jim stuck inside it. He unfolded both and took a deep breath.

After a moment, he gazed west toward the distant, jungle-covered mountains and that bare mountaintop. He recalled the firefight with Recon Platoon, and an image formed in his mind. The North Vietnamese soldier bursting into the clearing, his young face flushed, his mouth falling open and eyes widening—and that audible gasp.

Why didn't you drop your rifle? I wouldn't have had to kill you.

Brandt shook his head, and his mind flitted to another image. He stood at a fork in a jungle trail. He glanced down at his compass, but it had no needle. Lines from a Robert Frost poem appeared and faded.

Yeah, which path? But why did this come to mind? Frost wrote the poem as a joke to a friend who was always questioning his decisions.

He sighed.

A joke? Are the Fates laughing?

He stared at the ground.

How will I look back at this decision?

Brandt took another deep breath, refolded the form and letter, placed them in his pocket, and looked up at the sky. After a long moment, he whispered, "O.K., You're the real Big 6. Lead the way for me."

"Hey, Bill."

Brandt started. "Oh, Captain Johnson."

"How about going to the mess hall and getting some lunch?"

"Sounds good to me."

He hopped off the wall with a flourish. "No pain, sir."

After the meal, Brandt stared into his coffee cup.

"A lot on your mind, soldier?"

Brandt looked up. "Huh? Oh, sorry, sir."

"Got a lot on your mind, Bill?"

"I guess I've been lulled into ennui by light duty." He paused. "Miracle drug that it seems to be. I haven't had any headaches lately."

"Yes. I noticed your theatrical demonstration of that before lunch." He sat back and gazed at Brandt. "Maybe I can come up with a cure for ennui."

★ ★ ★

After breakfast the next day, Brandt trudged up the steps to the S-1 Office. *One more time.* No bounce in his step. As he entered, Brandt looked to Johnson's desk. No stack of papers. He looked to his own desk. No stack of papers there either. Johnson and Wilson wore curious smiles. Brandt hesitated, then sat.

Johnson cleared his throat. "Well, Bill, I seem to be all out of light duty today."

"Uh, well, would you like me to run up to Brigade Headquarters and pick up the mail?"

Johnson shook his head. "The clerk already did that."

Brandt looked back and forth between the smiling men.

Johnson stood. "Would you accompany me to the Battalion Commander's office?"

"Sure, sir."

Brandt followed Johnson. Lieutenant Colonel Everett sat behind his desk and gestured for them to sit. Captain McCarthy sat on Everett's right beside the desk.

"How are you feeling, Bill?"

"Fine, sir. Haven't had any headaches for a few days."

"That's what Captain Johnson tells me. And the Battalion Surgeon has taken you off light duty status." He paused. "That's why I have Captain McCarthy here."

Brandt looked at McCarthy. "A platoon leader position?"

Everett shook his head. "That's not what I had in mind."

"Sir?"

"Captain McCarthy is due to make major soon. I just made him my executive officer." Everett paused. "So there's a company commander position open. I want you to be one of my company commanders. What do you think of that?"

Brandt sat back. His jaw dropped.

"Sir, I'm not due to make captain for a while."

"I know, but Captain Johnson thinks you're ready, and Captain McCarthy concurs."

Brandt rubbed his chin and knitted his eyebrows.

Captain Johnson leaned forward. "Bill, an early promotion to command would be a feather in your cap. Just the kind of thing a career officer needs."

Everett reached into his desk, pulled out a piece of paper, placed it in front of Brandt, and laid a pen on top of it. "I understand your service obligation is ending. Let's take care of the paperwork now."

Brandt took a deep breath and let it out slowly. He leaned forward and picked up the pen in his right hand. With pen poised over the signature line, he hesitated. In the long moment, a mosquito landed on his left hand. He raised his right hand, slapped down, but stopped halfway, brought the hand down slowly, and shooed away the bug.

Brandt placed the pen on the desk, sat back, and looked at each of the three men.

He let out a deep sigh. "I'm tired of killing."